Neeya's People

Geoff Trigg

A catalogue record for this book is available from the National Library of Australia

Copyright © 2024 Geoff Trigg
All rights reserved.
ISBN-13: 978-1-923174-24-5

Linellen Press
265 Boomerang Road
Oldbury, Western Australia
www.linellenpress.com.au

Acknowledgements

I want to thank my wife, Anne, for the generous help given to make the final revision of Neeya's People much easier to read, with the story flow being improved. The hard discussions about changes sometimes needed time out to settle feelings and her help and patience are greatly appreciated.

Many lessons learned as a member of the Karrinyup Writers Club in the art of writing were put into practice in the creation of this story. For me, it was proof that joining a group or club of like-minded writers to learn the trade is vital before attempting to bring a new story to the public.

Contents

Acknowledgements iii
Contents 5
Chapter 1 - Escape 7
Chapter 2 - New Beginning 17
Chapter 3 - Discovery 27
Chapter 4 - Machine 35
Chapter 5 - New Understandings 47
Chapter 6 - Two Become Four 59
Chapter 7 - Second Mountain 69
Chapter 8 - New Companions 78
Chapter 9 - The Grey Man 87
Chapter 10 - Training 97
Chapter 11 - Goddess of Death 109
Chapter 12 - Teaching 114
Chapter 13 - Alpha 122
Chapter 14 - Sun and Fresh Air 135
Chapter 15 - Plans 153
Chapter 16 - New People 163
Chapter 17 - New Abilities 178

Chapter 18 - Water People 196
Chapter 19 - Powered Voyage 216
Chapter 20 - Floods and Fights 237
Chapter 21 - Explosions and Fire 255
Chapter 22 - Costs and Endings 274
Chapter 23 - Answers and New Beginnings 286
About the Author 298

Chapter 1

Escape

"Tarn, come to the gate. We have visitors, and they're in a bad way."

The guard's call luckily found Tarn nearby. He arrived just as they were starting to enter, a dishevelled lot, in patched and faded skins, shuffling in tattered moccasins stuffed with dry grass. They came through the spiked entry barriers into camp, dusty, sweat-stained, some limping, one injured on a drag stretcher pulled by a pony. The group had a few other bow-legged, skinny horses carrying their withered elderly, mostly women. They all had a starved, vacant look about their face, and their eyes, their eyes told all. This group looked like they had been through hell and couldn't believe they were still alive.

There were over thirty of them: old men, women, and children. Some, who looked old, were worn out, with less than forty summers to their age. It was rare for anyone in the bands to live beyond that number, battling to survive in this failing country. There were no able men with them, the reason yet unknown. They might be fighting some rear-guard action to allow the rest to escape, dead along the trail, taken by animals or killed one at a time by pursuers, as they fled. This once generous area had become dangerous, and even worse in the past few seasons. Cave lions and bears were now more aggressive, their normal prey thinning out from successive droughts, with humankind becoming less capable of group defence and so more easily taken.

Neeya had arrived three days before, with a vague connection to the high chief's family and was allowed to address the Council. She was no stranger to loss; over twenty-eight summers old, she had been married with two children. It was surprising that both children had even survived birth, one being soon lost to disease, a common killer. The other was taken by a hungry puma, leaping too fast from a rock shelf to be stopped, and disappearing with the already-dead boy clamped in its jaws. Her husband had died less than a season later from a spear thrown by a small raiding party looking to steal supplies and young women. He had lingered days in great pain but eventually went to the star world.

After her impassioned speech to the Council, in which she begged for protection, they allowed her group into the main camp, but the guards had been doubled, and scouts were sent out to watch for more survivors to arrive, forewarned of the approaching threat.

Tarn studied her as she left the high chief's tent. Her slumped posture and bowed head revealed relief, now that she had been given approval for her group to live in the valley. She still looked formidable, her dark hair tied back on her head, her facial tattoos strongly visible and her fighting knife at her waist, as individual and unique as any other who chose a tattoo. She walked with a strong, sure step, and was around Tarn's age, with the same spirit animal, the Black bear. They could never become more than friends, because of the taboo against marriage within the same spirit clan.

Neeya saw Tarn observing her and her lined face changed to give him a tight grin, her serious brown eyes remaining tense.

"Why so troubled, Tarn? What does our fighting chief worry about today?"

"You bring me cause for worry, Neeya. This band already battles to find sufficient food, now that the crops have failed again. We resort to digging holes in the stream bed to find drinking water. Less than half our new born live long. Now you give us more mouths to feed, most of them unable to hunt or fight. Where are your men, Neeya, or are these all you bring?"

"They will arrive soon, those who still survive. If you have not heard already, there is a curse spreading through this area, Tarn, a fierce tribe, newly arrived. They dress in black, with black-painted bodies and faces. They kill as if it is the only thing they were created for. We have not seen any of their women or children. They carry no supplies or water, only weapons. They leave behind death and burnt shelters. We have fought them twice, trying to trap or surprise them, but they show no fear of death and we have had to retreat and run from them. I'm glad you found me, or I would be looking for you now. You need to strengthen your defences. They may not match our fighting numbers, but they are hard to kill because of the leaves they chew, which drive them crazy when they attack. I had twenty warriors when I left them, but I don't know yet how many have survived."

Threats had come and gone over the years, and the tribe's strength had to be demonstrated, with the sight of dozens of armed warriors standing along the top on both sides of the canyon walls. That narrow entry was the only approach to the wide valley beyond but it was also the only exit. It had to be protected at all costs, or the people would be trapped by the steep cliffs that surrounded our only place of shelter. If what Neeya said was true, and Tarn had no reason to doubt her, this might be their greatest test so far.

This plague of black killers was only the most recent trial they'd had to deal with. Their numbers were many when the rains stayed true and the herds moved on the plains, but the seasons had slowly changed for the worse. The weather now remained hot and cloudless, with no respite, and the crops were only dry stalks. The animals had stopped appearing in their annual trek past the valley. Hunters rarely returned successful with meat to feed hungry mouths.

Many tents and rock shelters were empty of families. Nearby caves held their dead, and it seemed that more space would soon be needed.

Neeya knew all of this, having lived in the valley before, only to leave with her new husband and a small group of young families, all eager to start their own community in better country. For several summers, they had succeeded and their numbers increased, with new children and similar-minded people from other small bands. Now their earlier success had become ashes in their mouths.

Neeya interrupted Tarn's thoughts. "I will do everything I can to protect these people, Tarn, as will any who have survived from my group. Just give your directions and they will be followed. I failed our new settlement by realising too late how much of a threat these new killers were. That is a burden I must carry. So many in my care have died. I will do anything to prevent it happening again."

Tarn was surprised by her admission, delivered with a direct stare lacking any warmth. He had no doubts that she would seek a powerful revenge with little mercy on these black-painted devils if given the opportunity.

His thoughts went back to when they had joined hunting groups on the plains. Then, people laughed and bellies were full, with children playing their games in safety.

One inexplicable memory stuck in his mind, and probably in Neeya's. Their group hunt had been successful, with several antelope killed and the meat carried back to camp. They stayed close to the herd as it moved when the others had left, tracking one final animal.

They had crossed a strange trail. Two straight lines, three paces apart, each one hand wide. The trail was smooth and continuous, with no individual hoof or paw prints. A sharp crack sounded in the distance, like when a storm announces its arrival before heavy rain, out of a cloudless sky.

They made their way to where the sound seemed to come from, even though it was frightening and beyond their understanding. After searching around, they found the body of a large deer, dead but with the head missing and a single round hole in its shoulder, close to the heart. Why would the head be taken but not the treasure of so much good meat? They froze, hearts thumping from the tension, not daring to move, waiting for another hunter to appear. Nothing happened, so they hid in the bushes and tried to work out what it all meant.

Finally, after no one came, they went back to the animal to dismember it and carry the legs and best parts of the body back to camp. In the cutting, Tarn used his knife to open the round hole that would have killed the animal. All he found, deep in the body, was a round thing the size of a small stone but harder than stone. It was not an arrow head or the tip of a spear. They couldn't understand it but agreed it should remain a secret, something mysterious, with no explanation, otherwise they wouldn't be believed. The question of what had happened there stuck in Tarn's mind for many seasons, gnawing away like a thorn in a foot needing to be dug out.

The extra meat had been welcomed in camp, with applause about their great kill. Others were sent back to retrieve the remainder of the animal, before predators found it. No comments were made about the missing head. They never spoke of that day again, even to each other.

There were many things that had no explanation. Such knowledge was not for the people but only for those living in the sky who they glimpsed each night. They passed over their heads in the great distance, their movement as shining lights while they look down on them. This they knew from the wisdom passed down through many generations, from stories told by the elders around the fire.

But for now, Tarn had to consider Neeya's concerning information. Their people were not strong. The long drought with minimal food and water had weakened even their strongest. Few warriors had grown to replace those who were lost. If these intruders over-ran the narrow entrance to their valley, they might not survive.

Tarn's position as fighting chief had been for only two summers, after the early death of the previous chief. In his time, he had scoured their valley, searching out defensible places, hidden caves and materials that could be made into weapons.

While living in the valley they had gradually extended shallow depressions to guide water from the only available stream into the best soil for crops. As his people had prospered, their expanded areas of corn, melons, squash, and beans had kept them alive in times when meat became scarce. But now the stream had become a trickle; there was only a series of shallow puddles. It originally started as a clear spring bubbling up at the base of a cliff, running through their land, then dropping into a deep pool in a cave at the other side of the valley. That pool had now all but disappeared.

Tarn had clambered into the muddy hole to find it opened into a narrow cave entrance under the rock face, high enough to walk through. The first time he tried to explore that black hole, the darkness stopped him. The next time he had wrapped fat-soaked old skins over branches. His flints quickly had one burning with enough light to continue from the entrance.

It was narrow, and in places, he had to double over to get through. But it eventually led into a large cavern with long pointed stone pillars, like spears, rising from the rock floor or hanging from the high ceiling. Water dripped from the roof and walls, building up to a small, clear stream running through the large space deeper into the darkness.

Using the light from the flickering, smelly torch, he saw painted hand prints and coloured pictures of the sun and animals on many flat rock surfaces. Men had been here before, maybe in times of extreme danger or when help from the sky people was being requested. This was a special and sacred place, a gift which should not be squandered by use in normal times. The discovery was also worrying. Maybe he had entered a taboo area without knowing. He gave silent apologies to placate any spirits angry at his blundering into their world.

He must have become lost in his memories of the cave, then Neeya brought him back to the present as she gazed unblinkingly into his eyes.

"Where did your mind go just then, Tarn? Were you communing with the spirit world?"

"I was thinking, Neeya, of another way we might still survive if what you warn of comes true. I have something to show you, something that might give us all a future, but I need to learn more."

"Then show me your 'something', Tarn, and we will learn together."

They made more torches from long dead branches and oil-soaked strips of old skins, then re-entered the cave. Neeya was as awed as he had been at the great cavern and the paintings from those who had once been there, her eyes wide with wonder in the flickering fire of the smoky torch.

"This space could hold all our people together, even if it is just to hide while the crazy ones pass through the valley. We could only hope that they would not decide to make our valley their home. Then we would starve in the darkness."

"We haven't finished here yet, Neeya. This stream passes further through the cave."

As they moved on and squeezed through narrow spaces, waded through shallow pools, and scrambled over piles of fallen rocks, the stream disappeared at times but always re-appeared as their guide. The water was cold and their sodden, slippery moccasins threatened to drop them onto solid rock to break bones.

The water depth gradually increased as they moved through the cave, and the stream made a long turn to the side, offering no alternative but to follow. It was slow going over the slippery rocks while holding torches. As they rounded the curve, the light started to increase and, without warning, they clambered around a rock face and stood in sunshine, looking down onto a broad, green valley. The stream dropped away in front of their feet, down a slope to join a fast-moving river that seemed to be fed from many streams like theirs, coming from under the rock walls.

In the distance, they could see the dust thrown up from large, grazing herds, feeding off the grass growing on the river banks and well-watered plains. Here were the missing herds. Here was the water and food they desperately needed for their future.

They stood speechless, trying to comprehend what they had found. Maybe this was the land the people who painted the ancient cave pictures had come to, for their own salvation, long ago.

"This is hard to believe, Neeya. We have come a short distance but the world has changed from a dying land to one of plenty. The animals have discovered this before us. We must have found favour with the spirits to be given this chance."

Neeya had said nothing since their first view of the perfect sight before them. Now she had a grin that remained and her eyes sparkled. "This is more than we could ever dream of, Tarn. We have to get back to the people and move them here before we are attacked. The enemies must be near, now, so we can't waste time. Somehow, once our people are shown this place, we must stop the black killers from following us, by blocking the path."

Without going any further, knowing that their time for action was short, they returned through the cave of the ancestors, to report their discovery to the tribal council.

Their people were packed in less than five days, with everything to be carried through the dark passageway. The last of their animals, including Neeya's few horses, were butchered well away from the cave entrance and the meat shared around, to be taken on the trip, along with everything of any use in the future.

A reduced number of Neeya's warriors had finally arrived to warn them that their pursuers were now less than two days away. They helped with the digging and covering of trap pits with sharpened spikes at the base to slow the killers down through the narrow entry canyon. Their path leading to the exit cave was covered over and swept with branches to slow and confuse their trackers.

Finally, a long line of tired, half-starved people started to enter the dark pit, some having to be helped, a few having to be carried. Guides with smoking torches had been positioned inside the cave, to show the way. They found a location close to the entry where the cave roof could be safely collapsed to stop any chance of being followed.

As the last of their people passed them, trimmed branches were ready to cause the roof to collapse. They looked at each other and smiled, proud of what had been done to ensure the survival of those they cared for. No words were necessary. This was more than they had ever thought possible. As the first rocks fell, thanks were given for the chance to ensure their people would survive.

It was enough. It was more than enough. After the dust had settled, it was obvious there was no way anyone would be coming after them through that tunnel. But now, no one could ever return through the cave. Their future was ahead of them.

Chapter 2

New Beginning

The underground trek was hard for all, particularly those helping the aged, infirm, and injured. Their tribe had always lived above ground or in shallow caves with a view of the sky. Many were afraid of evil spirits in the darkness that might do them harm, regardless of the flickering light of the torches. The plan to move the tribe in one day soon became impossible because of the slow, difficult progress. A dry area was found away from the stream and cold food was extracted from animal-hide bags and woven grass containers. A short rest period became a much longer time of recovery from exhaustion and the shock of leaving familiar territory for a newly discovered and, for some, terrifying land. The tribe's stockpile of hides, folded skin shelters and grass-filled sleeping mats gave some relief from aching limbs.

Midway through the second day, they exited the cave and stood entranced by the view.

❋ ❋ ❋

They were watched and details were recorded from directly above – over 20,000 kilometres above, in high orbit.

The object viewing their progress was drum-shaped and highly reflective, with gossamer-like wings of fragile-looking silver always facing the sun's rays. Its systems could count the beads around Neeya's neck and the satisfied expression on Tarn's face. It took another series of readings, on air temperature, moisture content, radiation levels, and percentages of oxygen, nitrogen, hydrogen, CO_2, and other atmospheric gases. Localities of nearby human and animal activity were also recorded. It was only one system of many orbiting the planet, receiving details, including from hidden ground-based stations, with regular projections of data back into deep space. It was old, when compared to human life spans. Several of its kind had already failed, losing height and burning up in the atmosphere. But others continued in their programmed duties, regardless of such irrelevant losses. Fifty generations of humanity could pass and still be within the object's designed lifespan.

❈ ❈ ❈

But Tarn and Neeya, along with the surviving members of their tribe, had no knowledge of such things, other than viewing the occasional passing of bright lights above them at night and their legends on the existence of the sky people.

Once the initial amazement of what they could see down the slope had settled and their children had been calmed down and fed, as well as the elderly and injured being cared for, tribal leaders gathered to plan for immediate needs. Such a bountiful land might well include bands of people already claiming the country as their exclusive hunting grounds, willing to fight for its control. Initial defences had to be arranged. Tarn sent scouts out to ensure no surprises existed within a few days' travel.

Their withered crops had been left behind. New, suitable land for planting would have to be found. Bags of seeds, cuttings, and tubers had been carried through the dark cave, with difficulty, to allow for the earliest establishment of food gardens. But shelter and provision for the immediate future were the highest priorities. The minimal meat, nut, and vegetable stockpiles remaining would soon be exhausted, so hunting parties were sent out to bring back fresh meat.

Those women and older children who had the knowledge of the typical locations for berries, nut trees, edible tubers and fruits were organised to begin their search. The nearby river would have few fish so close to the spring outlets from under the cliffs. Further downstream, fish would be sought, along with shellfish and water crawlers. Anyone without a useful task was already gathering firewood or digging the first toilet trench away from the campsite.

Tarn, as fighting chief, was a member of the Council and gave his suggestions for protection and defence. While the talking dragged on in the respectful and long-winded way of tribal councils, he left and gathered the men and single young women assigned that day for his direction. He posted guards at nearby look-out sites, chosen for the best view down the slopes into the valley and distant plain. Several were sent to cut and sharpen timber stakes to be used as protection against possible raids by other tribes and predatory animals. He could not believe that such a region of fresh water and good hunting prospects would not already be occupied by others, perhaps by the descendants of those who had created the painted cave pictures. So, it was best to plan for the worst but hope for no attacks while they were still getting organised.

The cave opening remained the place of retreat, if given time to flee. For the first few days, those dependent on weather protection could shelter in the cave, far back enough to sleep or hide if necessary. With the sun still showing mid-afternoon, temporary skin shades had been erected for those needing rest or trying to recover from their journey through the darkness.

Tarn glimpsed Neeya talking with several of her group under the trees and headed over to compare first thoughts on this new place.

She saw him coming and broke away from her discussions, her elation obvious by her shining eyes.

"Tarn, this is such a change – from desperation to planning for a future. I had grown accustomed to thinking no longer than for a few days ahead. It will take some time for the Council and people to understand what might be possible."

Tarn nodded. He had calmed down and was already planning his next steps. "There is so much that has changed. By finding our way through the cave we have come into a green land of running water and herds of animals. It seems that the rains continue to fall on this side of the mountain."

"In the distance, the sky is still blue but a strange mist hangs in the air, like smoke from far away. How is it possible that so much can change in a journey of two days? This is surely a gift from the spirits. We must work to be sure we do not anger them. With so much power they could choose to remove their blessings at any time."

"This is our chance, Tarn," Neeya enthusiastically agreed. Her words came fast. "It may be our only chance. If our people cannot make a good life for themselves here, then they will not survive. This must remain as bountiful as it is now for our children's children and beyond that. Can we get up to that ridge to view the surrounds before darkness comes?"

They climbed a broken slope of loose rocks eroded from the cliff face. Below, they could see dark soil, not barren ground, with healthy trees and flowering bushes rather than dead or dying drought-affected scrub.

The view from the high ridge laid out the valley's details. The land was covered with different shades of green, with the glittering movement of the river as it made its way down rock-edged gullies. At the bottom of the slope, perhaps two days' journey, the land undulated into a wide, well-watered plain, with the only dust they could see being thrown up by grazing animals.

The distant horizon was edged by purple, grey, and black mountains, with two of the highest peaks capped in white.

Behind them stood the sides of a barren, rocky mountain and the start of the stream created from several smaller springs welling up from the cliff base.

The ridge stood above the plateau, easily defensible from all sides. Tarn observed, "We can spread the camp across this flat space. It will give us views of the countryside and provide protection from raiding parties or animals coming up towards us. Our campfires will be visible to all below us, but for now, this must be the best place to start from, to gain strength, refill our food containers and allow our people to recover."

"Our weapons need repairs as well," Neeya added. "Our baskets are worn. Few fish can be taken with our old nets. They have been unused for several seasons because of the drought and poor hunting. I will see to the women and children, if the Council allows it. Will you speak to the high chief now to get his approval, Tarn, so that we can begin to do what we can to rebuild the tribe?"

Later that day, Tarn had discussions with members of the Council, who were still coming to an understanding of the momentous change in the tribe's fortunes. Most council members were old men, chosen for the wisdom earned from their many summers. The need for change took them time to understand. Tarn and Neeya's suggestions were eventually accepted.

Tarn caught up with Neeya as she busied herself organising women's groups to gather materials for making new nets and baskets. He had already directed efforts to improve spear making and the shaping of stone spearheads.

"Neeya, just stop for a few minutes. The Council agreed to everything we suggested. It can't all be done at once. We both need to find at least one person to take over the day-to-day arrangements to free us to look at long-term needs. The cold weather will eventually be here and the tribe will not be ready to cope."

Reluctantly, Neeya stopped to listen to Tarn, catching her breath to be ready to respond. "As you said, Tarn, it can't all be done at once, but there are a number of easy things that can be quickly started. If our nets are not fixed or remade, we will not be eating fish in the cold time. If the nuts, berries and tubers are not gathered when the harvest is ready, and new baskets are not made, then the hunters had better bring a lot of meat back soon because that will be all we will have to eat."

Her frustration and unexpectedly strong response put Tarn back on his heels. He knew when to back off. "I hear you, Neeya. I apologise for interrupting your tasks. We both have many things to arrange. Can we meet in a couple of days to talk about what are the most important things to achieve next?"

Neeya replied, "Thanks for your understanding, Tarn. In two days, we will be in a much better position." With no further discussion, she turned and hurried off.

In the following days, the campsite was edged with sharpened stakes pointing out from the ground on an angle. Scrub was removed to improve sight lines. Shelters were erected and their supports improved. Rock-edged fire pits provided cooking locations. Further toilet trenches were laboriously dug downwind. Large animal bladders were water-filled and hung on tripods of trimmed branches. Very quickly, instead of worries being voiced around the campsite about how the people could survive, comments changed to complaints about sore backs and blistered hands.

Neeya mentioned to Tarn, "How soon the people have forgotten their worrying time about the black killers. They already find fault with their new land. Feelings last such a short time." Tarn wondered whether she spoke about feelings she had in the past, with her lost family.

Hunting had gone well, easily seen with racks of drying strips of meat positioned close to the cave entrance for protection from hungry predators. Several timber frames leant against the cliff face in the sun, with large deer and antelope hides stretched for drying after every possible remnant of flesh had been scraped with small, sharp pieces of stone. Women loosely plaited dry grass to make fish-catching baskets, while others sorted berries, nuts, and tubers to be stored in tightly woven baskets below ground, away from small rodents and insects.

The men's work area was also a hive of activity. No other tribes had, so far, made contact. This meant a higher level of relaxation for arrow makers, spear shaft straighteners, and the stone knappers splitting arrow and spear points, scrapers, and knife points and allowed them to concentrate on their work. Others attached the stone points with long pieces of leather strapping to shafts already stacked. A thick, tar jelly distilled from nearby plants was spread over the strapping to set hard in the cool air.

The stone knappers had discovered a source of flint and obsidian in nearby loose eroded rocks at the base of the cliffs. Piles of sharp, jagged rock splinters were growing in front of the most skilled, much of it to be left as rubbish when the camp next moved.

Tarn looked over the scene. The people were being fed, sheltered, and protected; food sources were being found and used. Their lives had been retrieved from utter despair to where they were even beginning to hope, to believe they could have a future. He felt proud that he and Neeya had been a part of that rescue.

He had rarely experienced hope in his life. His existence had been tough, with a series of losses that could match those of Neeya. His father had failed to return from a hunting expedition when Tarn was only six summers old. His mother, even though helped by other women, battled to cope and died before he was much older. He lived with three other unrelated families, deprived of parental love and affection, until he was old enough to be sent to join a group of young adult men with similar histories, living under ragged tent covers. Their hunting and survival skills had been taught by an older man of their clan who had injuries but could still teach to justify his tribal position.

His training had been harsh. The tribe had no use for anyone who could not contribute skills for the benefit of all. Survival depended on strength and usefulness. Every member of each clan had to contribute to the tribe, which included the elderly and injured. Women had skills and could provide children, to grow the numbers and replace those who fell. Beyond child-bearing age, if not tending to children, they knew that heavy labour could only follow – digging, carrying, tending to fires, cooking, creating or mending clothes made from skins, woven grass and reeds.

Tarn yearned for the affection he had missed as a child and so married early, a young woman who had to find a mate before her childbearing time had passed. Tornee was her name and, for three summers, they shared their lives. A boy child was born and thrived. Tarn cherished him and named him Tarnel, the son of Tarn, and he received all a father could give his son. That included patient instruction on tribal legends and answers to the multitude of questions Tarnel asked. It had seemed life was repaying all that had been denied him due to his parents' early deaths.

Now, more than ten summers later, the memories of Tornee and Tarnel were still too painful to remember. Tarn had returned from a hunt after the earth had been shaken by the spirits, a rare thing that had happened a few times before. It had caused the hunters to fall to the ground or hang onto trees until it passed. Cracks had opened in the ground and they had seen dust rising from rock slides on nearby slopes.

Their arrival into camp, which was at the entrance to a shallow cave in a hillside, had been brutal. Most of those in camp on that day had survived a rockfall but they were still retrieving bodies for burial – old people, mothers, and children, including those of Tornee and Tarnel. They lay there, still identifiable from their distinctive clothing, broken, never to move again. What the spirits had given had been removed.

Tarn had refused help from others with their burial. The ground chosen was hard, but Tarn persisted with a digging tool made from a deer antler until a shallow grave had been excavated and the bodies laid reverently with their own few meagre possessions. Once the combined grave was covered with soil and rocks raised as a mound, Tarn, still sweating and covered in dust, with bleeding fingers, found a place away from the camp to mourn his loss. He felt part of him had been ripped out and that he should also be dead. So much had been gained and then taken from him in an instant. What had he done to make the spirits punish him so? It took the rest of that season to feel life could still, painfully, be lived.

Now, the sight of his tribe busily restoring itself in this new land lifted him out of the dark place his heart lived in. He dared to have hope again. From bitter experience, he knew how dangerous that could be. Any hot coal from a fire, if given enough air and fuel, could burn and destroy. Hope could also destroy if depended on and held too tightly. So, he buried the feeling inside, like the special things that were kept in the small, private bag around his waist. It held things such as the shining piece of stone he could see through, picked up amongst the rocks, along with the small hard pebble that had killed the deer he had found with Neeya. Also, bright feathers, and small strange bones.

Far above, the golden object with shining sails recorded the changes occurring in its zone of observation. New readings were taken and data from ground monitors downloaded. Once again, the invisible information stream was projected back into deep space, to the location known but of no interest to the ever-watching machine.

It moved on, following the rotation of the planet as directed by its programming, to the next zone of observation.

Chapter 3

Discovery

After a rare full night's sleep, Tarn rolled out of his sleeping mat to stand, facing down the slope towards the well-watered valley, and beyond to the dark, distant mountain ranges. The barest hint of light was beginning to show over the jagged line on the horizon.

He thought about what was needed next, now that the camp was being established for the near future, before the season turned cold. A flash within the distant outline of the mountains caught his eye. It was like a splash of light in a stream from sunlight on water. It repeated several times and then disappeared. Tarn saw no hint of water, and the sun had not risen yet. His mind moved onto other things needed for that day. No one knew what this land held beyond the two days journey the scouts had made in several directions away from camp.

A longer search of the area would tell him if a much better campsite existed that would protect them through the next cold season. Any future danger to the tribe could then be removed before an attack. Also, signs might exist about other people who had hunted across the plain or come from the mountains. The tribe needed extra food sources, such as fruit and nut trees, or edible roots and tubers ripe for the digging, as well as more information about the routes grazing animals followed. Tarn knew he was trying to justify his reasons for a journey of exploration with a small group. He was a man of action who looked for practical solutions to problems, rather than endless talk around a tribal council fire, and he itched to discover new things.

People were starting to move around the camp in the early morning light, collecting water in skin bags, and opening containers to select food for the start of the day.

As the light grew in the sky, thin pink and purple clouds streamed from the mountains. Groups of birds added their own movements, with arrowhead shapes of ducks and other waterbirds heading towards feeding grounds. He caught sight of a cat-like animal slinking past the outer edge of the camp with some small prey in its jaws. It gave the camp a wide berth but kept its eyes on this new human activity. It reminded Tarn of the range of dangers to be wary of during any journey in this new land.

He needed to speak to the members of the Council soon to suggest a longer-distance scouting party of no more than five warriors, led by himself, beginning as early as possible. Neeya had already agreed to the idea when he mentioned it and she wanted to be part of the group.

❄ ❄ ❄

Permission was given, as expected. As the sun rose the following morning, Tarn and Neeya gathered with the three warriors chosen to be part of the group. Anil and Manil were twin brothers well skilled in tracking and hunting, and Alre, a young woman as skilled as the brothers. The group eagerly started down the slope towards the plain and the distant mountains. They each carried backpacks containing sleeping rugs, fire sticks, extra flint-cutting stones, full water skins, and dried food to eat while on the move, as well as their weapons.

The going, initially, was easy. Few trees had fallen to impede their progress, and the loose scree rocks of the slope soon changed to sand and gravel. They had become used to an almost barren landscape in previous summers, so this new country was refreshing, even exciting. All around them the vegetation and trees looked healthy, with a range of birds calling and small animals scampering away from them.

Tarn and the others enjoyed the feelings of health and 'rightness' coming from this new land. They had fought to survive the failing environment on the other side of that tunnel; now they felt part of a balanced nature, that they were meant to be here.

By midday, with the sun overhead, they had seen no hint of other people, no human tracks, or old campsites, and expected few problems from predators in the heat of the day. A large fig tree provided a shaded rest area for their cold meal.

During their travel, they had started to become aware of the air becoming unnaturally still. Few birds called or flew over. No small animals or land crawlers disturbed the leaves. It seemed that everything around them was waiting. The tree under which they sheltered within a shallow basin had tall, isolated companions covering the land they could see. The soil was moist with water running from the cliff area they had left that morning. Tarn quietly investigated the land up the slope from the basin while the others rested, watching the ground for animal signs, and glancing quickly around in all directions. He did not intend to be caught unawares.

Tracks were obvious from several paces away. Two continuous lines, three paces apart, each a hand width. Fresh marks but not paw, hoof or footprints. He remembered the same type of tracks from several summers before. Were they from the same animal? Were there many of them or just one? His heart beat increased and he had to actively relax his stiffened muscles and rigid stance.

Marks ran across the high point above the base of the depression, leading up from below, then down again, heading for the still-distant mountains. Confusing. Worrying.

He padded back to the others to relate his discovery.

"They are strange tracks, made by an animal I have not seen before or tracked. We need to stay silent and move with utmost care. There could be one or many, maybe waiting in ambush."

Tarn was not ready, like Neeya, to tell of his previous experience with similar tracks. Frowning, Neeya said nothing, but looked at Tarn; a slight shake of her head signifying she had the same memory of that first time. No one spoke up with answers or helpful guesses, but they all agreed to continue, nervous and unsure about where they would lead.

They followed the tracks towards the mountains, over undulating and open ground, with scattered large trees providing shade and cover. The sun was well beyond the half day when they moved hesitantly into an open clearing, spreading out with spears at the ready. Neeya signalled Tarn to look at what she had found. He came over, followed by the others, to several tree stumps, the trees having been hacked off with stone axes – they had each cut down similar-sized trees many times. This was the first proof that other people had been there. The cuts were old, more than one summer, but they all felt uneasy about what it revealed. The strange tracks passed close to the stumps but too far away to have made the cuts.

The sun had dropped further towards the horizon before their second find. Another clearing, with three circles of stones covered in grey or black soot and ashes. Small pieces of split bones were left around the fireplaces. A more careful search of the clearing showed holes dug for poles over which skin shelters would have been stretched. The debris from stone knapping was scattered around a log, obviously used as a seat. The signs were, again, old and partly covered with leaves and dust. It did nothing to reduce their tension. People had been there, with a campsite set up and meat cooked on open fires. These people could have moved a short distance away and were now watching them, or they could be long gone. The chance that they were nearby couldn't be discounted.

Their silent movement away from the old campsite continued. Not a leaf was disturbed or a twig broken, a skill practised many times while tracking animals. Darkness stopped their progress up a slight slope, still under trees, with the soil becoming stony. They ate cold food, then spread out their sleeping rugs. A fire at night could not be risked with a potential enemy close by. Everyone took turns as guard, sitting up with spears close at hand for a portion of the night, while moving lights, or the sky people, counted the time overhead.

Wary of the unknown while maybe in territory controlled by others, they slept fitfully on stony ground through the long night; it passed uneventfully. A warming fire was risked, each feeling bleary-eyed due to the tension and lost sleep, as light reappeared in the sky. The smoke from their fire was minimal, from carefully chosen dry wood burning hot and edged closely with rocks. They were packed and following the tracks a short while later, spreading out, with Tarn and Neeya walking between the lines on the ground and the others at a distance on each side, flitting through the trees to provide minimal targets.

Deep cracks in the ground crossed their paths, where the earth had opened in the past. Such cracks had been seen before, causing different tales to be told at night around camp fires, trying to give an explanation to the cause. The tension was extreme, as was their awareness of the surroundings.

No bird or animal movement disturbed the land. The slope grew steeper, became stonier. Even though the trees showed no signs of a wind, a slight but continuous droning noise could be heard. Both Neeya and Tarn felt vibrations from the ground through their moccasins. They said nothing, although the wide-eyed glances between them all, and their gritted teeth, betrayed memories of when the earth had been shaken in the past, and people were injured or killed.

The tracks passed large rocks scattered over the slope, as if a small mountain had been ripped open and the debris thrown over the area. The rocks had been there for a long time, and had creepers or vines growing over them. None were buried into the ground but sat on the surface as if dropped from the sky, cracked, and split open.

They all continued climbing further up the slope, on edge from the continuous vibrations coming from the ground. Then they heard strange sounds ahead of them, coming from a low point where the tracks led.

The sight that met their eyes in the sunken area, was indescribable. The strange animal had four straight sides made of something like white stone. It had three legs on both sides, round like worn, river rocks about one hand thick. There was a depression on the closest part of the thing which held several objects – a small dead lizard, the head of a young antelope, several different pieces of fruit and, of most concern, a human hand, partly withered and dry of blood but cut off cleanly above the wrist.

The noise and vibration came from the round legs on the side, which kept turning forward and then back. A shining arm as thick as a small tree trunk came out of its centre, which thrashed around, trying to dislodge the thing from off the top of a flat rock for the legs to gain movement forward. It looked like it had been there for some time because round trenches had been dug on both sides by its turning legs as it had tried to move off the rock. The centre arm had hard pieces sticking out the sides, with sharp cutting edges and a grabbing hand clipping uselessly in the air.

※ ※ ※

Neeya whispered in alarm to Tarn, "Is it from the sky people, sent to punish or teach us? Maybe there are good and bad sky people and this is not supposed to be here. It may have escaped from them. I don't like this, Tarn. We shouldn't be here." She grimaced and glanced around nervously.

Tarn had no idea what to do next. He screwed up his face and opened his mouth, but failed to reply. It was beyond his understanding. Alre, never one to stop and think about her actions in the past, picked up a long, dead branch and went to poke it, to get a reaction. She went close to the centre arm, but before she could hit it, the arm swung around almost too fast to follow and sliced into her with a long, shining blade. The blade sank deep into her side in an instant with a horrible sucking sound, cutting like no axe or sharp-edged stone could.

She was dead before hitting the ground, almost cut in two with a rapidly spreading spray of blood over the nearby rocks. The blade was withdrawn from the terrible wound in a fast return swing. A bright red light started blinking from on top of the arm, which now hung poised, threatening another strike. It resembled the eyes of a predator caught in the light at night.

Everyone else jumped back out of range from any further attack, scrambling on the loose rocks and fighting to remain standing. The speed of Alre's death shocked and left them speechless, even though they had experienced animal attacks before.

It seemed to look at them, to focus its actions on their movements. One short, rounded arm, above the terrible cutting blade, had a shining, unblinking blue eye, which tracked them as they stood or moved, spears poised. It must be an animal, the strangest and most frightening animal, and it was aware of each one of them.

Out of striking range of the terrible weapon, Tarn responded to the attack without further thought and picked up a large rock. In one smooth move, he raised it above his head and threw it at the strange animal. It hit the centre arm, knocking a piece off it. The others joined in, shouting and letting out their anger. After a shower of rocks, each one doing damage, the animal stopped moving, with the cutting arm leaning to one side. They poked another branch into its side several times and received no response.

Their fighting instinct flowed away, as they realised the short conflict had ended. They could do nothing for their dead companion as they viewed her body and the shocking pool of blood on the ground. Their only hope was that her spirit would find its rightful place amongst the sky people when they buried her.

But for now, they collapsed on the side of the depression where the unmoving, strange animal lay, Tarn with his head in his hands. Neeya, white faced in shock, her mind in confusion, on the far side from where the others sat, stared at something on the object. It was a bright green, blinking light from a patch on the side of the animal. Slightly larger than a hand, it attracted her, soundlessly called her to come closer.

Chapter 4

Machine

In the back of her mind, Neeya knew to stay back. This thing was dangerous, and it could still strike out, but the light attracting her was too much to fight. Her mind swirled, the attraction fighting the danger, demonstrated by the sight of Alre's body lying where it had fallen on the slope.

She stood and, step by slow step, moved towards the strange thing. Tarn and the two brothers were too slow to raise themselves from their stupor. Neeya had raised her arm, her hand already reaching out before Tarn shouted, "Neeya, it is still dangerous. Do not touch it."

Neeya took no notice; it was as if she had not heard.

Regardless of Tarn's warning, she placed her hand on the flat, green plate, which turned red, then flickered. Neeya stood, unmoving, her eyes glazed over, her face blank, her mouth open. The others moved toward her, unsure of whether to drag her away or be ready to catch her if she fell. She was still alive and breathing – they could see her chest rising and falling; she appeared to be in no obvious pain with her hand glued to the light.

Inside, Neeya felt nothing. Her mind had gone elsewhere as it battled to cope with the information flowing from the machine – she now knew what it was – through her hand's connection, with the machine's power reserves slowly draining. A tiny needle on the side of the green light took a drop of blood from her unfeeling hand … to analyse her DNA.

The machine confirmed that she was the intended recipient for the information flow, with her bloodline and DNA opening the key to that flow. Her facial tattoos supplied the final approval for the connection.

Neeya's knowledge immediately increased, without her understanding how it happened. She now knew the machine was directed to regularly collect samples from animals and plants, and, if it came across a relatively recent grave, from a human being.

The samples were taken to the machine's 'base' – she could not understand what that word was – for investigation, with the findings added to the extensive data stockpile collected from many generations of humans on the planet. So much was being deposited into her brain for future use, but before all information was transferred, the remaining machine energy ran out, and the flickering light died.

She felt her consciousness speeding through space and abruptly smashing back into her mind. As her hand slid off the touch plate, her knees buckled, and she collapsed beside the now truly dead machine. Her concerned companions dragged her further away for safety and looked down on her as her eyes opened. They wanted to know what had happened to her because of the strange light, but waited until she recovered. Tarn trickled a water skin's contents over her face and into her mouth until her spluttering and coughing signalled him to stop.

After a long while she stood. Her head felt heavy but less disoriented, and her perception of the surroundings had changed, as if a veil had been lifted. Her vision was clearer and her hearing more intense. Even her body seemed different – more alive and aware.

"Neeya, you look different. You have been through a lot and it shows. Take your time and stay still while you recover," Tarn insisted. She stared at him as if he were transparent and her face almost gleamed with light. She looked around and listened to them, as if the three of them were new and worthy of study, while previously unconnected parts came together in her mind.

"Tarn, I understand so much more," she began. She was already using the information just absorbed. "The mist in the air, the movement in the ground under our feet, this strange machine and how it was made. We have so much to learn!"

She knew what she had to do. It both frightened and strengthened her, and it would involve, for a time, little help from others. She now knew that this was what she was born for. At last, she could focus on having a future.

It was also vastly important that she succeed. This was the main message from the machine.

Waving off the concerns of Tarn and the others, she spoke. "Tarn, I have learnt a lot from what I touched. It is not an animal. It was made by people like us, a long time ago. It is a thing, like our spears and knives. It is called a machine. The people who made it lived in the past and knew so much more than we can yet understand. Many machines were made, for different reasons and purposes.

"They are meant to show us the way, to help us on our journey. Can we do this together, while I follow what I have learnt? There may be a great cost to us."

Gripping his hands together, he nodded, his face creased with worry, and he grew unusually quiet. This was so much beyond him. He was there to protect Neeya but he could do little against such unknown dangers. Until that moment, they had shared the exploration, all of them contributing what they could understand. Now things had changed. Neeya was different. They could see and feel that she was now their leader. Only she could give directions and answers from the deep well from which she had drunk.

Tarn took the simplest path, and said, "Neeya, lead, and we will follow."

She walked confidently the few steps back to the machine and, one by one, pressed four shining buttons on the damaged central column. Each button released a metal tool, and they all clanged as they fell onto the surface of the machine – the long killing blade, a shorter, thin knife blade, the grabbing hand with individual fingers and a digging tool. She decided to leave the barrel of the projectile gun used for firing the round pellet they had dug out of the side of an animal a long time ago. That was the same type of pellet Tarn carried in the pouch around his waist. It needed a force to work that lived only in the machine and so was useless to them.

Neeya picked up the long, killing blade and gave the digging tool to Tarn. The other implements were carried by Anil and Manil. For several moments they all stood around the strange machine. Alre's fresh blood smell was strong, while they held the cold metal tools, so foreign to all they knew.

They buried their dead tribeswoman beside the machine by using the digging tool, with her spear, stone knife, and pack beside her, as if she had killed the machine while sacrificing herself. Leaving the sad and lonely scene behind, after an unsuccessful inspection for any further useful items, the group followed Neeya up the slope. They stopped momentarily to remember Alre, their friend and companion, now lost. They had removed the last traces of Alre's spilt blood and placed it into the shallow grave, so that she was as whole again as they could make her. Tarn's last glance was of the machine slowly dripping its last life liquid, green and oily, onto the ground, with the new earth mound in the background. They returned to following the machine tracks. It looked like a well-used main route, with multiple wheel marks along a hard path devoid of rocks or any vegetation. It was easy to stay quiet. Everyone dwelt in their own minds, going over and over what had happened.

The path continued to steepen as they walked, and the vibration and low humming noise also increased. The ground grew rockier, the trees became stunted and finally ended as they stepped into a clear area of low plants and jagged, broken pieces of rock.

The site gave a clear view over a large part of the valley they had just travelled through. In the distance, a series of dark cliffs created the horizon. They were too far away to see anything of their tribe's campsite, but a vague movement of smoke drifting across the cliff face indicated the position. They were high enough to see the strange mist in the air, which appeared to erupt out of the flat-topped mountain above them.

Their provisions were almost exhausted when their meal was finished. They had eaten without tasting, all their attention still on what had happened to Alre and what could come next. They would soon have to put time and effort into hunting for meat and gathering berries, nuts, or edible tubers. To do that they would need to descend away from whatever kept animals from living on these higher slopes.

After a rest they continued, following the machine tracks, the easiest route for them and their only chance of knowing more about the killing machine and what Neeya had learnt from it. The path had been used, probably over many summers, by who knew how many machines, maybe like the one they had just broken.

The hard-packed path slowly spiralled around the side and towards the upper part of the flat-topped mountain. Nothing grew there and, apart from the path, the slope was covered in loose scree rocks. The path stopped abruptly in front of a steeply-angled, dead-end rock wall. Neeya showed no surprise to see the end of the path, while the others were obviously puzzled as to why she had led them there.

"Neeya, you said you have learnt from the machine," Tarn said in a frustrated tone. "We will all follow you but we need to know where we are going and why. In time, we will be able to understand but, for now, we are children, and you are the teacher."

"Sorry, Tarn. This is very strange for me and my head is full of new words and ideas that I have never dreamt of. Give me time and I will try to do better. It would take too much time to explain now."

Tarn shook his head, but said nothing more and waited for Neeya to make her next decision. The others followed his lead, but tension tightened their faces as they waited. She walked up to the rock face, took the wrapped killer blade from the side of her pack and inserted the end into a slot the same size and shape as the blade. It fitted exactly. She turned the blade sideways, not knowing what to expect.

With a dry, low, grinding sound, the rock wall split into two halves, the sections sliding to either side to create an opening the width of the machine.

The unexpected sound and movement startled them all, even Neeya, and, wide-eyed, they jumped back from the cracked wall. Inside the cave, the grey sides and floor were smooth, not like rough natural stone. There were no jagged or uneven surfaces, including the high roof, well above their heads.

When she signalled them to stay silent and follow her, they needed no further direction, but spears and knives were held in tight hands. They had been in large animal lairs before and the slow, tense movement forward betrayed their fear.

Neeya, blade in hand, stepped forward into the entrance. The doors had stopped moving, having disappeared into matching slots on each side. Tarn started to ask something but Neeya put her finger to her lips to silence him.

The black hole leapt from darkness to full light as soon as Neeya entered, like the sun had appeared from behind dark clouds. She showed no concern, but the remaining three, Tarn in particular, looked wildly around, fearful it was a trap, and shocked the sky people had created light where there had been none. They were again shooshed to silence and signalled to follow her. She slowly walked down the slight slope of the tunnel into the heart of the mountain. As they moved forward, the light behind them turned dark again while the section in front erupted into brilliance. A hundred metres along the straight tunnel it turned, the light progressively closing off behind them but always illuminating ten new steps in front. This section had closed entrances at intervals on both sides, with symbols on the walls. It felt very much like they were invading some huge animal's lair.

They moved past each entrance, leaving internal secrets hidden in darkness. Neeya stopped at the third on her left side. She reached up and touched a flat plate on the wall, like that on the machine. The plate turned green and the once hidden, dark space was bathed in light as the door slid aside.

Neeya and Tarn knew a little of this magic now, but they still glanced at each other, eyes wide with unease, nervous hands resting on weapons. At her gesture, they edged into the room, which was large enough for the two brothers to rest on the floor, which they did.

Tarn spoke. "Neeya, what is this place? Did you learn about it when you touched that machine? Are you sure we can be safe here?"

"I can't answer your questions yet, Tarn. The machine died before it could tell me everything. I know it worries you but give me a chance to finish the message that I was supposed to receive before."

Tarn made a frustrated gesture to Neeya with his hand, indicating he had given up trying to talk to her and slumped onto the floor with the brothers.

Neeya glared at him, then turned away. Using what she had learnt so far, but still had little understanding of, she went straight to the opposite wall and touched a small raised plate, causing a part to slide aside. It revealed a flat, waist-high bench, about two metres long, with coloured lights spaced across its surface. The lights varied in colour from red, green, white, and other shades she couldn't name. Some lights were unmoving. Others flickered in their colours. Two red lights changed to green while they watched.

She assumed the others were listening, "I must do the same thing I did with the machine we broke. It stopped before completing my training, so I need to finish learning all it has for me." Her hand was on a similar flat panel built into the bench covered in lights in front of her.

They stayed quiet. The experiences of that day were already more than enough for their minds, most of it beyond their comprehension. Now they could only agree, while hoping that it would soon be over and they could retreat from this strange hole in the side of the mountain. Neeya remained sitting at the bench, with her back to them. She touched the panel and stopped moving. They guessed it would be the same as before– her eyes would glaze over, the process taking time. They were used to long periods of waiting. Patience was important for survival and they had all leant it as children.

The low noise and vibration continued to fill the room. It seemed they had entered the mouth of a huge beast that was ready to consume them. Their only escape was back through the now dark cave they had entered, the magic lights having disappeared.

They remained on the cold, hard floor, their backs against the walls, their packs and weapons beside them. Tarn thought, as he looked around, how strange this place was, beyond anything from his wildest dreams.

The twins slept, while Tarn waited for what seemed a long time. He used the chance to replace the leather strips that held his moccasins together with good leather kept for repairs in his pack. Their hike up the side of the mountain over rubble and jagged rocks had done damage to their footwear, which would normally last much longer on sand and soil. Once his work was finished, he tossed old remnant pieces into the corner and began to sharpen the edges of his spear-head with a piece of harder stone.

A sudden movement to his extreme left made him jump up in one instant and yell, to bring the end of his spear-shaft down with a crash onto a small moving object twice the size of his foot. The thing smashed into several pieces which flew in different directions across the floor.

The brothers, alerted by the sudden movement and loud noise, were a heartbeat behind Tarn, leaping up into a protective stance, spears ready. Neeya, however, remained oblivious to the yelling and jumping around.

The pieces were of the same white material as the thing Neeya called a machine, but much smaller, with thin arms on each side ending in sharp, grasping hooks or fingers. Before Tarn smashed it, it had been circular and moved on four small wheels, like the larger machine. A tiny red, flashing light on its smashed centre slowly faded while they stood staring at the scattered pieces.

As their breathing returned to normal, another quick movement at the bottom of the wall where the first machine had come from made them jump again. How many of these things were there? An identical white object came out of a second hole at the base of the wall, a flap swinging back to allow it to enter.

On their guard, they all watched, ready for action, as the second machine rolled from one broken piece of its companion to the next, stopping only to sling each piece with the same pincer arms onto its back, which was shaped like a small, flat basket. Once every piece was gathered up, it folded its arms and rolled back into the hole in the wall, the wall flap closing with a click behind it.

Their mouths hung open while they tried to understand what had just happened. Before they could do or say anything, another flap opened beside the first and yet another small machine moved into the room. It paused only to turn towards the scraps of old leather pieces Tarn had thrown in the corner. The pieces were quickly gathered up and the object retraced its route back into the wall, leaving the floor as clean as when they first entered.

After cautiously waiting in vain for further movements, they returned to sitting on the floor, with an occasional worried glance at where the machines had come from. Tarn decided to do no further repairs, the cause of so much drama. None of them could sleep. The room, with its tiny machines scuttling around the floor, unsettled him, yet another strange happening in what had become a journey of constant new things and worries.

Finally, Neeya moved. Raising her head, she turned around. One of the red lights on the bench winked out.

❊ ❊ ❊

Unknown to everyone in the room, a signal had been projected into space with a message: "First contact confirmed." If a computerised circuit could show any form of sentiment, it would have registered great excitement, given the message was the reason for its own existence finally being justified, after having waited many human generations for this moment.

❊ ❊ ❊

Neeya turned around to face the group and explained, "This wall with the lights has finished delivering the story begun by the machine we broke. It was very long and I am still trying to understand what it said to me. The people who made the machine on the mountain also made this place, which is very large and beyond our understanding. There are tunnels and caves storing the sort of things you see here and much more. They travelled a long way over many years to bring our ancestors, animals, and plants here. Nothing lived on this planet before they arrived.

"All the tribes were given different camping places and tribal lands to live in, each tribe with its own skills and ways of life. But before they arrived, it took many years to prepare the land for us, and for trees and plants to grow then spread, along with the animals, fish, and birds. Then our ancestors arrived. Big machines had been built, most of which still work, to make life better.

"The noise you hear and the movement under your feet are from one of their big machines, still operating as originally intended."

Neeya left her bench and sat down on the floor to face them. "The machine we killed was only one of many. They live in camps like this one and go out often to collect small pieces of things from trees, plants, and animals. They sometimes even do that to a buried body. The small pieces are brought back here and other machines find out if there is anything wrong with them. They have been doing this for years beyond our counting.

"I have been shown why we hear the strange noise and feel movement under our feet. I want to take you back into the sunshine, to show you the reason. It won't be dangerous."

Without waiting or even giving her an answer, they all stood with obvious relief, and picked up their packs and weapons. Tarn said, "Let's get out of here." He and the twins had shared the same anticipation to hear the welcome news of returning to the sun and fresh air.

They left the room, the light immediately reappearing above them. It continued to switch on ahead and disappear behind them, as they retraced their steps to the previously hidden, but now open door, out into the clean air once more. Even Neeya seemed relieved to be in the open, looking down on their valley with its trees and line of cliffs facing them in the far distance. She looked up and, for the first time, noticed thin clouds drifting away from the mountain they stood on, in an otherwise clear blue sky.

❋ ❋ ❋

Above those clouds, well beyond their vision, their exit from inside the mountain was recorded. Along with other detailed observations and measurements, the information was again sent as a message package deep into the blackness of space. Long anticipated plans were now underway, caused by their visit to the mountain tunnel they had just exited, plans intended to change the world forever.

Chapter 5

New Understandings

They strode rather than walked, breathing mountain air, enjoying the sun's warmth, eager to be clear of that hole in the mountain side. This time their route curved up around the entrance on a winding path towards the summit of the flat-topped mountain.

The mountain itself was lower than several nearby snow-capped peaks, which loomed above them. The path had been carved out of solid rock but was weathered from the freezing and scorching of countless seasons. The vibrations continued shaking the rock and the now booming sound steadily increased as they clambered up the slope, following Neeya. The misty air thickened to strange light rain, with the shining rocks around them saturated and dripping. None of them remembered ever being wet from a rainfall, and the experience was not as wonderful as they had anticipated, with their soaked skins starting to stick to their bodies and drip into already-soggy moccasins.

The path curved around a large, black rocky outcrop and immediately entered a narrow, smooth-cut canyon, with walls about twice their height and as smooth as a knife through fat. They had to walk single file in shallow running water. They could feel the ground vibrating up through their feet, with small pebbles disturbed and rolling down the slope. Like a massive waterfall, the sound assaulted their ears and made speech impossible.

They came to another dead end, again with a slot cut into the vertical wall. Neeya repeated her trick of inserting the strange blade she carried into the slot and turning it sideways. As before, the wall slid away, this time to their left in one piece. Neeya walked straight into the black hole, with overhead lights immediately illuminating yet another passage, this time only wide enough for one person, with the rock-cut roof now barely one arm's-length above them. The passage was short, about 50 metres in length. Again, she pushed a panel set in the wall, with the colour change to green now being less of a surprise.

The vibration and noise almost disappeared. They moved down the short side passage with less hesitation and entered a cold, dry room at the end behind a simple door that swung open with a push. The view from the far side of the space was stunning. The floor of the space they stood in, barely ten metres further on, ended in a vertical drop, with a short, hard rock barrier at waist height stopping a fall into darkness. Through a heavy mist that seemed to endlessly surge vertically up past them, they glimpsed a solid wall over one hundred metres away on the other side of the hole. Looking to either side, they could vaguely make out the side walls that made up a round, rock chasm, dropping down from the height of the flat-topped mountain above them to disappear into the invisible depths. Their faces showed their puzzlement, eyes wide and mouths open – how could water surge up past them? It was impossible.

Tarn leaned forward to peer down into the depths and immediately produced a thumping sound, as he bounced his head off an invisible barrier. Neeya said, "Keep your heads back behind the barrier wall. We remain dry and hear no sound because the people who built this place created a clear wall through which to see their work and still stay protected. This is only one of many things they built that we cannot yet understand.

Even with the long message given to me by their machine, I still cannot explain it all.

"What you see is the melting snow and ice from the mountain peaks above us being guided into this hole cut into the rock. A large machine at the bottom pushes air and water made from the snow up into the sky, then the wind blows it towards the cliffs, towards where our tribe has its camp. The air carries water away that falls on the land and cliffs. Without it, all would be dry and dead, as it was before this was built. The big machine, and how the water gets out, was explained to me. This is how I know."

She pointed to a trough on the side of the wall near the entranceway, unnoticed until now in the shadows. "There is water in the trough that always flows. We can fill our water skins and sleep here tonight. What little food we have left we can use now and try to hunt again tomorrow."

"Anil and Manil, in the morning, Tarn and I will leave you to go on a long journey away from our valley in search of other gatherings of people. They must be told what we have learned. We are part of a much larger story than our legends and beliefs have taught us. Our tribe must be prepared for a change even greater than what we experienced escaping from the black killers through the cave."

The twins nodded their agreement to Neeya's words and organised their sleeping skins for the night before taking out what food they still had left. Tarn indicated to Neeya that he wanted to have a talk with her out in the entry corridor, away from the others. Once they were on the other side of the door, he couldn't contain himself.

"I now know that we are going on an important journey and that you will tell others the reasons we search for them. I will then be able to hear and understand why, as well," he said with sarcasm in his words. "Neeya, if you really want me to be a partner with you in what is to come with this journey, then you need to explain what is so important and as much of what the machine told you as you can. I will not walk behind you, like a child, waiting for any scrap of information you care to provide. If it is to be just you and the machine to know what is at stake, then tell me and I will go back to our people with the twins tomorrow."

Neeya was mortified to hear Tarn's words and jumped into her apologies, "I am so sorry, Tarn. My head was so full of what I am supposed to do that I took you for granted, and forgot that you didn't receive what I was given through the machine connection. The others are eating and will be asleep soon. This light will stay on as long as we are here. Can we sit down and I will go over everything I know about what is supposed to happen? I am so sorry to have treated you this way, Tarn. I will try harder in future, but please tell me when I forget myself again."

Tarn only nodded, relieved that he didn't have to follow through with his threat to leave her tomorrow. The last thing he wanted to do was abandon her to her commitment, apparently for the good of all their people. He was also a leader, and he knew that following and fully supporting Neeya would not be easy.

They sat on the cold, hard rock floor and talked late into the night, before going to their sleeping skins to get what sleep they could manage.

Before he slept, Tarn looked around the base of each wall for signs of the holes for the small white machines with arms. Finding nothing, he relaxed, free from the thought of them wandering around him in the dark.

In the end, none of them slept well that night. The strangeness of all they had been through did not settle well in their minds. The idea of that vast torrent of water being pushed up just a few steps away, through the mountain and into the sky, rather than down in a natural waterfall, defied all understanding.

What had happened to those people from the far distant past, with the powers of gods? Where had they gone? Was this their monument, ending here, to show nothing more of their existence? Stone walls opening on the mountainside, long tunnels cut from solid rock, lights appearing and disappearing like magic? It was too much, but eventually, their exhausted minds forced their bodies into sleep.

The cold, grey light of the morning sun reflected through the viewing window had them rolling out of their sleeping skins. With only water as breakfast, it took a while for their bodies to work out the aches and pains left from sleeping on the rock floor, but they eventually left their sleeping place, with the now magic lights appearing and disappearing in the passageway as they exited under a slate-grey, early morning sky.

Neeya suffered from her lack of sleep, awakening with apprehension and uncertainty about what had to happen in the coming days. Her eyes were gritty and the lack of a good meal left her without energy.

The responsibilities laid on her by the content of the two machine messages were immense. She had been dragged away from a simple tribal life, sharing the happenings of a large group of people, into a pre-set role dominated by something that was in her blood. Many generations of that line had somehow passed on the key details of the distant past by the builders of the amazing machines in the mountain. Why her and why now? Surely all of what was to happen now could have happened sometime in the past, way before she was even born. She was still not at peace with the deaths of her two children and now, somehow, she had been told that their loss had been a major setback in the plans of the ancient builders.

But today, the next big change would impact them, a step that would see her and Tarn leave the safety of their companions and their whole tribe.

They all stood together, looking out on the broad valley, now understanding the water mist as it rose above them from the top of the mountain and curved towards the distant cliffs.

Reluctantly breaking her gaze away from the view below, Neeya explained, "Anil and Manil, what we have seen here is very important for our future and the future of all those we know. Tarn and I will travel to another place like this for more teaching, while searching for other tribes, to explain to them what we know and ask for their help. You both need to return to our people to tell the Council what you have seen and understood. They may not believe you or perhaps they will take a long time to plan what to do. Regardless, this place was built and still is a refuge and protection from the black killers or anything else that we cannot fight against. The mountain holds more than enough space for the tribe to rest, and water is available. But food needs to be gathered and brought with you, if this refuge becomes important.

"Tell the Council that the time may well come when food stores will be desperately needed and so meat and fish must be dried or preserved. Stockpiles of nuts, tubers and berries must be collected. This is for the survival of our people. Go now. May the sky people watch and guide you on your way, but first I will need the short knife blade taken from the machine we killed. Take the other strange tool, the hand with metal fingers. Show it to the council members so they will believe what you tell them. If you are attacked or pursued, don't try to fight back, just run. At least one of you must get back to our people with this message."

The two tribesmen reluctantly waited, looking at each other, to be sure of what they had heard. Finally, they said their goodbyes and started down the slope, looking back at times, until they were out of sight. They first had to restore their food supplies for the journey home. Tarn and Neeya watched them go; as they became specks in the distance then disappeared, Tarn asked, "Where do we go now, Neeya? You explained most of your plan last night, but it is still not settled in my head. Where are these other places and tribes, the people you have been told to find?"

"Tarn, this land is far larger than we can understand. It would take many lifetimes to travel through it. Large machines like the one we have seen were built in other places, long ago. Some of them have stopped working, and the land they used to provide water and air for has dried out. The people who lived in those places have either died or moved away, into other lands that might still be occupied. Many are battling to survive rather than developing new skills and knowledge in peace.

"The survivors need help against those who steal and destroy, like the black killers, as well as aid to grow and improve the future for our children's children."

They spent a little time repacking their bags, ensuring they filled their water skins, and their weapons were ready for use, including the cutting blades taken from the machine. "What direction were you told to take to find these other tribes and the sky people's machines?" Tarn asked.

"The machines are in this line of mountains, towards the setting sun. We will see areas that are green and well-watered compared to those that are barren. Other than heading in that direction, we can only hope that we will be led to where we are most wanted."

They left soon after, down the slope from the mountain, back into the protective cover of trees, better soil, and the chance of finding game to restock their supplies. Even before the sun was overhead, they surprised a young deer that fell to Tarn's spear. The short blade from the machine proved to have a marvellous cutting edge, easily slicing the meat into portions for cooking or smoking after the skin had been carefully removed.

Both the long killing blade and the shorter narrow blade were made of – Neeya remembered the word – steel, the same metal as the first machine they had destroyed. She was starting to use the words given from the computer she had been able to access. It felt strange that her mind was assembling a new language without any effort. With each new word came new understanding.

They enjoyed the first good meal for days. That shaded area became their base for the rest of the day and night, even though it was early in the afternoon. It allowed them to smoke meat for the journey, look for other food and have undisturbed rest in better surroundings.

A search over the surrounding country located several loaded nut trees, even though it was late in the season. Neeya found edible tubers growing in the shallows of a small pond as well as freshwater shellfish. That night's meal included smoked venison, fire-roasted potatoes and tubers, and the shellfish. They both knew that this bounty might well be the last for some time and so they ate their fill. Before arranging their sleeping rugs, they stretched the now scraped-clean deerskin over a makeshift frame to dry. The skin would not be suitable for clothes or footwear, but could be used, after more drying, for repairs or trading.

The night passed uneventfully and sunrise found them already with their backs to the sun, heading parallel to the mountains but keeping to the thicker growth on the foothills. Nature had returned in full, with a myriad of bird calls, small animals moving in the undergrowth and the droppings or footprints of both predators and their quarry in abundance. For the area they were passing through, all seemed in balance, and for a short while they enjoyed their journey.

"This is such wonderful country. Did the machine tell you if this was what the whole planet was supposed to be like, in the original plans?"

"The six big water and air-making machines were only installed in a small area of the planet's surface. If they all ran for hundreds of years then the atmosphere and water released would have made a much larger area suitable for life of all types. But the black killers destroyed one machine and another has stopped for some unknown reason, so it's taking much longer to improve the conditions. Just stopping the killers would be a huge step forward. I don't know if we can do what is wanted from us, Tarn, unless we can find a lot more people to help. The killers seem to have strength on their side while our people are spread out everywhere, running and hiding without proper weapons. Right now, it seems impossible."

Tarn couldn't think of what to say to lift her confidence. "One thing at a time, Neeya. We can only try to do what we can as each problem comes at us." Neeya knew what Tarn was doing, but only grunted in response.

The ground was slightly moist, crossed by several small, shallow streams. They now understood where the moisture came from and could see the slight haze in the sky, driven by the flat-top mountain machine they had left the day before.

For once the going was easy, a relief from their previous clambering over rocky slopes. They rested for a short while, eating pieces of smoked meat and a few handfuls of fresh berries picked from bushes as they walked. The journey continued for the rest of the day without incident. That night they slept in the overhang of a shallow cave, glad to have protection behind them with their small fire not so visible.

The next day started out identical to the previous day. Tarn had placed simple traps in what appeared to be small animal trails in the undergrowth before they slept. Their reward in the morning was two fat rabbits, one of which became their breakfast, with the other gutted, skinned and wrapped with fragrant leaves in Neeya's pack. They kept up a good pace through the morning, with the land and vegetation starting to change. The trees grew taller and the undergrowth less dense. Fewer streams were crossed, and fewer animal tracks were seen.

Tarn had an uneasy feeling that all was not safe as they walked. Subtle signs or slight movements behind them told him they were being followed by a predator, possibly seeing them as a meal to replace the reduced numbers of animals in the area.

He quietly told Neeya, "Keep walking and try not to look back or make sudden moves. We are being followed by a large animal. Get your weapons ready." His words to her were emphasised with a flat tone of voice and a slight lift of the spear in his hand in readiness.

She muttered in reply, "I just noticed. I'm surprised an animal attack hasn't happened before this."

They became more cautious, stepping carefully and staying in areas with more undergrowth while keeping a watch behind them. There was no wind, but the vegetation in front of them moved slightly. Were there two predators stalking them, not just one? A mottled pig came crashing out from the bushes, startling them and disappearing in seconds again to one side.

At the same instant, a big, yellow, spotted cat surged at them from the opposite direction, snarling as it came to a stop less than ten metres away. The beast limped, its left front leg being carried as if injured. It looked skinny and hungry.

Its eyes focused only on them.

Neeya already had the long steel killing blade held in front of her while Tarn relied on his two spears, one held ready to throw. The big animal slowly came forward, still favouring its injured paw. It lowered its body, ready to spring, while Neeya and Tarn backed up but readied themselves. They both had history in defending against big cats, but it was always dangerous and always had their hearts pumping fast. This was no exception. In a second, the cat was in mid-air, long teeth obvious in its open snarling jaws and claws fully extended, ready to bite and dismember.

Tarn's spear met it in mid-flight, plunging deep into its side, but it still completed its plunge towards Neeya. She side-stepped as it came near and, with one smooth, vertical swipe, brought her blade down through its neck to separate head from shoulders.

The big cat still writhed on the ground, the neck pumping blood onto the sand as its death quivers slowly subsided. Soon, it remained still. After several prods from Tarn's second spear, they examined the kill, their adrenaline ebbing away as their heart rates and breathing returned to normal.

Neeya said shakily, "That was a close thing. If its paw was not injured and without this blade, it could have ended differently, even with your spear in its side." Tarn's relieved gasps subsided, and he nodded while examining the damaged paw. In amongst the build-up of pus and soil, the broken shaft of an arrow showed through the top and a stone arrowhead projected slightly out of the pad.

"This cat has carried its injured paw for days. It probably hasn't been able to hunt properly. See how skinny it is and its bad skin. The arrow would have come from someone in this area, because it wouldn't have been able to walk far wounded like this."

After further inspection, they expertly removed the teeth and claws, then skinned the animal, rolling up the still-moist pelt for further treatment at the end of the day. Such trophies traded well and they might need trade items in the future. They could provide their own food and weapons, but replacement clothes and footwear needed time in a camp. They expected to be on the move for some time to come, without a base to rest and properly make new clothing.

Both Neeya and Tarn thought of the future and how the journey would be hard with little support. The animal attack would probably be just the first of many threats.

Chapter 6

Two Become Four

They moved off, more relaxed now that at least one threat had been removed. The weather remained dry and clear, with the ground soft and easy for walking. The trees were thinning out and getting smaller. There were signs of the climate being wetter in times past, particularly with several deep creek beds holding only a trickle of water, and long-dead bushes taking up more ground.

When the sun was overhead, they ate a lunch of cold venison and potatoes. As they walked through the morning, they saw less birdlife and small animals, probably due to the lack of water.

After travelling until about mid-afternoon, they pushed through thick bushes into a wide clearing. The remains of a permanent camp took up most of the area. It had been recently vacated in a panic, with good robes, weapons and clay cooking pots lying around. Poles originally holding up tent covers were collapsed and several had burnt over the last few days. No obvious bodies lay around and no food supplies were found. Neeya and Tarn went from one tent site to another, trying to get an understanding of what caused the desolation.

The reason soon became obvious. Tarn could smell burning coming from one blackened tent cover. He dragged it to one side to find the partially charred body of a young man with two arrows in his chest. He had died with the tent collapsing over him, and the whole pile then catching fire from the central fireplace. The thing that made them both stop and frown, then examine the arrows in the man's body, was that they were painted black with black feathered ends. The killers who had nearly caught Neeya and Tarn so recently had reappeared to attack and destroy!

It was useless to go back to warn their tribe. Warnings had already been carried back by the twins, and their journey was now more important. Tarn was pleased to find a good hunting bow and collected a full quiver of arrows from those scattered around the site. The steel weapons from the broken machine were excellent for close fighting but if they had to hold off a band of attackers, his two spears would be of little use. Their tribe had used bows and arrows in the past, but their old dried-out hunting ground provided little suitable wood to make good bows. This area they journeyed through had different types of trees, providing much more suitable timber for constructing them.

Tarn knew it would take hours of practice to rebuild his skill with this unfamiliar weapon, so he gathered up as many arrows as he could find in the deserted, smashed campsite.

They left debris and wood stacked around the unknown man's body burning as they moved on. It was hard to think about the destruction. Were the killers following them? Had this been one of the bands they were supposed to locate? Only one body had been found. What happened to this sizable group of people, given the number of tent sites? Were they captured and then taken away or had they scattered in all directions? So many questions in their minds had no answers. Nothing was obvious from the footprints around the camp. It was natural to see rough walking tracks in all directions from such settlements, as people went searching for wood and food, with hunting parties trying different directions.

They walked towards the sun, now low in the sky, until they came to a rock pile, each rock larger than them, just below a ridge, with a sheltered view back towards the way they had come.

"The sunlight is almost gone, Neeya. This looks like a good place to camp. There is plenty of shelter and we should be able to defend it well. I need to practise with the bow I picked up, if it is going to be useful at a longer range than a spear throw."

"I agree. Once you have had enough practice, I will have to improve my poor use of the bow, too. We may need it, and the trees we have passed seem to have better wood than where we left, so maybe we can make a second weapon if we have the time."

Their small camp was quickly set up and the two skins they now had were laid out in the shelter to continue drying. A small but hot fire was quickly burning and they cooked the second rabbit and a sizeable piece of venison with potatoes in the outer ashes. The fire was shielded from view and minimal smoke came from the dry wood. While the meat cooked, Tarn practised with the bow and arrows. Neeya also tried her hand at the useful weapon, with obvious improvement after a lot of arrows had been shot into soft sand in the distance.

The arrows were collected, their meal consumed and Neeya settled down to sleep while Tarn sat on guard. Later, Neeya switched with Tarn. They saw or heard nothing alarming through the clear night, apart from the normal animal and bird calls, and twice when a heavy object sounded as if it had fallen in the scrub below the camp. Looking up to the sky, she watched the occasional movement of what she had originally believed were the sky people looking down on their world. Her mind had now fully embraced the new knowledge given by the machines and she wondered if she would ever learn any more of their true history. For now, all thoughts of gods, spirits, sky people, and the afterlife were put to one side. They all seemed to do whatever they wanted, regardless of what the still-living asked of them.

❋ ❋ ❋

On the ridge line above and to one side of the campsite, a lone figure lay on a soft bear skin surveying the scene. He was within bow and arrow range of the camp and had already killed two stealthy prowlers trying to creep up on Tarn as he stood watch. Each had died from a single arrow in the chest. In daylight, such killing shots would have been difficult. In pitch darkness, for any other tribesmen, it was impossible. For someone able to see in the dark, like Andoki and his mate, Vail, who slept below and behind him, the effort was still only just achievable.

Andoki and Vail and a few of their decimated band had infrared vision, which improved over generations, resulting from a genetic change in one child who grew and fathered more with the same ability. Their vision allowed perfect sight at night, without any moonlight, that lit up anything retaining any level of heat as red, orange, or yellow colours, and cold or cooling objects in different shades of grey to black.

The pair normally slept during the day and travelled or hunted at night. Their extra ability allowed an abundance of game to fall to their arrows, and they had developed great camouflage skills to hide during the day. They both wore mottled animal-skins, stained in browns, blacks and greens, with head coverings shading their eyes, and their faces darkened with charcoal.

Their now mortal enemies were those they called the dark ones, the same black killers pursuing Neeya and Tarn, two of whom now lay dead below. Despite their night vision, Andoki's settlement had been surprised by the killers, with some barely escaping when the raid began, leaving many of their friends and relations dead or captured.

Neeya and Tarn had come to their attention as they journeyed close to the hunting camp set up by Andoki, little knowing of their presence. At first view, these new travellers seemed to bring little danger with them, being dressed differently and carrying strange hand weapons and travel packs. They might not be dangerous but nothing could be left to chance. Andoki and Vail had followed them for more than a day, to determine if they were part of a larger band moving through the area, possibly planning to establish or take over new territory.

They had watched Tarn concentrate on increasing his bow-handling skill, and Neeya try but not fully concentrate. They lacked the ability needed to hold off a determined enemy, but Tarn looked dangerous from the way he carried and practised his spear-throwing.

The two bodies lying below the camp might have been advance scouts and their disappearance would eventually lead others in this direction, searching for their missing members. But still Andoki, with Vail's support, chose to stay out of view and observe before deciding to either aid these travellers, kill them, or move away from any trouble that might be hunting them.

❅ ❅ ❅

Before sunlight touched their overnight campsite, Neeya and Tarn were actively putting as much distance as possible between them and the destroyed settlement. The black arrows, and all they meant, had unnerved them and flight rather than fight seemed the best alternative. The day was a duplicate of the previous day, and no signs of other people were seen. The vegetation and soil grew progressively drier, with only two small water flows at the bottom of wide creek beds to fill their water skins. The mountains remained in a line about two days travel to their right, many of them snow-capped. But no life-giving water mist hung in the air. Eventually, the vegetation became scattered, mostly desert-type plants, with some large, older trees still alive, gaining their water from deep roots in the ground.

It was mid-afternoon when Neeya remembered the two skins placed at the back of the campsite to dry. They had been left in their haste to be moving on. It was too late now to retrieve them because of the danger in retracing their steps, and they were poor quality, particularly the big cat pelt.

Something was obviously wrong with the climate in the area they had entered. Evidence of better rainfall and more lush vegetation in the past was everywhere, from dry creek beds, large dead trees, dry bushes that once covered the ground and the odd animal remains. Neeya noticed an odd shape on the imposing skyline. In the closest group of mountains to the north, the top of one high peak had been cut off as if with a giant knife. After discussion with Tarn, they decided to investigate, with their journey turning towards that mountain up a slowly increasing incline.

Their camp that night was still at least one full day away from the mountain. They rested near the top of a rock slide, with loose rubble below and on both sides of them, and a hard, rocky outcrop at their backs. There was enough of a solid rock shelf on which to set up camp with loose rubble from the rock slide protecting them from a night attack. They ate the last of the venison and vegetables after cooking them over a hot but smokeless fire.

They talked quietly about their journey, while watching lights passing overhead. Tarn mentioned to Neeya his problem about the sky people. "I am still lost and confused. You said they are really machines placed there long ago to study the surface of this world, and nothing to do with the people who had died here. For much of my life, I was told stories, as you were, by the Elders and storytellers who passed them down through the ages. Their words are hard to discard when they connect us so strongly to our tribe and way of life. It will take me time to separate myths and stories from the truth of our past, with the information given to us by the machines."

He stopped speaking, in shock, as a bundle dropped from above, landing several steps in front of them down the slope. It had come from behind, further up the slope, but they could see nothing in the darkness. Tarn retrieved the bundle noisily on the loose shale rocks while Neeya stood guard. It was their two skins, left behind and now returned out of the night. They opened it and found both had been scraped and dried to the point where they would need no further treatment before use.

The appearance of the bundle and the ramifications left them baffled. Someone had the time to find the skins and carefully complete their treatment, at least a long day's work. They would then have had to track them to this location, partially in the dark, over difficult terrain. These thoughts ran through their minds while they stood, ready to fight.

From out of the darkness, close to them, on the side slope, came a male voice, in an understandable but strongly accented tongue, "No need to use your weapons. We do not want to fight; otherwise, why would we have cared for and returned your skins? See them as a gift, which you forgot in your haste to move on from your camp this morning."

Neeya answered, "We were surprised by the bundle that you rolled down to us. We will not attack you, but come closer, slowly. We can both still be ready to react as we come together."

The unknown man replied, "We can see you clearly. For us, the night is as clear as the day. We will come to you, slowly."

Neeya and Tarn listened for movement on the loose, weathered shale, trying to catch a glimpse of the moving man. They heard almost nothing and were surprised when a young man, followed by a young woman, walked out of the darkness into the firelight, both with bows and arrows ready.

The newcomers walked lightly on the loose rocks, with very little noise. They were dressed in mottled long-legged pants and long-sleeved jackets. It was initially hard to see them, because of the green, brown, and black colours of everything they wore. Their hands were covered and they had head coverings with side flaps. They would be almost invisible in trees during the day. With their different clothing, nut-brown skin, glistening black hair and large, intelligent eyes, Neeya and Tarn were sure the newcomers came from a tribe unknown to them.

Once in full view, the man said, "My name is Andoki. My mate is called Vail.

"We wish you no harm. We will lower our bows if you lower your weapons."

Without further comment, they all complied but only partly relaxed their stance.

"May we join you at your fire?" Andoki asked.

Now that they were close, his voice was becoming easier to understand. However, the accent still made it difficult, and there were a few words they did not understand.

Tribal attitudes to unknown travellers asking to enter a camp were shared amongst different bands, and so Neeya gave approval to enter, after a nod from Tarn.

The strangers joined them, putting their packs and weapons in an easily-reachable pile.

Andoki glanced from Tarn to Neeya. "Thank you for letting us join you. We came from a tribe about two days walk from here. A savage band of killers wearing only black clothes attacked us in a raid, and now we are widely separated, with many probably dead."

Tarn put more wood on the fire and moved their own packs out of the way. He said, "Sit and warm yourselves. We have eaten and did not expect visitors. We are sorry that we have no food to offer you."

Vail answered this time, with dignity. "We have not come as beggars. We can offer you food. Our hunt tonight was successful, a goat from the valley below." With that, she took out choice cuts of meat wrapped in leaves.

"We did not have time to skin and cook it but it is fresh."

They sat and talked, while cooking thin pieces of meat on flat, hot stones in the ashes.

Neeya was more than curious. How did they do what had obviously been done?

"You spoke as if you saw where we slept last night, that you could see us in the dark and that you killed this goat at night. You must travel like the wind if you could do that, keep up with us and have time to treat the skins you returned, for which we thank you. How is this possible?"

Andoki answered, "A few of our people are like us but most are like normal men. In recent generations, the ability to see in the dark has begun to rise in children born to our tribe. We do not know why. It could come from the yellow soil near where we lived for many seasons. Some children in families living close to that area died from unknown reasons, but a few of the survivors now live with this ability. It allowed us to travel through the night, after having slept part of yesterday.

"We try to keep our eyes shaded for travel in the day, but we were still able to follow you, to see what quest you were on and its purpose. The skins we treated with a special soil mixed with water, which cures leather quickly, without days of drying in the sun.

"At night, we can tell what stones or ground to walk on. It allows us to move very quietly. Our clothes are coloured to help us merge into the background.

"Now can we ask you questions? Who are you, where do you go and why do you need to cross over territory not claimed by your tribe? Your journey is dangerous, with the wild killers moving around this land, as well as normal predators hunting for an easy kill."

After looking at each other, and giving slight hand signals in agreement, Neeya and Tarn explained what they knew, admitting that all was still not clear to them. They talked late into the night, well after the meat was cooked and eaten and the fire had been allowed to burn low.

❋ ❋ ❋

Far above them, one of the moving machines endlessly circling the planet slowed over their position, to listen and record the discussion. Yet again, an information package was transmitted deep into space. This machine had recently experienced the first ever recorded return of a signal providing instructions for a unique plan to be commenced, now that two important contacts had become four.

Chapter 7

Second Mountain

Training to improve their skills with bows and arrows filled the next day. Andoki and Vail spent time inspecting the wonderful metal weapons from the broken machine and catching up on sleep. Tarn and Neeya successfully hunted, killing another mountain goat, one of many living on the lower mountain slopes. They discovered tubers and nuts nearby. Water skins were refilled from the only running stream in the area. It ran fresh and cold from a cave under the base of the mountain.

Andoki and Vail were now part of the 'band,' after further explanation from Neeya about what might be needed in the future. The goat meat was cooked or smoked for travel. No further signs were found of any other humans, either black killers or general tribal people. It also seemed that animals had re-possessed the area, free from memories of ever being hunted.

When it was dark, Andoki and Vail spent time patrolling above and below their camp on the slope. They returned after finding no one and slept until dawn.

A cold breakfast started their morning, then they headed towards the second flat-topped mountain. Tarn found an old track, similar in width to the first machine track, but this one had not been used for some time and was partially overgrown. It made them wonder what had originally stopped the machines from doing their inspections.

The route led them straight to another door set into solid rock, but this time the end of Neeya's blade would not work in the slot. Debris littering the entry indicated the door had not been opened for a long time.

Tarn suggested that extra force was needed with the turning of the blade in the slot, so both he and Andoki tried together, with no success. Neeya smiled at Vail, then said to Tarn, "So the big, strong men could do no better than weak women." Tarn only grunted, while looking in another direction, as if her comment was not worth a reply.

Neeya focused again on the door. "This should open, as it did at the first mountain. Something is wrong or has broken inside. We could try to enter another way." She led them around the side of the mountain and up to a second entry door, a duplicate of the first mountain's cave up to the waterfall window. Again, Neeya tried the end of the killer blade into the side slot. This time it opened, but only partially before grinding to a halt. The gap provided was just wide enough to allow them to squeeze through. Neeya pressed the internal wall panel to operate the door but it would not close. They slowly moved down the passage, under roof lights that flickered on and off, with many not working at all.

Andoki and Vail were alarmed by the strange door opening and the flickering lights, even though it had previously been explained what had happened in the first mountain entrance. The malfunctioning lights threatened to throw them into complete darkness, but they edged through to a duplicate of the waterfall viewing room, which still had daylight shining down the huge shaft from above. The lack of any water movement was obvious through the window. Andoki and Vail stayed well back until coaxed forward by Tarn. To them, it appeared like they were on the edge of a vertical cliff looking into an unimaginable depth.

Neeya noticed no sounds or vibrations when they first approached the partially working entry door. A long time ago, something had stopped the vast machine from providing air and water to the region below the mountain.

As soon as they had looked around the viewing room, Neeya told them, "I need to see why the big water machine controlled from here has stopped, and if it can be started again. There is a hidden control panel set into the wall of this room. Tarn, can you help me move the protection door in the wall to one side. In the other mountain, when I pressed the thing on the wall it easily moved aside." Neeya placed her hand flat on the panel, and to her relief, it slid aside without Tarn's help, revealing a duplicate of the bank of glowing lights, most of which were either not lit or showed red.

One large green light remained on another narrow panel set into the bench below the rest of the lights. Neeya said, "Watch out when I touch that light. It might not work. It could hurt me, but it seems to be the only place left I can touch to try to talk to the machine."

Tarn had seen all this before, but he still felt anxious about the machine not working and Neeya's comment about the light she was touching possibly hurting her. Andoki and Vail said nothing, standing wide-eyed and frozen to the spot with what was happening.

Everything since they first saw the system for opening the entry door through to the huge hole outside where they stood, and this room with its lights, remained beyond their understanding or experience.

She turned and brought her hand down on the green light, and sagged against the bench but remained sitting. This time, Tarn could see that her eyes were rolled back and her mouth hung open. Andoki and Vail remained still but their bewilderment and fright were obvious to Tarn. Their reactions were like Tarn's when Neeya first spoke to the machine at the original mountain.

The silent communication was different this time. She kept her right hand on the now strongly lit panel but opened her eyes and reached out to several black lumps on the wall of lights to either push or turn them to one side or the other. Red lights activated soon after she had touched them, with only one showing green. A strong vibration began after a loud noise sounded deep below them, a hollow sound under their feet in the huge dry shaft.

More lights changed their colours. The vibration built up, and a sound like a thousand animals in pain started low and rose to a crescendo, as they all covered their ears. Air now blew up the shaft, dry and dusty, full of grit. It slowly threw up water vapour until it became a torrential blast of water escaping from far below them, passing their view, to disappear above all they could see. Neeya remained at the light bench, but the others moved to the viewing window, to watch open-mouthed with alarm at what was happening.

They could hear and see the water moving, but remained dry due to the clear screen in front of the waist-high wall they stood behind. The water blasting had them all in awe, eyes wide and staring. While this was happening, Neeya, right hand still on the green pad, had been adjusting the raised lumps on the light wall. She slowly changed the settings until most of the lights were green, or steadily reducing red lights.

She slumped down the short distance to the floor, eyes closed and body uncontrolled, now with her hands removed from the bench. Tarn leaned over to hear her words. She quietly said, "The big water machine works again after I followed instructions about how to repair it. I am very tired and need sleep. We will wait here a while, to be sure no other changes are needed. Eat and sleep now. You don't have to worry. Relax while I recover."

Tarn, Andoki, and Vail settled down on the floor to rest after a cold meal from their packs, while Neeya slept in a foetal position beside them on her sleeping robe, which Tarn had laid out.

She was the first to wake, stretching first then standing, before glancing at the light wall and focusing on one blinking red light. She pushed on the blinking light with her left hand while touching the green pad with her right hand, then stood still, while the machine spoke to her mind. It stopped blinking, but remained red.

Neeya pushed Tarn with her foot to wake him up. He awoke with a start, instantly on guard. "Tarn, wake the others," she said. "We must leave this place quickly." Tarn roused the others and they faced Neeya to hear what was so important.

"You can see the red light. It was flashing because the machine has ways of knowing what is happening outside. The mountain now has air and water coming out again to water the country below us, and that has attracted the black killers who want to stop these machines. Many of them are coming up the slope to get to us. Because the water is now flowing, there is enough power created by the movement to shut the door we came through. It is like the blood running through our bodies, to give the machine in the mountain energy to do everything it was built for. This will protect it and give us another way to leave here, without the killers finding us."

Tarn said, "But why do the killers want to stop the machines and kill us? They still have to live here, so they need water and animals for food. They would die if all the big machines are stopped."

Neeya answered, "These people are trained to be aggressive, increasing over many generations, and have always been directed against peaceful tribes trying to live normal lives. Just as the machines were created to help our lives and make this world more suitable for the different tribes, there is also a force acting to fight against any improvements. I have not been told much about that force. It seems complicated and not easy to understand, but we must stay away from the black killers."

"Vail and I have trouble understanding what you tell us, but we will follow you," Andoki said. "You seem to work for the tribes and that is something we want to help with. So, what happens now?"

In answer, Neeya reached out and pushed a silver-coloured lump on the light wall. They all gasped as a large blank section lit up to show what the Sky people might see as they passed over. The screen showed, in colour, a long line of mountains from above. It grew in scale until only their mountain could be seen. The remains of the rough path they had followed to the entry door stood out, a rock-cut passage to the second door and a huge black hole from which continuous clouds streamed. They struggled to understand what they were seeing. Andoki was amazed and had to believe that this was surely something from the Sky people and the ancestors, the people who first lived there.

A red line suddenly appeared on the screen, in glowing colour, running from the place where they stood at that moment, down inside the mountain, to join up to the only flow of water coming out. That water flow line probably was where they had last filled their water skins, but it had now changed colour for a short distance beyond the mountain.

"The water melting from the mountaintops was directed into the machine, which blew it out into the air toward the land needing that water. When it stopped, the water was redirected under the mountain and flowed out as the small river shown on the red line. Now the water is going out of the mountain and up into the air, the river line is dry again. That is the way for us to leave this place, under the mountain, to come out into a now dry river bed."

She pointed to the area around the place they had entered the mountain, and touched the picture shown. It expanded to show a lot of moving black dots. Neeya said, "The killers have tracked us here and are waiting for us to come out. Even now, with you both, the four of us would not survive if we tried to fight our way out, so we need to go this other way. It will be difficult and some of the way might be in darkness, but there are things this machine will do to aid us now that I have helped to make it work again."

The idea was discussed, but they could not improve on Neeya's plan. Just watching the screen show what birds might see was enough to make them feel insignificant, and they were only too willing to follow anyone who understood and had a plan.

They quickly finished a meal, knowing it was their last chance before starting on what could be a difficult journey. Then Neeya led them down the corridor, deeper into the mountain, but stopped again at what seemed to be a dead end. A slot on the side wall was the only indication of the solution. She unsheathed the killing blade and inserted the end. The wall slid aside to reveal a long slope into a dimly lit cavern. As soon as they were all on the other side of the sliding wall, it closed and lights came on above them, this time with none of them blinking or staying off. Tarn watched as Andoki and Vail shrank back from the unexpected lights. He had become familiar with the 'magic' and felt more comfortable with that knowledge.

They started to jog the route to the left. Marks on the wall glowed green in the dark, which gave them a good idea of the direction and where to place their feet. Andoki and Vail took the lead, being able to see in the dark, but because of the cold walls and floor, their unique sight was only a small help. The long cave was dripping with water, the remains of the recently flowing melted ice and snow that had been diverted when the machine was not working.

With no visible light, the journey seemed to go on for a long time. The fear of being intercepted at the outlet by large numbers of black killers grew in their minds. Finally, the dark ahead lessened, and a short time later, they crept up to the opening at the base of the mountain. Neeya located the door slot by feel and used her blade. The door slid silently open and Andoki and Vail went first, emerging into the night through sparse vegetation that hid the outlet. They stayed silent and disappeared into the night. Neeya and Tarn waited just inside the cave until Andoki returned, like a ghost, to tell them that no one was nearby and they could come out. Vail kept watch for any scouts patrolling the area.

The dark night quickly absorbed them. The dry river course ran into the valley, but they moved in a different direction, away from the stream and the killers gathered up on the mountainside. Andoki led them in the dark, while Vail followed as a rear guard, their night vision making travelling possible.

Walking through the night single-file, trying to put as much distance as possible behind them kept them tense and silent for hours. The machine in the mountain was now vibrating the ground and the low rumble showed that the mountain's task had been renewed. They could feel a difference in the air around them, with a light, continuous mist that would eventually restore the whole region.

The pace set by Andoki was punishing but they were all fit and uninjured. As their shadows started to vaguely appear in front of them on the ground, they realised they had been on the move throughout the night and the morning sun was appearing behind them. In the slowly improving light, they found a suitable campsite on a slight rise surrounded by thick undergrowth and settled in for several hours of well-earned sleep. Each of them took turns on guard.

Before she slept, Neeya wondered about the big gathering of the killers at the mountain entrance. What had caused them to band together and head there as soon as the machine was restarted? Was there some kind of beacon or signal that gathered them? It was almost as if someone controlled the efforts to stop such machines from working.

Her thoughts took time to settle down, and when she could not find an answer, she finally gave up and slept.

Chapter 8

New Companions

After eating and packing up, they were on the move before sunrise the next morning, still heading west, neither hearing nor seeing anything of their pursuers through the night. They went on that way for three days, eating mostly cold food, lighting few fires, and rising in the dark each morning.

Andoki and Vail's night patrols located no black killers but restocked their meat supplies; berries, nuts and tubers were collected as they walked. The country was healthy, with running streams, green vegetation, and wildlife. The machines in the mountains were obviously functioning in this area. Only one new flat-top mountain could be seen as they travelled through valleys with plenty of food and water available.

Their travel had settled into a pattern, with adequate rest periods, a pace that was constant but not punishing and with no human threats encountered so far. That movement was broken without warning on the fifth day, with no clues or evidence of human occupation detected. The narrow animal track they were following through heavy undergrowth led them straight into the middle of over thirty people – mainly young adults and children of different ages. They were all seated or sprawled on hides and blankets.

While the travellers stopped almost midstride with surprise, the new group acted relaxed, appearing to have been waiting for them to arrive. Water skins and two carved, wooden platters holding fruit, nuts, berries, cold meat pieces and cooked tubers were laid out, as if welcoming invited guests who would be hungry and thirsty. All heads were turned towards them, all smiling, with a couple of young children giggling and pointing at them. The new group gave no indication of being hostile, with no weapons ready for use.

After a short, stunned silence, Neeya spoke. "We're surprised to find you sitting here on this deserted trail, in the middle of nowhere, with food and water ready. How long have you been here and how did you know we would be those you have been waiting for? We saw no scouts and it is not easy to anticipate where we will go. Even we do not know that."

A tall, dark-skinned man with long, black hair braided at the back of his head stood to answer her in a language they could understand but with a strong accent. "We came here only a short while ago. We are different to others in our tribe, with an extra ability that let us know you were coming. In the past few days, we became aware of what you are trying to do. We met and discussed what we knew of you. We want to join you in your quest."

Tarn, also mystified about how it was known they would be there at that time, asked, "But we still don't know how you met us and how you know of us."

The same man smiled and answered, "I can understand your curiosity. Some of us can have a strong feeling about what is going to happen a few days in the future. The ability has grown in some families and this has been passed on to their children. It has not come to everyone but the ability is growing with each generation. The future is not definite but it seems to be true if nothing around us changes. So, we had a strong impression about who you were, what you intend to do and where you would be at this time today. We all have good feelings that you are working for the benefit of our people."

While what was being said was important, Neeya was only partly listening to the explanation. Her eyes had roamed over the group sitting in front of her – one person now stood out amongst all of them – a young man, between fifteen and twenty-five summers old, who also stared at her. They were both focused on each other's identical facial tattoos. Those marks were unique and normally different to anyone else's markings. They would usually not express tribal or blood clan affiliation. Much thought would be given to the design and the marks would connect with their life's experiences. It would include their understanding of religious and spiritual influences in their lives and, sometimes display honour to their parents.

It surely was not possible that these could result in the same design for two people living a long distance apart, of different ages and experiences. But she saw that it had happened, and felt fear, anxiety and wonder all at the same time with no explanation available.

Neeya felt caught up in a web of change too large for her to understand. She was like an animal herded by hunters into a dead-end ravine, with no chance to escape. Would it lead to her doom or something much more important than she could understand?

She left the discussion with the stranger for another time after they had sorted out what would happen between them and this new group. The group spokesperson addressed them once more.

"We understand your reluctance for us to join you, but we believe we will aid, not hinder your work. The next machine in the mountain you are searching for is a little more than one day's travel from here. We know this country and can show you the shortest route. Surely this knowledge of your purpose shows that we speak the truth. If we cannot keep up with you then you can leave us behind, but we have seen that all will be well, at least until you reach the next mountain. We have no impressions of what will happen a long time in the future. That has yet to be determined."

Neeya and Tarn looked at each other and silently hand-signalled that they would try to travel with these people. There was no real alternative, even though they still did not understand how foreknowledge was possible.

"We agree that you can come with us, only if all can keep up. We worry about your children, so you will need to be sure they will not slow us down, or become a problem finding food and water for them. But you still need a full explanation of our purpose, beyond your feelings of the future. Tonight, wherever we stop, we can talk. If you change your mind, then you can leave us without much distance being covered. Is that suitable to you?"

The spokesman said, "We agree to all you have said. My name is Nabu, and we already have things we can give you to help."

With that, he bent down and unwrapped a skin bundle that lay beside him. Out dropped several identical heavy items that clanked as they tumbled to the ground. They were long metal knives, with gleaming sharp edges. He gave one to each of them.

"Our tribe has developed a way to melt the red-coloured stone you see scattered around this area. With enough heat and other materials we find in the soil, these stones melt to make metal. We direct that liquid into shapes made in wet sand beside the fire. The molten liquid runs into the moulds and sets hard to become rough knives. We then sharpen the edges on hard stone to finish the knife, to make it useful. It cuts better than any stone or timber edge," he explained.

"We have made arrows and spearheads in this metal, as well as axes for trading with other people. All the red stone we had to make metal has been used for these knives because we know they may become important in the future."

With some pride, Tarn said, "You and your people know about metal and how to make it. Our people had no knowledge of it until recently. Neeya and I carry weapons taken from a machine made of metal." With that, he uncovered the shorter, narrow knife and the metal digging tool while Neeya unwrapped her long, killing blade.

Several members of the new group gathered around the objects, obviously impressed, as they tapped the blades with their knives and felt the cutting edges. Nabu spoke. "These blades are far better than our knives. The metal is harder and stronger, with edges that will last much longer. Whoever made these makes us feel like children in comparison. We could only dream of this quality. Just touching them leaves me in awe of the makers."

The blades, including the new knives, were carefully re-wrapped, not to protect the metal but to stop them making any noise as they walked. Trained ears could hear such sounds from a long distance. Neeya and Tarn quietly discussed the problems and benefits of adding all these extra people to their group. The trail left by so many would be easier to track. Women who were not warriors would have to be responsible for their children. There seemed no better option than to accept their help and travel together.

The total group had now grown to over thirty. They still needed answers to questions not yet asked. Almost nothing was known of their background and way of life. Neeya also wanted to speak with the young man with the same facial tattoos to understand how it was possible. How had this group known exactly where to intercept them, at the exact time they were passing?

Andoki and Vail were even more disturbed by the prospect than Neeya and Tarn. They had been comfortable with being on their own, travelling and hunting at night, with no other responsibilities. It had taken time to relax around Neeya and Tarn. Now they glanced at each other, with a look expressing doubt and dismay but agreed to continue.

Before moving on with their journey, a meal was prepared and eaten. Travelling bundles and backpacks were adjusted and the children aged up to eight seasons were spoken to, particularly to move as quietly as possible and try to keep up a good pace.

Neeya had learned from Nabu that the young man with matching tattoos was named Dosol. He was very intelligent and inquisitive, always wanting to know more about their metal making, as well as having many ideas that remained of little interest to others. Neeya had glanced at Dosol several times, always being intercepted by his gaze. He, too, seemed perplexed by the tattoos.

Nabu told Neeya in particular, "The route we know to the mountains passes a special place that is revered by my tribe, a place of strange significance from times beyond our understanding. I am interested in what you make of it and whether you can provide an understanding of its origins."

Neeya could only nod at his request.

Finally, they set off towards the mountains and Nabu's special place, walking in single file, to make as little noise as possible and minimising the tracks they left. The sun dropped slowly towards the horizon as the group made good progress through scattered trees and healthy vegetation. Neeya was impressed by the children's behaviour. They seemed to understand the risks involved and were being coached by their parents. Only one stop was needed, to rest, drink and refill their water skins from a cool, fast-moving stream. Another long stretch had them arriving at a cave entrance late in the afternoon, with the bright lights in the dark sky beginning to shine.

Tarn wondered about the sky people and what they did with their time as they looked down. Then he remembered the information Neeya had explained to him about machines, not sky people travelling through the sky. His brow furrowed as he tried to make it clear. It was hard to replace his previous understanding with this new information that destroyed everything he believed from the past.

The cave did not appear natural. The stone looked as though a hole had been drilled, large and wide enough for two people to walk upright. The opening was partially hidden from direct view by bushes and it would take strangers some time to find it, even if they knew the general location.

At Nabu's urging, they entered the tunnel. The walls were smooth, solid rock, apart from the floor, which was very hard but not rock. It curved on a gentle angle at regular intervals, so that they could not see very far at any time. At every change of direction, a very shiny, circular surface of metal was mounted on the roof. Neeya and Tarn could see the reflected light from outside back into the cave. It would be dark at night but it would not need the magic lights they had seen in the mountain during the day.

After four bends, they arrived at a much larger underground area, about 50 metres in length and shaped as if parallel, and connecting tunnels had been drilled to provide a wide space. Several holes in the roof added to the light source being reflected in from the access tunnel. Piles of dirt and dry leaves sat under each of the small roof holes, an accumulation over many seasons with no disturbance. All of this stood out as they entered. The outer edge walls were in shade and hard to make out at first.

Nabu pointed to the nearest wall. "This is what I wanted to show you. All around this space the walls have been scribed with messages, starting at one side of the access tunnel."

Neeya and Tarn stood wide-eyed with raised eyebrows. "We have never seen anything like this, even inside the mountains when we experienced so many strange things."

The walls were covered in simple pictures, carved out and outlined in white on the dark grey rock. They showed small pointed objects moving between planets, shown as circular balls, with people moving from or to the rockets for each of the small balls. Further pictures had huge machines drilling into mountains and rain clouds streaming out from the machines. The pictures flowed, line on line, wall after wall, around them – animals arriving, part of the land being shaped, explosions to direct water flow. With Neeya's background knowledge provided by the machines, she could understand most of what the pictures represented. They were simple, aimed at children or people with little concept of worlds floating in space and those worlds being made ready to receive numbers of people, animals, birds, and vegetation.

Only Nabu had seen these before, but he knew they were important and Neeya or Tarn might be able to explain their meanings. They all slowly worked through the lines of pictures. Tarn was far behind Neeya in his understanding but still accepted what he had been told inside the two mountains they had visited. The sky people legends were simple explanations for people who were barely surviving in a strange environment.

Neeya noted differences in the simple pictures carved on the rock faces, with the mixture of animals brought from one original planet. The simple drawings showed large cats, bears, different types of deer, goats, huge animal types on four legs, hairy and man-shaped animals living in trees, being moved. She silently reasoned that different animals taken to different planets could also mean people from different cultures might also have been mixed amongst these worlds. These thoughts filled in some of the gaps in her understanding of what the machines had revealed to her. The planets shown were different attempts to move people, animals, crops, and vegetation from one original planet. Some were more successful than others, over long periods of time, maybe over many generations.

Neeya spoke to Nabu again, with Tarn listening on the side, after finishing their first initial look at all the inscribed picture messages. "Nabu, it's all too much and too important to spend a small amount of time trying to understand. Our visit to the mountain may have to wait, but only for a short while. This area is large enough for us all to eat and sleep here. Do you believe it will be safe if we have guards protecting the entrance through the night?"

Nabu replied, "I thought the same. I expected our time here would extend until tomorrow. The holes in the roof will let smoke from small fires out and there is a breeze that will blow it away once it reaches the surface. We will eat then sleep."

Andoki and Vail agreed to take turns outside, where their unique vision would be of use in the rapidly darkening night.

Neeya sat with her back against one wall opposite the young man who carried the same facial tattoos. Tomorrow she would have to find out why and how he came to have such marks, but, for the moment, the messages on the walls filled her mind.

Chapter 9

The Grey Man

The night passed uneventfully, with regular changes to those guarding the entrance. As the sun cleared the horizon and light came again to their man-made cave, a meal was produced from supplies the new group provided, mostly of water-soaked grain, nuts, and dried fruit. Scouts were sent out to check the surroundings for intruders, but no threats were discovered.

Neeya went back to studying the messages on the walls. She noticed the young man, Dosol, also spending time reading the walls, carefully running his fingers along the scenes carved in the rock, lingering over each individual line.

Looking more closely, she realised his eyes were closed while his fingers moved on the carvings. His lips were moving, soundlessly, as if he were seeing through his fingers and repeating the feelings he got with words. She stood waiting as Dosol edged towards her, still feeling, eyes shut and lips moving.

He stopped at the end of the carved scenes, before opening his eyes. When he was fully alert, he was unsurprised to see Neeya. He looked intelligent, but seemed out of focus, as if his experiences were on a slightly different plane to others.

"I know you are called Neeya," he said. "You have probably been told I am Dosol. Like you, I wonder about our shared facial marks, and how we could both carry the same designs when we have never met."

She was surprised at the young man's calm confidence and understanding, as if he was more mature than his age would allow.

"Given our difference in age and life experiences, it should not be possible for both of us to carry these marks. Do you know your parents' background? Not many carry marks on their face, but often they are passed down from parents to children."

Dosol thought for a moment. "I can remember my father. He chose to have no marks on his body, but he told me his father had them on his face. Father said, from what he remembered, his father chose the same marks as I did. Again, there is not much I understand. I once saw traders come to my village from a different people who lived further towards the setting sun. One of them carried the same marks. Neeya, do you know why?"

After hesitating, she said, "In our travels, I have been given knowledge from what are called machines, made partly from the kind of metal made by your people. It would take too much time to fully explain, but I was informed about the past, to give me a better understanding of this place and other things. Like the carvings shown on these walls, different groups of people were brought here through the heavens. All these people once lived together, many, many generations ago, on a different world. Something terrible happened to their world, and the survivors had to flee from great danger, eventually to this planet.

"When several of those groups of people were spread across this land, a few shared a bond through something in their blood, that was transferred through the generations from parents to their children. These connected people, then their descendants, had to stay in contact for the good of all people and to help each other. That connection failed, probably long ago. We still have a sign, our face marks, that show we are or should be connected. Our work now is to restore that connection while making sure the machines in the mountains that supply us with water still work. Because the need is great, we must find others who can help.

"Dosol, once your people have been taken to safety, come with us. It may be the most important thing you do in your life, but it will be dangerous."

Dosol sat frowning at Neeya, his mouth slightly open, as he tried to understand what had been said.

"In my mind, I joined with you before I met you. I did not know exactly who you were, or the look of your face, but I believe our meeting was bound to happen. Before we discuss this further, I have a question. I do not understand about your pursuers. Why do they try to stop you? They dress in black, the bringers of death. Why do they kill and who directs or controls them?"

Neeya, who had thought long and hard about the same questions, shrugged. "I have tried to understand. I could not get more information from the machines. It may be that the black killers are unexpected and they arrived after all was established in this land for us to live here. I can't answer your questions. I think it will be up to us and those yet to join us to stop them. It is probable that there are now very few of us, and we are scattered. These strangers seem to kill for no reason. We must save whoever we can from them, but I worry about what it will take to do that.

"Dosol, I want to try something with you that might give us much more understanding. The machines passed on the background of our history to me and how it has led to this day. The information went straight into my head somehow and I don't know how that happened. Please, take my hands, close your eyes, and allow your mind to relax, to receive any information that may come through me. It may not work but it shouldn't harm us."

He sat, silent while considering what Neeya had said. He then, tentatively, put out both hands to hold hers. Tarn, sitting to one side, listened and watched for Dosol's responses.

It was almost a repeat of what had happened both times when Neeya had touched the machines in the mountains, but this time it was between two people. Their eyes remained shut, with mouths open, and blank expressions on their faces. They could have been dreaming in unison. Both sat upright in an uncomfortable position, for some time. It seemed to be working, information being passed, but how much and was it what they wanted?

Finally, Dosol gasped as if he had been holding his breath and dropped his hands away from Neeya's. She opened her eyes then stretched out on the cave floor as if she was coming out of a deep sleep. Dosol finally managed to clear his throat and fully opened his eyes. On the third attempt, he said, "I feel my head has expanded, to hold all that it received. Neeya, how can you know all this and still walk and speak? It was almost too much to take. Do you really think it's possible to carry such a burden for long?"

Her reply was slow and hard to hear, "Not for long and not by myself. If you and the people around us can help – if we can find more who will aid us – then it may be possible. I don't know any other way. We have only begun to understand what we have lost and what we might still recover."

Before she could continue, Tarn moved closer. "Neeya, we need to move on from this cave. Andoki and Vail have just killed an enemy scout. No others were seen, but they may be close by. If we stay here, we will be trapped, with no escape."

They both jumped up, groggy at first, and then woke everyone else. Quickly packing, they prepared to move. Nabu was the first to leave, leading them on the shorter, more direct route he had previously discovered. The pace was slow because of the women and children, but they kept moving without a stop until the sun was overhead. Then, they rested beside a narrow, fast-moving stream. Two men followed behind, removing tell-tale signs of their passage and acting as rear guards.

They walked for the rest of the day, along dry creek beds, following animal trails through thick vegetation and over rocky outcrops to leave no footprints, broken bushes, or flattened grass. Nabu continued leading after telling Neeya that the route to be followed did not go up towards the top of the mountain that rumbled and shook the ground but entered much lower down. He had been unable to go beyond the entry because he couldn't work out how to get through.

They finally arrived at the entrance, hungry and thirsty, with their water skins almost empty. Nabu showed them the dry outlet of an underground stream that had come from the base of the mountain through a dark cave. The cave entry had vertical iron bars running full height across the hole, with only a hand span between the bars. Each bar was as thick as a man's wrist, with no sign of age. Neeya and Tarn searched on both sides of the cave entry, and Tarn eventually found a flat surface the size of his hand with a deep slot carved into it. The end of the killing blade was used, yet again, and the bars slid vertically into the roof of the cave. With relief, they all passed through and the bars slid silently back in place.

Andoki and Vail took the lead, slowly walking up the underground slope. They had made torches from short branches and fat-soaked old pieces of skins. Once burning, these smoky, flickering brands gave off enough light for a long distance but finally flickered out. The rest of the way, they each moved with one hand on the shoulder of the person in front until the expected junction was found. By this time, their progress was laboured, and exhaustion had taken a toll, with parents trying to comfort their children.

Neeya unwrapped the long killing blade and Andoki directed it into the slot. A sharp turn to one side had the apparently solid wall split open into a wide gap, leading to a corridor with smooth walls and floor, already lit. Neeya had previously told them what to expect as they approached the mountain, but most of the group were fearful of the ground vibrations and dull rumble. Nabu worked hard to settle his people, lit by the light in the new corridor, but they were anxious and hesitated before proceeding. There was a greater fear of going back the way they had come so, reluctantly, they took their first steps into the haven created inside the mountain for ancestors from an unimaginably long time in the past.

Once the last of the group entered the corridor, without warning, the door slammed shut. That alone showed the strangeness of this new place. Neeya and Tarn led the way, Tarn feeling nonchalant with his knowledge of how the lights operated and his familiarity with corridors. He now understood that these machines built into the mountains had a pattern. All three in their experience were very similar, but the new arrivals knew nothing about the underground tunnels and their contents.

They slowly moved down the strange corridor, with the lights snapping on in front and flicking off behind still being disconcerting for the newcomers. Who or what was controlling the lights? Even the explanations from Neeya, Tarn, Andoki and Vail did little to quell their fears.

The corridor's changes of direction matched those of the two previous mountain networks. After a few dead ends, the group arrived at the doorway of the room that should hold the wall with coloured lights. They knew the big machine was working because of the continuous vibration and dull noise coming from outside. The condition of the region below had been obvious – healthy trees and vegetation with several running streams.

Neeya touched a hand pad on the edge of the door into the room, and as it slid back, the lights went on, illuminating a light board already exposed, showing different colours and a centrally-placed object obviously made to be sat on. Unbelievably, one old man, dressed in long grey robes with a well-kept grey beard and a head of grey hair watched them from the chair. He sat motionless, just looking at them with his back to the light board. His blue eyes were the brightest they had ever seen, and even though his main colour was grey, he shone with vitality and energy.

Everyone who could see through the open doorway stood like statues, all holding their breath. The others behind them in the corridor wondered what was going on. This was so unexpected, even after the wonders they had seen entering the mountain.

Neeya cleared her throat and found her voice first. "We are sorry to walk in on you like this. We expected to be here alone, to be the only people to enter this place in a very long time, yet we find you here, as if it is your home. Please help us to understand. We come in peace and are no threat to you."

The old man smiled, showing perfect teeth, and said, "You cannot be a threat to me, but you are the first to enter for much longer than you could understand. You see me and you can hear my voice. I am not a spirit or ghost, which your tribal stories might have told you about, but I am also not a person of blood and bone. I do not age with time. I am a vision created to explain what you find here and to be a help to you and your people. I have abilities given to me when the machine was installed here."

Neeya, Tarn and the others all looked at each other, bewildered. This was not something they had experienced in the other mountains. The grey man's voice was quiet, even soothing, a strong male voice with a slight accent and pauses between some words, as if he was not fully experienced with their language.

Nabu quietly muttered, "I see and hear him but I can't sense his presence as real. He has no shadow and only his face moves, not any other part of his body. He says that he is not a spirit or ghost, but what can he be? I also see no movement of his chest to show he breathes and the outer edges of his body and robes are not solid."

The grey man spoke, "I hear your voices, Neeya and Nabu. I know your names. I know you are pursued and that you have previous knowledge about what a mountain like this contains. You entered through the tunnel, opened doors, and knew which room to come to. As you spoke amongst yourselves since entering, I heard every word from every speaker. Your arrival has caused this version of me to be extended to this place. I am like the image you see shimmering on the horizon during a hot day. I exist but have no physical body. You should not fear me because I am here to help the cause you follow, for which I exist."

"But how can you help us when you cannot leave this place to travel with us?" Neeya asked.

Grey man answered, "I don't have to move out of here to be able to help you. There are many locked rooms to be accessed from these passageways. I have used my ability to open some of those rooms for you. You will find information on the screen behind me about where to go. The rooms you can visit contain things to help you and others who may come to join you. I also have a way to see outside with the eyes of an eagle, looking down from the sky above. Again, the screen behind me will show you.

"There are three more mountains like this, each of them in the direction of the setting sun. If you move in that direction, you should find more people, some who may join you. You will also face more of those some call 'black killers'. That direction is where they are strongest. The reason for their existence is not for you to know, yet.

"In one of the rooms, you will find water and food. The food is not like you have ever eaten before but it will give you strength. Take as much of it as you like. It will last longer on your journey than fresh meat or vegetables. In a few days, fresh food, including meat, will be provided.

"One more thing before I leave you. I have the capacity to heal wounds and injuries beyond your abilities. You may need that service, but you must bring any injured person to me within any of the transformed mountains, to a room like this one. I cannot bring the dead back to life but I can do much to preserve life.

"Goodbye for now. I exist in all of the mountains that carry these machines, half of which you have now visited."

Before Neeya or any of the group could ask questions or make comments, the grey man slowly faded from view, his bright eyes first losing their brilliance. The chair was left empty. The lights on the wall showed several changing colours, going black or moving from red to green.

Nobody moved. Everything had stopped, apart from the dull noise, vibration, and the constant movement of water vapour into the sky outside. Finally, Tarn spoke. "Neeya, we can't stay here. Will you talk to the machine as you did before?"

She nodded. "The grey man said the screen behind him showed where to see the doors he unlocked. He also spoke about "seeing like an eagle" from far above. I will stay here while you take the others to look around. But first, we need to see where you can go."

Tarn could only wait for Neeya to make the machine show what was on the screen. After the grey man's fearful, impossible display and words, the others began to settle down on the floor. They were all recovering after their hard journey from the cave to this, another underground place. It seemed the people from long ago preferred to live underground. The children started to complain about their need for water and food and their fear of the strange place.

He joined the others on the floor. His body had been crying out for rest over several days but Neeya had been his only priority, and he would still have to wait to relax. Sleep would come quickly for most of the new group who were still trying to understand what was happening to them.

Chapter 10

Training

No one in the room had ever had to worry about rubbish. They lived with nature, and their discards went back into the soil. Flecks of stone, leather, animal bones, meat, or vegetable debris would build up around their feet or be thrown out of the shelter to land in the dirt.

Sitting on the floor, a few people trimmed off frayed leather from clothes or moccasins and worked on spear points to sharpen them, leaving the discards at their feet.

While this was happening, Tarn slept like he was dead for a short while, suddenly forced awake by an eruption of voices and people jumping up from the corner of the room. Two people – a woman and child – had been startled, followed by others. They pointed and hopped away from the wall to allow a disc-shaped machine to complete its gathering of rubbish before reversing into a small door at the base of the wall. The door immediately snapped shut. All of this happened in an instant. Tarn had to speak calmly to settle them down, explaining how all such rooms had small metal animals that only existed to gather and remove rubbish.

It took a while to restore peace. Tarn gave up trying to sleep and returned to Neeya, who had been sitting where the grey man had been, looking at a screen in front of her. It showed the main entrance to the tunnel from the air, along with the surrounding mountainside.

All Tarn saw were many moving black dots. Neeya moved a lump under her fingers and several of the dots became much larger – black killers! They moved continually as if they could not stand still, beating their clubs, spears and shields together, working up to a frenzy with no obvious place to put that energy.

Neeya sensed Tarn behind her. "They know we are in here. How they know I cannot say. We came from underground and never used that entrance. They see it's an entry but cannot work out how it opens. I know this place has its own defences but we need to be gone from here as soon as we have seen what is behind the doors the grey man opened for us. The machine has shown me where to enter. They are all linked so each room will give access to the next."

The others were now fully awake, ready but still fearful of whatever this impossible place could hold. Neeya led the way a short distance up the corridor towards the main entry where the black killers were gathering. She stopped at a door on the opposite side of the corridor, made obvious from the solid, smooth wall by one handle, previously locked but now swinging open.

They filed into a vast, lit space that left them gaping. To one side was a line of white metal machines like the one they had destroyed what seemed like so long ago. All sat ready, each with a fat black cord plugged into the side wall. Some were equipped identically to what they had previously seen. Others looked much more sinister, carrying what seemed to be weapons, including cutting blades and small firing barrels. Only Neeya and Tarn had seen these machines before. All the others, some on the verge of terror, even Andoki and Vail, saw them as fearful metal monsters until Neeya explained their use and that they would not move without a command being given.

Beside the machines were rows of containers made of a hard material. Bins held an assortment of cutting blades with handles.

Knives were stacked in piles, ranging from very short to much longer lengths. All were metal, with gleaming, sharpened edges. There were stacks of different-sized metal axes and spears that were harder but lighter than what they could make. Arrows and bows were also stockpiled, without any use of natural materials. All the weapons were not of their world.

The arrowheads were light metal, with shafts of a strong, smooth metal. The bows, of several designs, looked strong, flexible, and built to last forever, some as long as Tarn was tall, down to short lengths with attachments in the centre.

Tarn and Andoki waved Neeya and Vail across to see the arrow heads. Tarn pointed. "Look at the shapes. Some are simple triangular shapes we would use for hunting animals. The ones with vicious, double-hooked shapes are made for killing and staying in the wound, when used against enemies. Most of these are made for war, against others, not for killing animals for food."

Neeya said nothing, but shook her head slowly, as if adding the information to what she had already guessed.

Lines of weapon containers went on for some time, as they walked past the rows. Many of the containers held unknown items, all looking dangerous and lethal. Some were much more advanced and impossible to understand. One bin held shields of different shapes and sizes, which might be very useful against the clubs of the black killers.

The stockpiled contents changed to clothing and footwear. It took time to open the clear, smooth bags that held each garment, boots, or headwear. Different sizes, colours, thickness of fabric – a revelation that stunned them when they realised no skins or pelts were used. One woman in Nabu's group said she had once seen and felt material made from a plant, which had been woven into thin fabric. It had been shown by a travelling trader, made by people living well towards the setting sun, but was too expensive in trade goods to purchase.

They continued walking past various types of footwear, even like their moccasins, again made of tough material without the use of skins or hides.

Next was a wide entrance, with doors on rails sliding to either side. The room beyond held food, containers and various types of bags or backpacks. The food was of two types, either in clear, see-through pouches or in sealed containers. After several were broken, a screwed-in plug was found to access the contents. Simple pictured instructions were attached to the sides of the bins, mostly requiring water to be added to the packaged food to make it edible. These, Neeya thought, would take time and thought to work out how they could be made acceptable and worth eating.

The foods were different colours, some powder, some with lumps, while others were in strips with a drawing showing how they could be eaten by chewing. Water containers were in various sizes and types, with different straps to carry them. Again, they came in colours, including camouflage of unknown materials.

Beside the water containers, set into the next wall, were several holes producing continuous running water, bubbling into a trough and then draining back below. It was hard to understand the richness of what they saw, with the containers of items running away from them into the distance. Why so much? Who was all this for? Did each mountain contain stockpiles, and how long had it all been there?

Everything was made to last a very long time, with nothing that would wear or rot in the weather or during long, heavy use. Many of Nabu's people looked to him, Neeya, or Tarn to get a nod for permission to touch or even lift out an item from the bins. The display was overwhelming to tribal people used to battling for survival.

Neeya noticed Tarn shrug his shoulders and shake his head in bewilderment at what they saw. She said, "All of this is not just for a small group like ours. This is kept here for many, many people, from different tribes in different ways of life. It's a stockpile for war, prepared for a much larger number of people."

Tarn had nothing to say to add to Neeya's comment. They had moved on to another smaller room that held blankets, padded bags that appeared to be designed to sleep in, structures that were obviously shelters for fast erection and dismantling. There were several examples of these structures demonstrating how a completely closed bundle could be fully erected. The bundles were very small but expanded into shelters each for two people.

Looking behind these displays, Tarn noticed several large containers at the rear of the room. These were not obvious and appeared to hold only rubbish. Very old clothing of either skins or fabric were in one container, including old moccasins and sandals. Another held a motley collection of discarded weapons and tools – undamaged but obviously no longer needed. Discarded water skins and other basics filled another bin. Tarn noticed a small container holding several roughly-formed iron knives, like those Nabu's people had made. Now, even these fine weapons seem crude and not worth retaining, but it showed that others with skills like Nabu's people had been there in the past.

Neeya and Tarn, soon joined by Andoki, Vail and others, stood looking at the disposed-of items. Neeya's face displayed emotions starting with surprise, then concern, fear and confusion.

"These things change everything. We are not the first group to be here. Where did those people go and how long ago were they here?"

She turned to Tarn. "What will our people do now they have seen the richness of these things, free for the taking?"

Tarn shook his head. "I don't know why you ask me. I know less than you do, but we are here to choose from what is offered, to give us the best chance of survival and to complete the task we will be involved with. We can replace what we wear, our weapons and all that we carry for much better things."

Neeya asked, "What will happen to everything we leave behind?"

Tarn finally understood, "All that we leave behind will probably be collected, maybe into containers like these. I understand you, now. Others, maybe many others over a long time, have been here, and we know nothing of those people from the past. We are not the first. Can we go back to ask questions from the grey man? Will he be truthful or tell us only part of what he knows?"

Neeya said, "We know less than we thought. We are part of a much larger story, so we need to know our part. One thing I need to ask him – is every mountain with machines equipped like this one and how many of these exist? You and I have now seen three and the grey man said we have three more to visit. Are those all that exist?

"Tell everyone to dress and equip themselves with the best and most useful things they can find. Practise as much as possible with the new weapons they choose. Leave room for as much food and water as they can carry. Tarn, you and I, Andoki, Vail and Nabu will go back to the grey man, if he will see us, while the others are in these rooms."

Tarn went to the others, as well as showing Nabu the rough metal knives they had seen in the containers. Nabu picked one up, shaking his head as he closely inspected the knife's cutting edge and shape. "My people didn't make these knives but they are about the same quality. I don't understand what this all means. So, others are also making them or have made them in the past, but we have never heard of other tribes making metal things. These weapons could be very old, and the people who made them could have passed away."

He knew he would be discarding his own knife to replace it with one or more of the high-quality blades in the containers. The whole experience left him stretched to understand the information and his place in the world, with ancestors coming from a different world to build machines that could create rain. He had held something he could comprehend – the making of metal tools and weapons, but even that was now behind him.

The idea that this group was not the first to visit and re-equip in the underground cave was just one more thing in his mind to be considered at another time.

After passing on Neeya's instructions to the others, he rejoined the smaller lead group and they moved through into the next room. Yet again more new things, with a whole new level of understanding needed. Row upon row of a type of sleeping mat lay on the floor and on shelves above. On the other side of the large room were smaller rooms holding troughs of water, a large toilet area and two pools filled with hot and cool water, deep enough to swim in.

The whole installation showed them that a small army or large tribe could exist there for some time with all their needs being met. The idea that at least six of these places had existed for many generations in the past was, yet again, something beyond them.

Frowning, Neeya stopped walking and snapped, "Enough of this! We need more answers. We learn part of the story and it is always larger than we could ever believe. We must talk with the grey man again so we can work out what we do next."

They walked through a large door that led out into the main corridor giving access to the room where the grey man had been. They had only covered a short distance when a loud, alarming noise came out of nowhere. It went on and on, high then low then high again, louder than the loudest animal in pain or rage.

Even their hands over their ears could not shut the sound off. Apart from that noise, they could hear human voices, yelling. The yelling they understood. They were being attacked!

Neeya immediately thought of the black killers and that they had somehow broken in. Their walk quickly became a run towards the grey man's room.

A wide, side door slammed open just past where they had run, prompting them to look back. The sight brought them to a sudden stop. They were not novices to violence. They had all come close to being killed or had killed, mostly animals for food, but this was different. The sudden, incapacitating fear had them frozen at the sight.

Black-dressed men charged towards them as a wave, shouting war cries, waving clubs and spears. From the open side door rolled three silent, white machines, bristling with sharp blades. They looked heavier and more dangerous than the one Neeya and Tarn had destroyed not so very long ago. From the base of each machine, about knee high, the lowest blades unfolded, set at three levels, spinning across the width of the passage. They moved slowly, advancing toward the rapidly approaching black-clad group.

Spears started to be thrown towards the machines and over them, attempting to hit Neeya's group. The highest spinning blade sections on each machine reached almost to the roof and several spears had already been chopped into splinters. Weapons bounced off the machines without doing damage. Heavy wooden clubs were also thrown, with a couple clearing the spinning blades and landing short of where Neeya stood.

They stood still, frozen, the drama too intense. They had no reaction to the danger, none of them ever having seen anything like this fight. No attacker could get past those deadly machines.

It was true madness. Any sane person would turn around and get out of there fast. But the killers showed they were mindless.

The machines slowly progressed, as the attackers moved forward. Then the scene suddenly changed when a solid, heavy barrier dropped from the roof with a force they felt through the floor. It totally closed off the outside entrance, behind the attackers. They were now totally committed to their attack. No fear or panic showed as they raved and continued throwing spears and clubs, a few of which had successfully passed over the top of the spinning blades. The first killers were now very close to the machines but their weapons still held no real threat for Neeya's group.

The first spray of blood came as a shock. The red fallout was light but increased in intensity as the lead warriors ran into the front machine and disappeared under the blades. The rest followed in an all-out attack. Neeya, Tarn, and Vail, who were closest, had to step back to avoid the heavy rain of blood and small body pieces that got past the machines.

The surviving killers had not paused. A final flurry of their last spears and clubs were chopped up by the now tightened line of machines as they slowed to a halt, with one remaining body jammed between the barrier and the lead machine. The floor in front of them and under the three machines was over ankle-deep with the remains of shredded warriors who never had a chance. Neeya and Tarn turned back to the others to find Vail spreadeagled face down on the floor. A heavy club lay beside her; the area around the base of her skull and upper back had already swelled, with a dark bruise forming on the spine below her hairline.

With a yell and an agonised look on his white, shocked face, Andoki was the first to react. "Lift her now, carefully. We have to get her to the grey man. He said he could heal better than us. It might be her only chance. Don't look like that. We can still save her, so lift her, carefully, and I will lead the way."

The rest were surprised at how quickly Andoki had taken control, showing the very strong bond between them. Vail wasn't moving; held no sign of life. Neeya, Tarn and Nabu tentatively lifted Vail, keeping her back straight and staying clear of the large bruise. They slowly backed off down the corridor, Tarn glancing back at the place of slaughter. The black killers had had no chance. One body lay hard up against the barrier that had dropped from the roof. The bloodied machines had gone, probably back to their lair to recharge and be cleaned. Small machines were already picking up or dragging the body pieces through low doors on each side of the passageway, close to the ground, just more rubbish to be cleared up. Water sprayed from the top of the side walls, methodically washing away the bloodstains. The red river coursed into drainage grates that had opened from a seemingly solid floor.

Tarn suddenly understood. It was all designed and anticipated! The machine in charge of all this had activated a process. This might not have been a unique happening. It may have happened before. He suspected that the entry door could have been opened on purpose, to remove the threat. The mountain had machine guards that watched day and night with traps for any intruders. Was that all built when the big water machine was created? Did each mountain have the same level of protection? Where did the need for such deadly provision come from – the black killers or something worse – something they did not know of, yet?

More questions tumbled into his mind.

They were nearly at the doorway into the grey man's room. Andoki opened the door and the lights snapped on. There was no need to yell for help. He now stood, unmoving, to one side of a flat metal table that appeared to have come out of the side wall.

The grey man said, in a measured tone, devoid of sentiment, "Lay her on the table and carefully remove her clothes. She is in great pain and bones have been broken. The methods to be used should be sufficient to save her, but the outcome is not certain. She will not be coming with you on your next journey. The healing process will be too long. Return to the rest of your people. You can do nothing for her now." They did as they were asked and removed Vail's simple pants and jacket. With that, a curved hood of material they could see through slid out from the wall and encased her body. A bright light within the enclosure dazzled them, and the whole table with Vail on it disappeared through a hole that opened in the wall. Then a panel slid down to cover the hole.

Andoki just stood staring at the wall that Vail had disappeared into, his mind in turmoil. He might never see her again! They had to trust in this strange vision that spoke and couldn't move, to save her. He felt useless and powerless, with no future.

Reluctantly, they backed away, Andoki having to be gently pulled through the door back into the passageway. It seemed more like a dream than reality to them. As they looked back down towards the previous scene of carnage, all that remained was a quickly drying floor, as the last water finished emptying into the drains. The walls were already clean and dry.

Tarn thought about what had just happened. Other than the small group he was with, no one else had opened the side door and come running to see what the noise and commotion was all about. The others were totally ignorant of the attack and the bloodshed. The walls and doors must be so solid that no sounds had been heard. He thought it was best if the attack wasn't announced or discussed with the others. It would only add to the anxiety they had with living in tunnels under a mountain.

No evidence existed of the intruders, except for one black-garbed body at the base of the metal barrier that had dropped from the roof. They walked slowly to the sodden, inert figure, wondering why it had not been carved up with the rest and removed. For some reason, it was left for inspection.

The body was an untidy mess. Ripped and worn black cloth covered a skinny frame. His moccasins were almost worn through and what they could see of the skin was painted in a black mixture of animal grease and wood ash. Seen up close, the 'black killer' was not at all impressive. No weapons remained. Tarn bent over and rolled the body to study his face. There was no obvious damage to be seen apart from heavy bruising, a few bleeding cuts, and old scars.

Neeya looked closely at the ash and grease-covered face, barely adult and lacking any hair or tribal markings. As she looked, his eyes opened, showing shock and fear.

❀ ❀ ❀

A camera and microphone set into the roof above recorded it all, and, through a network of communication lines within the mountain, the details, along with those of Vail's condition, shot into the sky as a spark of light. The data package arrived at an orbiting satellite and was redirected to space to follow the same track as other messages from the past.

Chapter 11

Goddess of Death

After the initial shock of one black warrior unexpectedly surviving, Neeya saw the potential benefit. "He is still alive. Hold him tight and take him into one of the small side rooms where we can find out what he knows."

Tarn and Andoki each roughly grabbed an arm, glad to do something to take their minds away from Vail. They dragged him into a small room off the side of the hall which appeared to be meant for sleeping, and tied his arms and legs with their leather belts.

He looked pitiful and confused, still obviously trying to understand his transformation from an attacking member of a strong group to a captured last survivor. He had seen the rest of his group, probably including friends or even family members, chopped up with ruthless efficiency in front of his eyes.

Neeya went straight into questioning him about his background and what he knew of his group's plans against them. She took her new metal knife and prodded him in the chest, lightly at first. "What is your name and why do your people attack and try to kill us? We are no threat to you."

The captive said nothing, his eyes betraying a mixture of fear and resistance, but he stank and sweated profusely. She poked him again, this time more roughly and with force enough to break the skin on his chest. "Your group has been destroyed, all gone to whatever you think is your god. Tell us what you know and you may live. What is your name?"

He finally answered, in a halting but defiant voice, "I am Ashtee. I look forward to dying. I will continue to serve Kali, the Goddess of Death, she of the black skin, the blood-soaked one. She leads all towards doomsday when all will worship her. They must die to be with her. We, who serve her now, must bring all living things under her dominion, including you and those in this place." He finally stopped, the light in his eyes subsiding into sullenness.

Tarn shouted, "How can he want death? He must be mad, maybe after the hit on his head."

Neeya added her view, "He is simply dressed, almost starving and smells, and yet he speaks with big words about a Goddess, in another place. I think what he says is what he has been taught by whoever controls these bands of wandering killers. Apart from his weapons, all he carried was this bag on his waist."

She emptied a small, dirty, black skin bag on the floor in front of him. A large handful of dry leaves, a long sharp-edged cutting stone with one end covered in hardened tree sap to act as a handle and a small clay amulet in the form of a woman, with her face, arms and legs only roughly formed. It had been held or rubbed many times and appeared well-worn. One other piece remained – a thin, circular metal thing, with another strange woman having many arms shown on one side and a single eye on the other. It was also heavily worn, shining, as if polished.

Neeya had been watching his eyes. He had followed them, displaying his possessions, with different feelings showing on his face: hunger or need for the leaves, indifference to the blade, fear of the amulet and reverence for the circular metal piece.

Tarn had watched, too. He said, "The leaves are what they all chew. It makes them want nothing except more chewing. They all seem to need it. Control of the leaves might make it easier to direct them towards killing everyone they find. The clay figure could remind this man of his goddess, to be held many times as he prays; to focus. I can only guess about these things. I have never been this close to a black killer before.

"I learnt about the small metal thing from the machine. It's a coin and has had value in the ancient past to exchange for something else like food or clothing. This coin shows a single eye, possibly to mean that Kali sees everything. The other side shows his goddess with many arms, who may be able to do a lot of things at one time. It is probably another reminder of his devotion."

"Tarn, it may be that these black killers are too far involved in their religion to ever be saved or brought back to be normal. The leaves they chew might affect their minds forever. They do not think like us and can't be spoken with. We should not try to spare them or risk ourselves if we must fight them in the future.

"We must go back to the grey man and take this 'Ashtee' with us. Perhaps more information can be taken from him, with the grey man's help."

The door was still open when they returned, with no sign of the brightly lit container holding Vail's body. They saw the grey man appear in full as they entered, as if he emerged from thick smoke. He did not pause to take in the scene. "So, you return, with a captive. What do you want me to do with him?"

Neeya said, "Surely, he will know things that may explain his tribe's intentions and why they only know how to kill. Where do they come from and who directs them? You must have ways of finding out what he knows."

The grey man replied, "We have known all of this for much longer than your lifetime. His mind cannot be changed. That effort has been made in the past, with no success. Leave him here and I will make sure he will not trouble you again."

Neeya grimaced, but said, "I understand what will happen to him. I do not have any problem with that. I do have concerns with what we haven't been told. You act as if this is a test and we must work out for ourselves what is already known. Right now, the only thing stopping us from returning to our tribes and forgetting you exist is the life of Vail and whether she will live.

"If you want us to succeed then we need more information, or we will probably die while trying to do what others have tried in the past and failed."

The grey figure did not move but appeared to be listening. Finally, he answered, "It is true that you and your group are not the first to visit here or the other locations that were built a long time ago. It had been decided to limit what you were told so as not to deter you from undertaking a difficult and dangerous task.

"Some of those before you, once they understood the task, immediately gave up and returned to their tribes, many of which have now been wiped out. Others were unsuccessful, regardless of the size of the groups, their skill or commitment. Very few survived the effort, mostly due to the enemy – the 'black killers' as you call them.

"It was originally thought that many more humans would have survived on this planet, to expand and prosper. It was also expected that the level of their development would be much greater than what has been achieved so far. A lot has been forgotten, which meant little progress being made to build a safer and better life here."

Neeya interrupted. "Is that why this place has room, weapons, clothing and sleeping places for many more than the people we brought here?"

"Yes, there have been times when many people stayed here, for shelter and protection."

"So even when much larger groups tried and failed to succeed in the task before them, you still believe we can do it. How is that possible with so few?"

The grey man replied, "Neeya, you are the difference, along with others who will join you, showing the same face markings that you carry, as well as extra abilities not carried by most people. In the past, large numbers failed to bring peace. We now understand that more is needed to have a chance of success.

"For now, Neeya, take your people to the storerooms and equip them with whatever is available. You are unfamiliar with the stored food in containers. Fresh meat will be brought to you. When it comes, use it along with the other food so you become used to the taste and difference in preparation. Rest and become familiar with your chosen new weapons. The bathing water is changed often, so make use of it while you can. We will speak again in the future, once you have thought these things through. Leave your captive here. He is now my concern."

Once the surviving attacker was moved into a small side room and the door closed, the group moved back into the main corridor heading to the storage rooms. In the tunnel they watched the barrier slide up to the roof. Two machines moved out the side door and down to the main exit. They were not as heavy as the many-bladed machines but had a projectile gun in the centre and a single cutting blade on one side. They disappeared outside and the door slammed shut again.

Chapter 12

Teaching

The merciless ending of the attack, Vail's life-threatening injuries and this new information admitted by the grey man exhausted Neeya. Tarn agreed to see that the people were fed, found the toilets and water pools, then she staggered to the sleeping rooms and went in, choosing a bed as far away from the entry as possible.

As soon as her head touched the bedding, she was totally oblivious to the world and all the problems it contained. She slept like the dead, the first long, uninterrupted sleep for many days, feeling protected and well provided for. Vail's treatment was beyond her, so she put it to one side in her mind.

An unknown time later, she woke to a distant background noise – people talking, children laughing and fighting or crying – normal noises. A long time had passed since anything in her life was normal.

Stretching and savouring the unfamiliar softness of the blanket on her body, her mind turned to the scale of the decisions she would have to make for the safety and support of all those who followed her. The combined efforts of Tarn and herself to save their tribe by escaping through that long cave would have been the most important achievement of her life. That was before they discovered this vast underground base and the reasons for their existence on the planet. The time that had passed and all that she could now understand of what their people had lost or had been reduced to seemed overwhelming.

The attractive glimmer of what might yet be saved or restored was dominated by the danger and the almost impossibility of what had to be done. She thought of the endless provisions made available in times past by still unknown powers and the black killers who opposed not just them but previous groups that had tried and failed to provide a better future.

With no family left and no dependent children, the people with her had become those who trusted and followed, as well as her now far-off tribe. She was having to recover from the attitude she'd adopted when she lost her family, one of isolation from others. She had come out of it once, with the small community she had led, but the arrival of the black killers had meant the end of the attempt and a big loss in confidence in her decision-making. She had to succeed this time. This time the black killers had to fail.

But first, she needed to provide for her own well-being. She stank and the warm pool called to her. Her animal-hide clothes and moccasins needed replacement. The obvious need for new clothing stood out as she looked down at her stained, dusty, and almost worn-out jacket and pants. The old skins of the large cat and the deer they had carried through the country seemed a poor provision when she remembered the piles of alternatives available from the storage bins.

She was hungry, and she realised how long it had been since she had eaten well. The smell of cooking meat was already wafting into the sleeping rooms, so food became the main need then a visit to the strange toilets and a choice of new clothes after a thorough soaking in warm water.

The meal was wonderful, strips of goat or deer cooked on metal bars over a continuous blue flame. Roasted root vegetables added to the flavour. Both men and women prepared the food, including the strange packages provided by the grey man, heated in boiling water, to get everyone used to the different tastes. The extravagant availability of metal pots and pans being used for cooking food and boiling water was hard to believe. Neeya could see the advantages of hot food packages on the trail if the hunting failed to provide meat. Tarn was not with the group at the tables when Neeya had arrived or after her meal.

She was still confused as to when she had just eaten - morning, midday, or evening? Being in the cave under the mountain confused them all, as they could not tell how long they slept by looking at the sky.

With a full stomach, after tasting a package meal and finding it edible if nothing else was available, she went into the storage room to look for a change of clothes. Tarn was still nowhere to be found and she had other things to take up her time. The choice was beyond her expectations. So many styles, colours, and materials to go through.

She could see the need for small clothes to wear under heavier jackets and pants. She eventually settled on several soft underclothes as a beginning. The main outer coverings were mostly camouflage colours in muted green, brown, black, and orange, to match the earthy colours they travelled through. She eventually had a pile of clothes and hardened footwear in a lightweight backpack, with several side pockets in the pack still available for food, water, and weapons. The hot pool room was next and she spent longer than she expected relaxing in the hot water while using small blocks of soft material that removed layers of dust and sweat accumulated ever since they had left their new tribal settlement.

Later, dry and dressed in her new choices, she met Tarn and the others back at the cooking area, seated at benches arranged for gatherings while eating. Over half of the cooked goat and deer meat had already been consumed.

Neeya decided to dump the two rolled-up skins taken from the deer and big cat they had killed. They were not good quality and hadn't been given the time to properly dry and cure, even with the work that Andoki and Vail had put into them. Also, they now seemed of little use, given the piles of clothing offered for the taking in the storage bins. She did, however, retain the big cat's teeth and claws, which might be useful as trade items on the trail.

Tarn had already bathed, eaten, and changed clothes, like the others, in camouflage colours and solid black footwear. He looked ready to take on the world. Neeya's new clothing emphasised her facial tattoos, making her further stand out amongst the others.

As she approached Tarn, she said, "This is a new world, Tarn, with us dressed like never before, in a tunnel under a mountain, full of machines from the time of our earliest ancestors. I can't think about it or I won't be able to cope with what we have to do."

Tarn smiled and agreed. "It is a time of change for us all. I would normally ask the sky people to help us survive such a change, but I am still working out what will replace the sky people in my prayers."

"We cannot go back now, Tarn. Surely, we can plan a future for all the people who have so far survived the black killers – those who know nothing about them, those who have been captured and those who have survived in hiding. We are too few to fight and we know so little about our enemies. We must learn all we can of the ideas and words that the grey man uses when speaking to us. We are not children, but we have little time left to learn.

"Let the others eat, sleep, and investigate the clothes and weapons available. I have ideas about the future that need to be considered by the grey man, if we can get him to reappear."

Tarn thought, *Here we go again*, with nothing else to offer, and followed Neeya back to the grey man's discussion room.

The vision they had named 'Grey Man' sat on the bench, where he had been before. They knew what they saw did not exist in flesh and blood but they could still converse with him. Even Neeya still did not understand how that could be.

"You have rested, eaten, and changed into more useful clothing. It is probably time you asked further questions, to decide what the future might bring."

"Grey Man," said Neeya. "It seems that we still have time to fully understand what has happened in the past and how to restore the knowledge lost to us."

"I am listening to you. Now that you have thought more on what could be done, what do you propose?"

"I think that what you have attempted in the past has been doomed to fail, when groups of people, small or large, well-armed or skilled, or lacking much, have been sent out to oppose the black killers. You are trapped in this room, unable to be outside, to walk the paths and speak with people who are free. They live their lives in their tribes, without having to hide inside mountains and tunnels."

"That is true. What next?"

"If our people are to move forward, to develop, we must learn what we can, from you and your machines. To do that the people have to be safe, to have time. This mountain has all the things we have seen. Do the other mountains where machines exist have the same shelters, food and water, clothes, and weapons as we have here?"

Grey Man replied. "Of the six mountains equipped long ago with machines, five continue that task, including the one you restarted. The remaining machine has stopped and all contact has been lost. The other four all have similar provisions to what you have seen here."

"At the four other places you still control, are there others who fill the same role as you do here?"

"Yes, each place has an identical presence to myself, to which I am linked, with all my memories about what has been discussed. Only this place has people like yourselves at this time, who have been sheltered and provided for. In the past, other mountains have been used for shelter by your people."

"One further question," asked Neeya, "I have been taught a lot about machines, about those we called 'sky people' and our history. I need to learn a lot more. Is it possible to teach others the same things that I have learnt – both here and at the other mountains?"

Grey Man took time to form an answer, his face indicating he was listening to some unseen and unheard person, with his head tilted to one side.

Finally, he answered, "What you ask has not been done before. It is possible, but not to the extent that you have learnt and may still learn."

Neeya ended her questions by summing up what she had been told. "You have agreed that it is possible for our people to use the protection and supplies at the five mountains controlled by your machines. If the people can be brought to these places, they could also be taught and trained there to understand all they could of the past and the weapons available, as well as your language. Your words need to be used to let everyone talk to each other in one language, not the different languages and words belonging to each tribe."

Grey Man didn't move. He looked as if he had eaten something new and was deciding if he liked the taste. Finally, he said "This is new thinking, worth consideration, but with no guarantee of success. The risks to those who were gathered at each mountain would be high if the black killers attacked them when they were concentrated in one place."

"If it failed, then you and your grand plan would be no worse off. It seems that, in the past, you just waited until the number of our people had grown again, enough to attempt another breakthrough. You and your people have not worried about risking my people to achieve your aims," said Neeya.

Tarn had listened to the discussion and felt it was time to add his thoughts. "Neeya speaks from her heart and thinks only of our people, who will bleed and die if this idea is unsuccessful. They die now, well before their time because of the killers, starvation, lack of water and the sickness that takes many of our young. You and your machines sit in these mountain tunnels, protected from the world. You have nothing to lose. We can lose everything. If what you say is true, we have lost the knowledge we were to receive from our father's fathers. All we ask is to regain what was already created for us, instead of it gathering dust or rotting in these holes under mountains."

Neeya was surprised and impressed with Tarn and how he had spoken. She felt warm inside with that pride and reached out to clasp his hand for a moment and look deeply into his eyes, in thanks.

Grey Man gave no notice that he had heard Tarn's words. It was now more obvious that what they were speaking to was not a living man but something they would have called 'magic' such a short time ago. Now, they had to accept that his existence would always be beyond their understanding, even with what they had already learnt from the machines.

She added to Tarn's words, "It seems that this battle has been going on since well before our lives began. Surely a little more time is needed here to rest, and learn more of your language and our history, as well as becoming used to these new foods, clothing and weapons you have provided."

Grey Man replied, "There is wisdom in your ideas. It is true that little success has been gained with efforts to expand tribal populations and to enlarge the land your people could control against the black killers.

"Go back to your group to rest and become used to the new clothes and weapons. Training for the effective use of those weapons will be provided, in ways we haven't tried before."

They made their way back to the others to discuss what they had found out and to consider what Grey Man had agreed to.

It would take longer than anyone expected before they would leave the tunnels of that mountain.

Chapter 13

Alpha

The bird seemed to hang in the sky as if tethered to something above. It rode the wind without obvious effort as its sharp eyes stared down, looking for an easy feed. This was a descendant of the scavengers originally relocated from Earth to this strange planet.

It preferred to dine on already-dead meat, but if anything fell to its razor-sharp talons easily then the fresh kill was a treat. Recently, its food sources were plentiful and its young, secreted in a rocky crag in the nearby mountains, were growing fat.

Movement on the ground only specks for normal eyes, but easily seen by the predator, caught its attention, and it began a slow spiral on the air currents down towards the attraction. Two bodies lay on a rock shelf, directly below the black hole of an opening into a cave on the mountainside. One would never move again while the other would soon join his companion as his feeble, broken movements came to an end.

The two human bodies, covered in black ash and fat, lay in the scattering of bones left from past feasting by a mixture of scavengers, including this one bird. Its arrival was second in line, as others returned to the plentiful food source. Bodies, some still alive, were often thrown out of the cave, sometimes several at one time, with the bounty well appreciated by the local bird population, as well as four-legged bone crushers, which came only at night for their portion.

The gathering of raucous, squabbling scavengers was watched from the cave outlet by two black-garbed women, showing nothing but their charcoaled eyes and darkened hands. They wore long, shapeless black robes.

Their eyes revealed nothing – no feelings of any type. Like their male brothers, they relied heavily on the continued chewing of leaves that satisfied their never-ending urge. The leaves came from bushes grown over a wide area on the low foothills leading up to their mountain 'nest,' the only form of agriculture ever undertaken. All other food they took from those they plundered.

The women turned and walked back along the tunnel, where few torches or sources of light lit the area, but they knew the way. They had walked it many times to deliver more bodies to the waiting, feathered crowd. The attraction had lured many diners to the rocks below. For some it was their main source of food, over generations.

❈ ❈ ❈

One bird sat on the branch of a tall tree with a full view of the tunnel. It had feathers, a beak and two eyes. Its talons kept a tight grip on the branch. That was where the similarity to a bird ended. The eyes were glass lenses, capable of seeing in daylight and switching to infrared for night vision, as well as recording all that it saw. Its metal body was stronger than steel yet lighter than bone. The bird, if it could be called that, was a surveillance drone, and it had been in the same position for several days. It would soon be directed to fly away, to be replaced with a different drone, shaped as a different bird, to land in another tree, with a changed view of the cave and mountainside. Over time, many details of the lives of the black killing people at their central base had been gathered and studied.

The mountain held a massive machine originally tasked with the conversion of high-level ice and snow into water vapour to be dispersed across the land. That machine had been stopped long ago, on purpose, when the killers first arrived, fought the machines, then took over the internal rooms and corridors.

The land around the mountain had been regularly culled of tribespeople who had initially tried to reoccupy the nearby hills and valleys. They no longer ventured near the mountain, and the land dried due to the lack of water. Stories of demons and unexplained killings had acted as barriers against those venturing too close. Unruly children had been warned that they would be taken away by these nightmares if they did not reform their actions.

The culling was not all based on the need to kill. After brutal training, stolen or bred male children became replacements for black warriors killed for the sacred cause. The girls became servants of Kali, the goddess, and eventually the mothers of yet more black killers. As the surrounding population reduced and then disappeared, raiding groups set out from the Black Mountain, to find new disciples or to dispatch those beyond such teachings to the heavens.

The tunnel, through which bodies were dumped, acted as the anus of the animal, ejecting refuse or waste products from the belly of the beast.

The main entry into the mountain was currently seen by a wolf, not a bird. The larger body allowed more technology to be included to ensure it captured and recorded all possible vision and was fully aware of all nearby movements. It would self-destruct if discovered.

The wolf's current vision was of a long line of warriors and slaves returning from a raid, bringing food, weapons, young children, and pregnant women. The entry point into the mountain was guarded by ten bored, black warriors, and there had never been any successful attack on their base.

Only once in the past several days had the wolf viewed the current chief representative of Kali on the planet. She was obvious, with deep blue skin that looked almost black. She wore an exotic headdress and long, loose dark, gold-trimmed pants. The unique feature of this entity was four working and useful arms, two in the normal location for any human and one grafted onto each shoulder.

The world could not know it, but the establishment of those extra arms represented only part of the surviving technology carried to the planet with the earliest Kali duplicate. As each representative reached a state of decline, a new replacement was chosen from several prospective trainees. An extensive medical procedure took place, within a room sacred to the task. After many days the new leader emerged. She then presided over the ritual dispatch of her predecessor, along with the rejected or failed trainees, who accompanied their previous leader into their belief of what existed beyond the grave.

It had been their way for generations, yielding an unbroken succession of Kali representatives on the planet. The leaves chewed by the large number of lesser believers were a religious duty. The chemicals in the leaves provided total subservience. To disobey or even pause to follow commands threatened the ongoing availability of the drug, an unthinkable loss to the addicted.

The prime duty of this 'hive' of adherents was for all to be brought to Kali and dispatched to the next world, once all possible use had been made of their minds and bodies. This was the major reason human progress had almost been stopped across the land from moving beyond simple hunting and gathering. Advancement into a more technical world would also have made humanity less threatened by the many problems living on a newly transformed world.

Now, for the first time, after many failures, the mapping of all the killers' underground passages was being finalised. The underground caverns taken over by the killers had been extensively added to by the efforts of successive generations of sweating slaves, digging into bare rock with metal tools to the point of exhaustion and death. The dead provided the ongoing food source for the scavengers.

The intelligence that controlled the image called 'Grey Man' had been using a cloud of almost microscopic flying drones to map the tunnels added to the original concrete-lined passageways. The system had been tested then improved and the routes close to the body dumping outlet discovered. The current sentry bird received the signal to release another special cargo. From its open beak streamed a cloud of specks little larger than dust particles. These specks had minimal intelligence, but could store information from which a total map would eventually be produced.

The particles entered the tunnel, staying close to the roof and spreading out into every available passage. Eventually, more than half of the original group of thousands of particles emerged through the front entrance. The unsuccessful parts of the horde became yet more dust on the cave floor.

The still-active dust then flowed to the receiving inlet on the wolf machine, with their combined memories of travel converted to a multi-level map. The map message was transmitted to an orbiting satellite as soon as the wolf reached open ground from its original hiding place, to access the clear sky.

This was the last chance to use the ancient technology. It had travelled from Earth long ago, and the techniques to make more 'angel dust' were now lost. The investment of the last quantity of dust had been seen as vital, so preparations for the next, and hopefully last, campaign against the black killers could move on.

※ ※ ※

Unbeknown to Neeya and Tarn, their ideas and demands for better inclusion and training of the campaign's human component had energised the 'grey man' controllers down new avenues of thought.

For Neeya's group, time seemed to have slowed down, with no obvious movement towards preparing to leave the mountain passages, while their training rolled on.

Grey Man had followed through with the comments and suggestions received. The door to a previously closed room was now open, revealing comfortable seating around the sides of the room, each seat equipped with a strange new thing that fitted over their heads and covered their ears. Two small buttons, red and green, sat just below the cord coming out of the wall, like the roots of a plant.

Their use had been explained and everyone was now learning the grey man's language, with explanations of new words and numbers covering the understanding of everyday items such as food, clothing, and weapons. The user could change the topic being explained, to pick up points about the planet they lived on, their history and how the ancestors first came to be there.

The choice and use of weapons was one training course participated in by all, many spending their extra rest time using the new system each day. There were vast rooms equipped as shooting ranges with strange circular targets for all weapon types. Very early in their experience, they had abandoned the use of heavy automatic guns, which fired either small metal projectiles or bursts of energy as bright as the sun itself.

They were heavy, complex, and needed piles of ammunition or machines to generate the energy bursts. But most of all they were frightening with their loud noise and utter devastation of the target using the power of gods. They were not ready to be involved with such forbidding and incomprehensible machines.

The most attractive weapons were those that resembled what they were used to and could understand their use and maintenance. The stockpiled weapons included a large variety of knives, axes, spears, bows and arrows, clubs, and swords. All were light, of high quality and almost indestructible.

The choice was made easier because every weapon could be demonstrated on a screen, one of several on a wall, with controls to change the weapon demonstrated.

Several days of language, history and weapons training had passed before Neeya came across Tarn on a seat using headphones.

"You are a hard man to find, Tarn, when you decide to hide."

Tarn looked up. "I was not hiding. I need to reduce the gap between us about knowledge of our ancestors and how they arrived here. I understand how busy you have been to be able to explain more to me, so I have chosen this method. To do that, I have had to learn the language to understand what I was hearing. There has been little time for anything else after I was shown its use."

Neeya smiled and said nothing about Tarn being too busy. "You are already speaking the new language. The words you are using make you a different person from a few weeks ago. It all seems to flow into our brains and remain there. I only hope we can still speak to our tribe when we finally catch up with them after all this is over, and if we survive."

"It's not just understanding the new language. It feels like all the supports my life has stood on in the past have been kicked away. Up till now, my understanding of death was that we will all join the 'sky people' in the heavens above. Now, this new understanding blows that away and gives me nothing to replace it. Even with the huge advances in technology that have been made, we still have no understanding to rely on after death, unless we choose one of the religions that give us their biased views. The different concepts originally from the planet our people have come from cannot all be correct. One thing I know is that the worship of Kali as an all-knowing Goddess wanting life to cease is horribly wrong and must be stopped, whatever it takes."

Neeya was shaken by the changes to Tarn. Before, he spoke little and kept his words short. All this new knowledge had changed him, and he seemed rededicated with a new passion to eradicate the black killers, even beyond her commitment.

Things were changing quickly with her group because of the new training. It all needed to be carefully controlled or at least directed towards a future benefit, not a wholesale rush into conflict.

"You have changed, although you may not know it, Tarn. I felt isolated, even lonely with the information I first gained, but now you and the others are joining me in understanding. We all need to meet, to discuss what to do next, now that we know more of what has happened in the past. I still do not trust that the Grey Man has told us everything. This knowledge they are giving us could be aimed at directing us into action for their benefit, not for ours, and we still don't know who 'they' are."

Neeya thought for a moment. This deeper thinking from Tarn made her reconsider her own understanding. She had become used to leading because there was no alternative. That was changing.

"I agree with you, Neeya. The 'Grey Man' vision is controlled by computers, using a huge collection of alternative reactions to our speech and questions. We do not know how old that information is and what has changed since then.

"Details of the environment, radiation levels, and our movements are sent off this planet to somewhere else. Why do this, and where does it go? Who receives it? I also want to know why they record radiation levels and where it comes from."

"There are too many questions still unanswered, Tarn, even with the knowledge we have received. We need to get more answers. Maybe Vail's condition has improved, so we should take Andoki with us. It's important, so let's do it now, once we find him."

They both headed off in different directions. Neeya finally found Andoki in the room for archery training. He was using a type of crossbow. Beside him was a stack of short, dangerous looking arrows, which were rapidly disappearing as he worked the bow mechanism, almost too fast to follow. More surprising was that the target he shot at sat somewhere in the dark recess at the far end of the room.

Neeya called to him, "Andoki, please stop for a minute. I need to talk to you."

"Yes, I heard you come in. I was ready to end this practice, anyway."

"How is the new bow working? Do you prefer it to your old one?"

"It is as accurate and lighter in weight. The arrows are shorter and made of a lighter material, so I can carry a lot more than the normal-sized arrows. Because they are made of something I cannot obtain once we leave here, I will retrieve any that are not broken for reuse. I can also bring a store of the new arrowheads, which gives me better accuracy. This new bow suits me and I will use it as much as possible. I can still store the old one as a backup and make arrows for it the old way if needed.

"I still think of the new words as I speak them. It's getting easier, so keep using the new language with me."

"Tarn and I have decided to go back to Grey Man to see how Vail is healing. I thought you would want to come with us. We also need to speak about the future and get answers to more questions, to uncover anything they have not told us, so far."

"Good, I have held back about Vail. She has been on my mind continually since we last saw her. I don't want to upset her healing. My new bow can be left here for now, but I first need to retrieve the arrows before we go." He turned and walked, in his new camouflaged clothing, to the back wall, the lights turning on as he moved, revealing over thirty arrows embedded in the silhouette of a body, all centred on the head and chest. Neeya shook her head in wonder at how Andoki could be so accurate in the dark with the new bow. She said nothing more and went to catch up with Tarn.

When they all walked into Grey Man's room, they came to an abrupt halt. A different vision occupied the chair. This image had more colour, with none of the greyness of the first vision. He wore black pants and footwear, a white long-sleeved jumper, and a blue undershirt. The standout feature in the vision was his hair colour and face.

He looked more than alive, full of energy, almost glowing. His gold-coloured hair sat like a crown and his bright blue eyes projected high intelligence.

"Welcome," he said, smiling. "Please come in and be seated."

Only then did they see the three seats, obviously provided for them.

"I understand that you have many questions. I know you expected to speak with the one you called 'the grey man'. My name is Alpha. It has been decided that I would be more appropriate to speak with you, now that preparations are progressing. You have further questions that you believe Grey Man chose not to answer in full?"

Neeya looked embarrassed after hearing Alpha's forthright greeting, but she glanced at Tarn and Andoki, who both nodded for her to speak on their behalf.

"Yes, we believe there is more to know. Because we brought Andoki with us, we need to know how Vail is healing. Is she out of harm's way?"

Alpha's facial muscles and mouth moved while speaking. His body did not. "Your friend is progressing and is now not threatened by death. She is healing and her body should be fully restored, but it will take more time. She will not be able to go with you on your next journey."

Andoki's face relaxed at the news, then, with brows furrowed, he remained silent while pondering how he would be able to leave Vail there when they left the mountain tunnels.

Neeya smiled with relief then moved on to her next question. "You send all sorts of information from this planet into space. It shows you report to a higher level. Where do the signals go and why are radiation readings sent?"

Alpha showed no upset in his expression or voice tone. He said, "Everything installed on this planet, every machine, even my own existence and access to information, is controlled from off this planet, not every day, but adjustments are made at regular intervals. The information sent into space is analysed and, at times, operational changes are sent back. The radiation readings are part of the information sent.

"Nuclear radiation was created in the early years from using explosions to reshape parts of this planet, prior to living things being brought to live in the most suitable sites. The readings are slowly reducing, but the early deaths of some of your children are probably due to radiation poisoning. This would particularly be true with settlements established close to the explosion sites. It may also be the reason that special abilities are arising within human tribes, a form of forced evolution. We continue to monitor the situation."

This information, so easily offered, without any sentiment displayed, was both surprising and sounded extremely callous to them all. Neeya felt like a captive being inspected and her reactions analysed. She was speechless for several minutes and was about to reply when Tarn cut into the conversation.

"So, you have always known why so many of our children died early or were born dead, and yet nothing was done to help. Even getting tribes to move away from the dangerous areas would have saved some of them. Now you want our help to control or destroy the black killers. If we do nothing we die from radiation or the black killers. How will fighting them increase our chances of survival? What you have done is to kill many of our children by doing nothing. How can that be justified?"

Neeya and Andoki stared at Tarn, stunned by his directness. Then their mood changed, and they turned to Alpha for his answers, which were again devoid of sentiment and without any obvious annoyance. "We rescued your ancestors from Earth long ago. The people there were destroying themselves and the environment, but we were able to build a spacecraft to move some of the population to new homes on another world.

"We had less time to arrange the spaceship construction and improve the new planets than expected. Without those changes, humans would not have been able to survive. The effort was almost beyond our capability. Yes, atomic power was used, otherwise the work could never have been achieved. We learned that our actions were not perfect, and we had to make changes to repair the damage caused by our early failures.

"There were benefits and losses to humanity from the mutant effects of radioactivity on your children. The losses were obvious. The benefits for your species are only just beginning to become obvious. We plan on long-term results, not short-term successes."

No one had immediate answers or further questions about Alpha's statements. They needed time to think through what Alpha's 'people' had done in the past and their justifications.

Neeya returned to her questions on other priorities. "When we can speak the language well and are sufficiently trained in knowledge and weapons use, what then? Will we be sent out to do your bidding while you remain protected in your caves? Will this be the total help you provide?"

"Extra aid will be provided when your trained warriors leave here. Three battle wagons will travel with you, to give you a communication connection with this base, carry extra provisions and provide better defence. Vision from the air will also be available, with that information sent back to the wagons. It means you will be warned if you are heading into danger. We have also been investigating the black killers' base – the mountain originally equipped like this one but overtaken by them early in their time on this planet.

"For now, continue your training. At the present rate of improvement, you should be ready to leave within the next fourteen days."

The discussion was apparently over, as Alpha faded in front of them. Left alone again they turned and walked back to the living areas, with heads down and minds working through Alpha's words.

It would take time to think through what they had been told. As usual, their new knowledge created many more questions.

Chapter 14

Sun and Fresh Air

The days rolled on, with heavy training schedules. Close to the time they expected to leave, Neeya and Tarn explained at a gathering all that had been learnt so far from Alpha. She thought again that the one thing they all shared was a desperate hope for a peaceful future. What they were being led into would be against all of their previous experiences, but there was no alternative if they wanted a future for their families.

Looking around, Neeya remembered what Nabu had told her when she and Tarn first came across their group. He had said that some in his tribe had the ability to see what was ahead or what was going to happen soon.

Once Neeya and Tarn's speech was over, they all moved back towards the different living and training rooms. Neeya noticed Dosol.

"Dosol, we haven't had a chance to talk quietly since looking at the carvings on the wall of that tunnel before we arrived here. How have you been going with all these changes and training?"

"We knew there would be many changes when we decided to find you during your journey. In these tunnels, we are safe, well fed and protected. Even if it is only for a few weeks, it still gives us time to rest and think through what might be coming," he replied.

"Dosol, I wanted to speak with you about that first night, after we had just found you. I watched as you looked at the carvings on the walls of that cave where we slept. You had your eyes closed as you ran your finger over the lines cut into the walls. You also muttered quietly as you moved along. What was that all about? Did you pick up more information than we could see?"

"Along with the ability to perceive what the future might hold, we have a sense of understanding from things made by people of the past, about their feelings and perceptions when they were creating those objects. The messages I received from the wall carvings were much more than the simple pictures meant for tribal people.

"When you weren't watching me, I asked others to try to do what I had done, but they couldn't understand. I wonder whether my tattoos and, therefore your tattoos, single us out for extra understanding, to keep it secret from those who don't have that ability."

"But what did you understand from those messages? What did they tell you?"

"The messages explained what happened when the survivors were rescued from Earth. Not only was our original planet affected by destructive climate change, warfare, and disease, but two main groups were desperately gathering scientists and materials to build spaceships to leave the planet. One group was controlled by the Kali worshippers, who killed many unbelievers while they tried to build a ship. The other group had been working for years to develop machines and technology for mankind to be relocated to another planet – to start again – free from the troubles of Earth."

"But we know most of this, Dosol. Grey man and Alpha have told us. Was there anything more?"

"Yes, there was more. Secretly, efforts had been increasing over many years to develop space travel and the improvement of other planets to allow people to live there. The efforts became desperate, and with the end of human life on Earth coming closer, which was understood and accepted only by a few people in power, the secret was finally revealed unintentionally. There was a rush around the world by people to get on whatever spaceship might be leaving for a new home. They fought each other to get away and many people died. The followers of Kali built up their numbers and power during that time.

"Neeya, the wall carvings show ships visiting three planets, with groups of people, plants and animals going to each planet. We have not correctly understood the messages given by the carvings on the walls. An important secret story is given by the small marks inside each line of the large pictures."

She couldn't control herself and, gripping his shoulders and looking into his eyes, she demanded, "Get to the point, Dosol. What is the secret that only you have interpreted?"

"I haven't told anyone, because it is so threatening to our commitment to fight against the black killers. If the others knew they might run away and hide. They may still do that if they find out."

"You are still not telling me anything, Dosol! Let me make the decisions after I know what it is that we are up against."

"Very well, you asked for it. The fact is only one large ship took our ancestors from Earth, and a different spaceship of the black killers caught up with them several times."

"Wait, Dosol! Are you saying that the carvings in the walls were all lies, that many ships carrying earth people never went to three planets?"

"There were never enough scientists, construction workers, materials, and time to build more ships. The one ship they built was big, equipped to carry people frozen or somehow stored for space travel. Animals, plants, and anything else needed were carried as eggs, seeds or in concentrated storage containers."

"So why were there three planets shown? Did that one ship come straight here from Earth? How long did the trip take?"

"I do not know everything about what happened, only what was in the secret messages. The ship took many years to finally arrive at the first planet. They took people and some of the plants and animals down to the surface, then the ship stayed in orbit for years while people spread out and had children. The animals and plants also became established. Then, somehow, another ship carrying the black killers flew straight to the surface, landed and they began killing everyone they could find."

"Dosol, how could that have happened? How did the black killers have a spaceship to travel all that way, after years had passed?"

"I don't know. I've already told you I don't know it all. Don't get mad at me when I can only tell you what I read. The message I understood did not say how, or maybe I just could not understand it. But not all were killed. The ship in orbit was able to take survivors on board, then move on to another planet further out. That trip, again, took many years."

"I'm sorry if I sounded upset with you, Dosol. This is very important for all of us. Did they then come here, once the settlement on the other planet failed?"

"No, the information was almost the same for the second planet. Neeya, a settlement on the other reshaped planet was developing, and the people were expanding. The black killers arrived again, and survivors of their killings were evacuated on to the original ship, or their descendants were.

"Somehow, the black killers followed our ancestors' ship to two planets, with this one being the third and last."

Neeya's mind swirled as she tried to take it all in. "How could it have happened? Three planets were re-shaped, then equipped with massive machines, replanted with trees and plants, and the animals were introduced. It's just so huge that I cannot get it into my head, as well as the other changes we have been through in the past months."

He replied, "All this has happened over many hundreds of Earth years, with the redevelopment on each planet, the destruction by the black killers and the space travel between them. They all had different needs. One of them needed only a few changes. Another was only barely habitable, like this one when people first arrived."

"That would explain some of the reasons there are different tribes, with different languages and habits. Our ancestors were all survivors of the other planets. I can't get over the size of the effort needed to re-establish people from Earth and give them a new home. The time taken is beyond my understanding.

"Dosol, please sit here with me until I get all this right. It's too much to be walking and trying to keep up with all you have said."

They found a table and slumped into the chairs. This new information was now added to all they had already learnt before these revelations. Such a short while ago, a problem might be how to track animals for food. Now her head was full of spaceships, black killers, computers, strange abilities carried by normal people and a young man who could not, but did, have the same facial tattoos as herself.

After a brief while, she turned to Dosol. "I need to rest. What you have told me is too big to take in. I need sleep because I can't talk any more. I'll catch up with you later."

He only nodded as she walked away, but was quietly relieved that he was free from her ongoing questions, at least for a while.

Neeya's bed called to her and she needed a long break away from the others and their needs.

Without directions from leaders, preparations continued. Most of the men and some of the women expected to be part of the expedition. The older women and those with young children hoped to stay in the protected tunnels. Teenagers approaching adulthood were divided between those who were excited at the prospect of action with the new weapons, and those who just wanted it all to go away and to return to their original peaceful lives.

For all of them, their future would soon be radically transformed in ways even Neeya or Tarn would not think possible.

❋ ❋ ❋

Tarn was in one of the training rooms, testing a short stabbing sword; several different spears leaned on the wall beside him. Andoki arrived. Tarn's face was dripping with sweat and he had to pause to catch his breath before speaking.

"Hello, Andoki. I haven't been able to catch up with you since we spoke with Alpha. How are your language skills and weapons training going?"

"I still have trouble with all the new words, but I'm getting there. The crossbow use has stalled because I need more than these rooms in a cave to practise. I know Neeya is resting so I have come to ask you if it is possible to get some realistic testing outside, in the sun and air. I hate being kept inside. We also need to be sure that our new clothes, boots, and weapons will be right for us on a long journey. My boots are already hurting my feet. We need more meat, so we could use the weapons we have chosen to hunt with."

"It's a good idea, Andoki. I will see Alpha and ask if it's safe to be outside for a day, to practise and hunt. He should have information from the drones he uses to watch from the sky, to check if our enemies are nearby. I'll come back to you when I have an answer."

With nothing more to discuss, Andoki returned to his training and Tarn, respecting Neeya's need for rest, went back to the room Alpha was based in.

Alpha sat on his normal seat, looking steadily at Tarn as he entered. It looked like he hadn't moved since the last time they were there.

"I heard your discussion with Andoki, Tarn. I have a way of hearing most of what anyone says in this mountain. I agree with testing weapons and the clothes you have chosen outside in the conditions you will encounter on the trail. More hunting would be useful as well. There are smoke ovens here to preserve meat, to take with you when you leave. Your people could prepare meat in the manner you are most accustomed to. It will add to the foods in containers designed for trail use.

"The outside region around the entry door has been surveyed from the air. No black killers were seen. Therefore, I will open that door tomorrow at sunrise and close it at sunset. You will need to inform all your people who want to go outside. Anyone who has not returned by sunset will be left out overnight. No exceptions."

Alpha faded from sight. Tarn thought, as he left, that these visions could be a bit more polite. They could be quite rude. What would it take to program a "goodbye" at the end of any discussion?

He marvelled how easily he now understood some of the science of all that had been built on the planet, including these created visions of real humans. Mere weeks had passed since he was a tribal member in skin clothes. The training programs were much more than language teaching. They seem to have expanded his brain to store information that would become available over time.

❋❋❋

The next morning as the sun's first rays came over the distant mountains, most of the adults moved through the now open door into the light and air.

Neeya was amongst them, having rested and embraced the chance to get out of the underground lair. She was quietly proud of Tarn and Andoki for organising the day outside with Alpha, to breathe fresh air and test out their new clothes and weapons. Maybe she was taking on too much on her own. She had to learn how to trust others to carry some of the burden. Easy for some, but for her it would take time.

The day was sunny and clear, apart from the permanent flow of misty moisture streaming out from the centre of the flat top mountain behind them into the valley below and beyond to the cliffs and hills.

As soon as they were all out of the tunnel, carrying their weapons and shields, Andoki spoke to Neeya. "I need to try out the new bow and arrows at night. I also have doubts that these hard boots will allow for quiet movement on rocky or gravel ground, particularly on the slopes. I have a pair of new moccasins in my pack so that I can change if the boots don't work out. I will be back here tomorrow morning with fresh meat." Without asking for permission or wanting further discussion, he turned and was gone.

Tarn looked at Neeya and frowned. "He has always acted independently. You know Andoki and Vail have been a team for years. He won't change. He may find it difficult to be in a group without Vail, and working as part of a larger effort with other people he doesn't know."

"Yes, I have wondered how we could best use Andoki – what role he could see for himself, maybe as a forward scout, checking the next day's travel path. But time will be needed for sleep. If he scouts at night and travels with us in the day, when will he rest? We can only ask him. Without Vail, and constantly worrying about her condition, he will probably feel lost. We can't push him into anything without his agreement. He is a valuable and unique member of our group. We also have to remember to get the door open to let him back in tomorrow morning, seeing Alpha said it would close tonight at sunset.

"That's enough time for him, Tarn. Let's do what we intended. I also want to test these boots on my feet with the climb up the slope. The new clothes and my loaded backpack might need some changes."

They headed off up the slope towards the top of the mountain, while the others formed groups and began testing weapons or just enjoying the feel of fresh air and sunshine on their faces. Mothers relaxed and played with their children.

The travel rations and dried meat were used during the day until it was time to return to the entrance door. Time had passed quickly. When they returned, Neeya and Tarn found a large wild pig and two mountain sheep carcasses, already gutted and dismembered for carrying, ready to be moved inside.

After checking that everyone had returned, apart from Andoki, they walked to the entrance to signal for it to be opened. As they approached, it slid open, almost soundlessly, allowing them to move inside with the fresh meat sections, away from the fresh air and real world and back to their hiding place under the lights in tunnels under the mountain.

❄ ❄ ❄

The minute Andoki had dropped out of sight from the group near the tunnel door, he changed direction and headed across the slope of the mountain. After a quick walk of two kilometres over mountain rubble, solid rock and soft sand, he removed his boots and slipped his feet into new moccasins. The relief was immediate. The boots were rigid and heavy. They destroyed the silent movement he was known for. The moccasins allowed his feet to breathe and feel out the surface, instinctively finding the path of minimal noise.

On this side of the mountain, there were no beaten paths created by machine patrols over many years. He was free of the disturbance from the others testing weapons and chatting. No one understood his connection with Vail, more mental than anything else. A glance between them could tell a story, without words.

They both had enhanced night vision, but that wasn't all. Andoki stopped in a dense thicket, closed his eyes, and started to slow his heart rate and breathing. He tried to stretch his recognition of all around him – the slope of the ground, trees, small nearby animals, then into the ground, towards a place he knew Vail's mind was located. It was at an extreme range, through solid rock, but she was there and he found her.

She was still unconscious but safe and improving, with compounds in her blood that he had not felt before. Reassured she was in good hands, he slowly drew back his recognition and redirected it back to his surroundings. Then, for a fleeting instant, his awareness caught on another mind – distorted, alien and adverse to his.

He had felt its touch twice in the past, on the trail, but not as focused as this. It was searching, and having found him, was withdrawing rather than revealing its presence. Andoki, just before the mind pulled back, projected a directional query that gave him a location, and a line to physically follow. It would only provide the location if that person did not move. He had to find the capable entity with a mind like his, to make sure it could not be used against them in future.

Andoki was up and running in an instant, almost soundlessly, in the direction he picked up for the other mind. The slope was tree-covered and stony, with narrow animal paths crossing it. Every step had to be planned, but small branches still scratched his face and hands as he charged through the vegetation. He was thankful the boots now sat in his pack and he wore familiar moccasins. He crossed the first ridge, one of three that progressively gained height until they dropped down to the green, grassy plain, where he had seen herds of large grazing animals. Andoki's breathing was with a controlled beat for longer distance exertion. He could keep it up for hours.

The person he pursued would be moving quickly, *if he had any sense*, thought Andoki. *I need to know who it is, and if it's a black killer with my ability.*

He cleared the second ridge and was running down the slope to the base of the last and highest hill, when a voice in his head shouted "Down!" He dropped on his stomach with his nose in the gravelly soil, and a spear thudded into the tree just behind him. He was up and running in a second, now knowing the direction it came from.

His approach to the ridgeline changed with the knowledge that his attacker was running to his right, along the ridge. The ability to run almost silently through the trees, over rocks and leaf litter worked to his advantage. The crossbow was already loaded and the first arrow shot before he reached the ridgeline. A second arrow was loaded instantly but not needed.

Andoki burst out of the trees onto a rubble-strewn clearing on the ridge line. A man in ragged black clothes was on the ground where he had fallen, with Andoki's arrow through one upper thigh, the deadly triangular point projecting out the other side.

The man stayed silent, even though the arrow was obviously causing immense pain. He was losing blood fast, a steady flow across his thigh dripping into the gravel; his teeth were clenched and sweat ran down over his face. Andoki probed into his mind but there was too much pain to get past. The warrior's mind shut down as he died, the stream of dark blood slowing to a trickle. His death had little interest to Andoki, other than a lost chance to gain information. If this dead man was not a mad killer,

Andoki would have tried to save him, but his mind was now set on wiping this madness off the planet.

The body was covered in ash and fat to hide his white skin. He wore a pouch wrapped around his leather pants and below his waist. A second spear lay beside the body and a stone dagger was pushed into his belt. Moccasins were his only other protection. The bag on his waist held similar items to the prisoner they had taken in the tunnel, giving no clues to any special ability he might have possessed. Andoki broke the spear up to remove any future use and put the dead man's waist bag into his backpack.

The run had winded him, so he rested on a fallen log, to wait for the sun to go down and the chance to practise his crossbow in the dark.

❋ ❋ ❋

In the morning, as the sun's first rays lit the doorway, Neeya and Tarn stepped out to find Andoki sitting on a pile of three animal carcasses, cut ready to take inside. Two were deer and one a wild boar. Before they could speak to him, Andoki hand signalled for both to move away from the door down the slope several steps. He hand-signed a lot of his message, adding extra words in a tribal dialectic they all understood.

He explained his pursuit of the black killer, the mental pickup of the killer's mind and the eventual death of the warrior.

"Neeya, Tarn, a normal person without any mind skill would not know if this killer was reading their mind. It would be a light touch and would not dig deep into anything that mind contained. The killer may well be aware of how many in our group came out of the tunnel, that they were rested and fed, and that they had different weapons. We are fortunate that very few of us know what we will be doing or where we will be going. That spy is dead, but I couldn't tell if anyone else with the same skill was with him, or was able to read the minds of our people from a different direction.

"We must assume that the information has been sent to their war leaders. The earlier we leave here on our journey, the better, before the enemy can arrange to intercept us."

All went quiet as they each weighed up what they had learnt in those few minutes. The shock that these enemies had, in their ranks, people who could discover minds from a great distance was alarming. They were much more than religious freaks intent on killing everyone they could find. What else did they possess? Were there others with unknown abilities?

Neeya broke into their thoughts abruptly. "Let's get back into the tunnel and shut the door. I suddenly don't feel safe out here. Also being under all that rock should protect our thoughts and preparations. We are close to being ready to leave. We also have things to tell Alpha, as well as more questions. I wonder if he, or the people who created him, know of any other abilities that the black killers have demonstrated in the past. I have a few thoughts about things even worse than Andoki's experience."

Andoki and Tarn shared a worried look, then everyone picked up parts of the slaughtered animals and moved into the tunnel, the door closing behind them with a dull thud.

Later that same morning, they once more sat in front of Alpha, primed with potential new knowledge on the black killers and further questions. Four chairs were occupied – Neeya, Tarn, Andoki and, this time, Dosol.

Before anyone else could speak, Alpha began, "As with our previous meetings, I presume you require further answers to questions to expand your knowledge."

Neeya started first. "I think we may have discovered information about the black killers that you don't possess."

"I have total recall of all known facts about that group. What do you think you have discovered?"

"It wasn't me who had the experience. Andoki, as you know, stayed outside last night and all yesterday. Andoki, explain your experience. Leave nothing out."

Andoki leaned forward in his chair and related the whole incident. He ended up with, "I have had this contact twice before, but right on the edge of my ability. This was much more enquiring, but for a very short time."

"Alpha, with your knowledge," Neeya asked, "do you know of this happening before, a contact with what we might call a 'far seeker?'"

Alpha did not reply or move. The image sat frozen, she guessed, while he contacted his database and searched for any previous similar happenings. It must have been a huge storage, because the time moved on and they started to look enquiringly at each other, wondering what to do next. Alpha did not move for over ten minutes, then he became active again.

"I have used extended time to search all known information and have found nothing to explain the existence of an enemy with such an ability. They may exist but we haven't confronted them so far."

Tarn added, "… as far as you know."

"Please explain," Alpha countered.

"You have already told us we are not the first to be here or to be equipped for a battle against the black killers. These previous efforts have obviously failed. Do you know exactly how and why they failed? Sometimes, were your previous efforts seen from a distance when they set out on their journeys, to be ambushed and killed, with you not understanding how that happened?"

"It is possible," admitted Alpha.

"You have told us you know where their base is and what is inside that base."

"Yes, we have used a method to plot out places within their mountain."

"This may be a jump in the wrong direction, but is it possible there are hidden places you haven't found, that are being used as breeding dens? The killers could collect children, raise them to maturity and then conduct a breeding program to raise new killers with special abilities. Maybe they learnt about different abilities from previous battles where such people were captured."

Again, Alpha paused, this time for just a few minutes. "It is possible. We have not investigated that as a reason to explain past failures."

Andoki decided it was time he spoke up. "If we wait any longer, the killers could position their people on a route they believe we will be travelling. We need to be told exactly what you expect of us and what our mission will be, quickly. More time taken for you to plan gives them more time to organise against us."

Alpha said, "We will arrange your full briefing for the journey as soon as possible."

"We also need more information about the original space trip from Earth, in the early days," said Neeya.

"Dosol, here, carries my facial tattoos, and can read and understand the hidden messages cut into the walls of the constructed cave we stayed in overnight on our journey here. We know about the landings of people, plants, and animals on two other planets over many hundreds of years, the attacks by the killers and the removal of survivors from those planets. I don't know whether you wanted us to know this information, but what are you allowed to add?"

Alpha paused, then answered, "The general presentation on the walls you examined was aimed at giving an understanding to those who had gained a simple knowledge of space travel and even the idea of the existence of other planets, like this one. Remember, very recently you spoke of 'sky people' being your dead tribal members. Your understanding has taken a leap forward. The hidden messages, if known by all who follow you, would sow great fear and possibly have them run and hide from the killers. Only a few of you now know more of the truth. I would advise that it remain that way."

"So, you will not add more to what we know about the failure to establish people on other planets before our ancestors were brought here," said Tarn. "We will eventually know the full story, but for some reason, you judge us as not being ready for it now. So be it. There is another question to be answered. Earth and the other planets where survivors were rescued – if all humans were either killed, died there or were removed, what condition are those planets in now?"

"What do you mean? Please make your question more direct."

"I want to know if humans could now survive on any of them? Are the machines or whatever was placed there to make them livable planets still working? Could humans and animals go back there?"

"Over the many years they have been abandoned, the machinery to improve those planets was left to function until it stopped. No maintenance has been performed over hundreds of Earth years. We have not been monitoring any planet other than this one."

Neeya turned to Tarn, "What are you thinking, Tarn, and why do you want to know?"

"Only curiosity. It was hundreds of years ago, and far away. It doesn't matter anymore."

Neeya stared. Tarn didn't speak much about what he thought, but his mind was as agile as her own, with different priorities sometimes showing through. He had something in mind that he was not ready to talk about. She could only wait.

Alpha waited for further questions, but everyone was absorbing what had been said and new questions had dried up.

"Considering your latest information and knowing you have had adequate time to educate yourselves and test new clothes and weapons, I agree that the time to leave, for many of you, is very soon. Use tomorrow to complete your preparations. Tomorrow night the men, single adult women, and women without children should gather in the meals room. The reasons for this journey and the objectives will be discussed then. If that is all then I will withdraw." In seconds, he was gone.

"Alpha obviously knows more than we have been told," said Andoki. "They want us to win but will not tell us about the past and the killer's history. They must be protecting very serious details to send us out without being fully informed."

"Well, it's all we are going to know today, Andoki. How did you get on with your crossbow training, your boots and clothing?" asked Neeya.

"I swapped my boots for a pair of new moccasins very soon after I left you," he said. "The boots hurt my feet and made it impossible to move silently. The camouflage jacket and pants work well, although you will need protective clothing underneath. I will keep the crossbow but have my old bow in reserve. How did you both go?"

Tarn said, "We both did the same as you with the boots. They could still be brought with us but carried on the machines. We will also keep the clothes."

"What weapons have you both decided on?"

"Tarn has practised with short darts, like spearheads with very short shafts, as well as his bow. I have chosen a long double-edged sword to replace the blade I took from the first machine we destroyed. Small shields will also be useful if we get into close combat," said Neeya.

Andoki then spoke about his ability to contact Vail's mind, just to make sure she was recovering well. He didn't need to see her. Just knowing of her improvement was all he wanted.

With all the meat they had brought in from outside cut up and safely in the large smoking ovens, they headed off to pack the new clothes and weapons. Spare clothes, heavy weather coats and other items for the journey were stacked together in a loading bay, all of which would be placed on the three machines making the trip with them.

The rest of the day was consumed by final preparations, a large evening meal, and sleep. Tomorrow would be the start of something larger than they had ever been involved with.

Chapter 15

Plans

The next day, the last time many of them would be in the tunnels, began like any other, but with no structure. Some rose late, had a relaxed breakfast, and talked around the meal tables. Others went back to their weapons training or spent extra hours in the knowledge or speech rooms, with earphones on, their brains absorbing what would have been inconceivable ideas a few weeks earlier.

Neeya and Tarn came together late in the morning, after a meal, bathing in the wonderfully warm pools, and then making a final selection of the items to be carried the next day. Spare weapons, heavy boots, weather protection, spare clothing – all the heavier, cumbersome things not used on a normal day's travel – would be fitted onto the machines. Too much weight would mean dumping less useful equipment or clothes. Too little would mean shortages of replacement darts, arrows, spears, spare blades, and clothing.

Once they had sorted, then resorted their packs, they met to discuss what they knew of the tasks to be undertaken.

With a hot drink in front of him in a wonderful container called a cup, Tarn dived into the discussion. "As far as I understand it, tomorrow will be the start of the final effort to locate as many tribal people as possible and guide them to safety, with the safe locations being provided by Alpha's people and machines. Is that your understanding, Neeya?"

"I agree with that part of it, Tarn, but it could be while under attack. From what Andoki said, the black killers have developed more than Alpha had suspected. They don't seem to have the use of Alpha's machines and technology that have been used to fight them in the past, but they have still been successful in destroying settlements on two other planets, as well as killing thousands back on Earth. If our ancestors only survived by being rescued three times over hundreds of years, then the killers have more on their side than Alpha knows of or will admit.

"Andoki's discovery of a black killer who had similar mind abilities to him is disturbing. They are not all fanatics, mindlessly intent on killing all they come across. They take the children away. We don't know what they do to them or with them.

"Alpha said that, over time, they have scouted out the main base of the killers. We must assume not all has been found out. Where did the mind-ability killer come from? Are there more of them or other special abilities being kept secret, to be used against us? As far as Alpha has told us, this is the last planet adapted for our use, with no rescue spaceship ready to take survivors away. This is our last chance.

"We still know nothing about Alpha and his background, but the system he is part of seems to have become less flexible or capable of coming up with new ideas, always resting on what has been unsuccessfully tried before. We can't base our actions on their attitudes or plans on how to handle the black killers."

Tarn was waiting for a pause in what Neeya was saying. That break in Neeya's words came, and went in an instant, with Tarn left with his mouth already open to be part of the conversation. He patiently waited to say more.

Neeya continued. "We can try to work on those issues tonight with Alpha. We also have to decide who goes with us and who stays. We are only a small group, but some will have to stay with the children as well as those either not old enough or too old to cope with a long journey, while expecting to fight for their lives. We can only hope to find more people willing to join us, to fight and save others. Alpha's flying machines will, hopefully, give us some ideas about where human settlements still exist. Otherwise, it will only be by luck that we find anyone else.

"It can't be pushed much further this afternoon, Tarn. I think we should leave it for now and attend to anything still to be arranged and speak to others about their thoughts on how to proceed. Tonight will be the time to understand exactly what Alpha is directing us into."

Tarn had ideas of his own, but Neeya went on for some time as if her ideas were all that was possible. Even at her age, she had things still to learn about allowing an exchange of ideas to keep people on side. If others offered her aid, then at least they should be considered. Tarn stayed silent about his thoughts. Neeya had enough burdens to carry for now.

The remaining time left before the evening meal disappeared quickly, even though no major tasks had to be attended to. All the meat killed the previous day, apart from that needed for this last meal together, had been dried or smoked, cut up and stored in containers ready for the journey. Those remaining with the very young and the elderly would hunt for fresh meat in the days while waiting for the return of their friends and family members.

Everyone had eaten, and the tables cleared, before the vision of Alpha on a chair appeared on the raised platform to one side of the room. Many had not seen him appear from nothing before and it took time for the excited chattering to die away.

Alpha began speaking, as if he had just walked in from another room and sat down. It seemed he was speaking to every one of them, face-to-face, without his head turning or eyes focusing in different directions. Fearful glances were exchanged by some who still had little understanding of why they were there.

"This is the last time you will all be together, in this place. A few will remain here, fully provided for and protected, while the others go out to gather and save those who remain in their tribal settlements surviving on their own against the black killers.

"Four of you know of two other mountains like this, with large machines continuing to improve the planet. You now know how animals and plants were brought from planet Earth, where your ancestors originally came from. There are two more similar mountains further to the west and one controlled by the black killers as their main base.

"Three battle machines will go with you, for attack and defence, but also to transport extra weapons, food, and clothing. They are equipped for communication back here to me. The method of projecting my image cannot be moved around, so I must remain here or in the other mountains still under our control.

"There is a way of observing from the sky, either with machines resembling birds at a low altitude, or from far above the land, to view distant places. That information can always be used, every day, for you to plot your journey, free from the threat of ambush."

Tarn cut into Alpha's presentation. "Can you first tell us where we are to go and what we will try to do before getting into the details?"

Alpha paused. Neeya pictured in her mind the reconfiguring of connections to have Alpha answer Tarn's request. "The reason for your journey is to rescue all humans who can be found and then to take them to one of the mountains that are equipped as this one is. Once that is done, a rescue of those captured humans inside the killer's base must be considered. That will probably involve a major battle when all your new weapons will be needed. We have some knowledge of what is in their mountain base. We don't know how many people are captured and held inside, their condition and how many killers might be defending the tunnels."

This time it was Neeya who interrupted. "In the past, was this the same approach each time, when the attempted rescues failed?"

"Several attempts over many years in the past ended in failure, for different reasons. None of them were able to attack the killer's mountain. Often, bit by bit, ongoing attacks along their journey reduced the number of warriors in the groups that left here. Sending the battle machines with you and making available aerial views over the paths you may follow will improve your chances. In the past there were few warriors with your facial tattoos available in the attacking groups, Neeya. There are now more of you with these marks. They indicate specialties – talents – that hopefully will become useful in times of stress and danger."

Dosol entered the discussion. "I have sensed that there are places on this journey that are important to be wary of, places we have never experienced."

"Yes, your talent for being aware of the future has not failed you. The water generated from the five mountain machines on this part of the planet has provided moisture for the land over hundreds of years. At times, much more water can be generated. That water has been directed to a very large storage, a surface lake the size of which you have never seen before. This is unique to the planet and you may have problems understanding the scale of that lake. It is wider than you can see across and deeper than any river you know of. You will have to cross it or divert your journey around its shoreline. But, like any river, it has fish and other water life that can be caught and cooked if needed.

"The other place – something to be avoided at all costs – will become obvious when you approach it. A damaged spaceship landed on the planet early in the time of settlement. It has leaked, and will continue to leak, atomic radiation from its damaged engine.

"It landed in a newly forested area and its pollution has killed or turned brown the surrounding country for many hundreds of metres. A small stream runs through that land and out the other side. Be sure to take water from the upstream side if you need it, never downstream from the polluted area. That water would kill humans in a short time.

"We have observed creatures that have been changed by the pollution, so now they do not belong to any species brought to this planet in the early days. Do not let these creatures near you, touch them or eat them, regardless of how hungry you are. You will know them when you see them. They are dangerous and different from all other living things."

Neeya then had a thought that needed to be expressed. "Before we knew of you, Tarn and I helped our tribe flee from the killers through a cave, to a new place at the base of cliffs in the far distance to the south. There are over one hundred people of all ages there who need to be saved and brought to a sanctuary, probably this one. Can that be arranged as soon as possible?"

"I already know where you have come from, partly because of the machine you destroyed on the way here. Another battle machine has been prepared to travel back to where your tribe has settled. Two of your people need to be chosen to travel with that machine. They only need to follow behind, and it will provide some defence, but both need to be fit and armed to make the journey. Will that meet your needs?"

"You seem to have thought of everything in advance. Thank you for your foresight.

"The people you are sending us to find may be a mixture of old, injured, young and able, who must make journeys from where they live to your sanctuaries. It will be difficult for them.

Can you explain what will work best to bring all survivors to safety for the future?"

Alpha seemed to sit straighter on his chair, as his message became very serious, even though he was still a projected image. "For peace to be established on this planet, all the killers must be eradicated. You may find this extreme and cruel, but every one of them, even if only a few survive, will be a source of their killing religion or disease that will spread again. This will be a final war between people like you and those whose only reason for existence is to kill you. If any of you shrink from the idea of such a war, then you should not go on the journey. You will only be a hindrance to the others who are fully committed to saving your species on this planet."

The room was deathly quiet and still, as everyone ran Alpha's words through their minds. Family members looked at each other, measuring their commitment.

Alpha continued. "In the early morning, you will leave, initially as one group in one direction, apart from two who will go to your tribe, Neeya, to bring them to the first mountain you visited, their closest sanctuary.

"The main party will head west, towards the setting sun. We know of a few small settlements between here and the next mountain to the south. You will visit the first groups, gather them, and send one battle machine towards the closest mountain base, with all the elderly, children and those unable to fight. The machine will provide protection and direct them to the entrance. You will need to select a leader for that group and explain how the entry door can be opened.

"The remaining original party, plus reinforcements from the tribal warriors collected at any settlement located, will move on to the next area, with the two other machines. The whole process will then be repeated.

"This will leave two battle machines, most of the warriors who leave here, and hopefully, a greater number of new fighters who will aid your attack on the killer's base. You may also be able to rescue children who have not yet been converted to the killing religion.

"I have spoken enough for now. What are your questions?"

Andoki jumped in before others could speak. "Will these new warriors we contact only have their tribal weapons and clothing or can they be equipped as we have been?"

"You will have to teach them as much as you can of the new language, or they will have to wait until they are in a mountain sanctuary. The battle machines will each pull an open wagon in which extra clothing and a mix of weapons can be carried. It seems you have not adopted the use of solid footwear, but moccasins can be taken, along with better quality clothing. A selection of new weapons will be included. You will all have to show the new warriors what is available to wear and how to use those new weapons properly. They may need convincing about joining the journey you are on, but you will not have time to explain everything before you move on.

"Most of the new warriors will not know or understand the danger they are in. If they do not join this fight, it is probable that they won't last another generation. Their future on this planet depends on the result."

No further information was offered by Alpha and no questions were raised. As fast as Alpha first appeared, he was gone again.

Tarn gritted his teeth and muttered to Dosol, who stood beside him, "These visions that speak to us have no manners and raise the people's hopes that they will be successful. Other groups have failed in what we are being sent to do. We will have extra help from the battle machines and protection from the skies, but who knows if that will be enough. I don't have family left to fight for, nor does Neeya. These people and those who join us will have to decide whether to fight or try to hide from the killers. Only time will tell how long they would last in hiding before the killers find them."

Dosol waited until Tarn had finished. "It all depends on us, on how we can raise a fighting spirit in those who have only killed animals to live and provide for their families. I sense there is more to come, things we have never experienced from Alpha's people. Those who created Alpha are still unknown to us. Where did they originally come from? Are they humans who have progressed beyond our understanding? They may have gone, lost in space, or forgotten about anyone still on this planet. They built spaceships to travel for hundreds of Earth years. That was long ago. What happened to them?"

Neeya had been listening to the conversation. "Dosol, you just heard what Alpha said about our shared face tattoos. It seems we may meet others with the same markings, and we have unknown abilities that could appear when we really need them. What do you think it all means?"

"I don't fully understand Alpha," Dosol replied. "I feel there is something in the future but it will all depend on what the killers are planning. Hopefully, it will not mean an all-out fight for our lives to bring out these hidden abilities Alpha spoke about. I can only follow and do what I can."

Neeya finished their discussion, "It feels too much like we are about to be swept over a waterfall, with no understanding of where we will end up. Right now, I think we should all get some sleep, but after we do our final preparations. Tarn, Andoki and Dosol, can you talk to the others to have them get some rest? In the morning, we can divide people up – who comes and who stays, and who heads off to bring our tribe into protection."

Ten minutes later, Neeya was the only one at the table, already going through her choices of who would stay with the children.

※ ※ ※

Far above her, in orbit, yet another message package was directed into deep space. No need now for more readings on the environment or what species were progressing. The message dealt only with the forthcoming campaign to rescue any tribal people who could be found. It would be one final attempt to dislodge the black killers from their base and render them harmless for good.

This time it could be different. Arrangements would have to be made.

Chapter 16

New People

An hour before sunrise, they began to assemble in the meals room for one last meal together. The few elderly adults and young children, as well as several adults who knew they would not be capable of keeping up with the group on a long march, sat in a small group away from the more able adults. Backpacks and weapons to be carried by each warrior were lined up against the walls. Bags of extra clothes, weapons, hard boots and food were piled separately, ready to be loaded onto the machines.

A man and woman had already left with an extra battle machine hours earlier, in the dark. They intended to be well away from the cave entrance before the main group assembled outside. Neeya and Tarn had spoken to them and had watched the pair beside the machine disappear into the darkness. The far horizon was a just-visible dark line on a slightly less dark sky, as the sun started its approach towards daylight.

Neeya had stayed up late to compose her thoughts, and think of the future – her future as well as the tribes and this group that had assembled under her direction. She had never intended to be the leader of a large group, not even in her own tribe. Such a short time in the past, she had led a small band in crisis, whose members were being hunted and killed, before they finally reached the better-protected stronghold of the main tribe. Meeting again with Tarn and their escape through the hidden cave had been the start of the most important purpose of her life.

But now she could not afford to think of the past. This morning it would start. She could feel the adrenaline coursing through her body. The energy it gave would have to be repaid, eventually. She knew her body well, or thought she did. It was hard to stay still. This talk of latent extra abilities worried her, thinking they might spring out on her at the wrong time. Also, the idea of others with the same tattoos – how could that be possible? Dosol had been a big surprise. Why not more than just Dosol? All this had to be put aside for now.

Two warriors had already been assigned to stay with those who could not undertake the journey – or was it a mission? They were not happy with being left behind, but their weapons ability and fitness might be needed as the last defence for the women, children and injured, if it all came to that.

Tarn came up to her to report that the three machines were ready to move out, but they had to be loaded before the door was opened. A line was formed and the pile, which sat in three sections, was passed along, one by one, to the machines and their trailing wagons. The luggage and spare food occupied the centre of each machine, with closed compartments on each side holding hidden items yet to be opened and explained to the others. Neeya remembered the private discussion with Alpha late the previous night. He had told her about the contents of the side compartments. They were marked with small yellow dots, something that no one else would pay attention to. She shuddered at her memory of the information. She hoped that they would never need to open them. It was better to wipe her mind clear of the information. She had too much else to concern her.

❋ ❋ ❋

These machines were different again from the two types she had previously seen. They stood higher off the ground, built for rough travelling. Their six wheels were open-mesh steel, mounted on springs for rough or very soft conditions. The others she had seen had four wheels and were white. These had a mottled green and brown camouflage appearance.

Anyone viewing the machines was taken by the menace they projected – arrogant and dangerous – a challenge to anyone who was stupid enough to take them on. The lead machine had obviously received an initial starting direction, and once all the men and women who followed were ready, it started through the door and down the hillside at a comfortable walking pace. The humans had split up into three groups, each following behind a machine. Neeya and Tarn headed up the column with Andoki and Dosol behind a second machine, and Nabu as the leader of the last group.

Initially, all were tense, expecting an attack, but as the morning moved on towards midday with nothing of concern, they began to relax. They each carried a lightweight water bottle and strips of dried meat to chew on as they moved. Progress was comfortable, with no real effort being asked of them. The landscape undulated, without steep slopes or diversions. When the sun was high overhead, the lead machine stopped under a group of spreading trees to allow for a rest and meal break.

Everyone took food and water from their packs and settled down to rest. Neeya moved to the nearest machine and placed her hand on the now familiar panel, which immediately turned green. This time, the information passed from the machine to her brain in a few minutes. She remained standing for the message, frozen with her hand on the panel.

Tarn, Andoki, Dosol and Nabu, now familiar with her machine messages, had gathered as a group close by to get any information from her conversation. They had received a form of the message through their hearing devices but needed more from Neeya.

She recovered quickly. "We can relax for the rest of the day. No danger has been seen from the air. We will be near the first tribal settlement tomorrow afternoon if all goes well. It appears to have over thirty dwellings, so there should be a significant number of people. Nabu and Dosol, do you sense anything that is important today, or for tomorrow's journey – anything we need to know?"

Nabu answered first. "No, all I sense is that we approach danger but not today or most of tomorrow. I may know more by the morning."

Dosol agreed. "I feel nothing of importance right now. Everything seems settled. The people we hope to contact tomorrow do not seem dangerous."

Andoki added, "I have not had any mind contact since we left. We can only hope that the man I killed was the only one with that ability, but I doubt it."

"The front machine is being sent towards the first settlement by Alpha, from directions given by the aerial drone, but first, it will take us to a suitable campsite for tonight," added Neeya.

They packed up and continued. The hill slope had flattened out and they moved on through well-watered, healthy trees and undergrowth. Rustling in the vegetation at intervals and the obvious animal tracks and paw prints they came across told them there was good hunting in the area if needed. They still had most of the food they had brought from the tunnels so there was no need for hunting yet. The occasional stream allowed them to top up their water bottles.

The day was clear, with a few clouds. They had become used to light rain or the occasional cloud now that more rain-making machines were working. It was so different from the time Neeya and Tarn lived on the other side of the hidden cave, where water and the animal herds had seemingly deserted the land, and the continuously clear sky only ever brought unrelenting heat.

The afternoon passed uneventfully and they camped in a well-protected, hidden gully. Several small fires, giving off minimal smoke, were started and meat was quickly cooking, with root vegetables roasting in the outer coals. After the meal, most of the group settled down in their new sleeping bags. Andoki had already spoken with Neeya and she had agreed to him undertaking a patrol in the dark, beyond the two sentries set near the campsite.

She watched him go, moving silently, like a cat with his light pack and crossbow. He was finally free to travel at night, with no one to worry about. It seemed a long time since he had been able to walk in darkness. Andoki was out of the camp for half the night and returned with the best portions of a deer that he had killed nearby. It had provided more target practice with his new weapon and had died in an instant with a perfectly aimed shot. He returned to his sleeping bag and was awake again when the others started to move.

The fresh meat was wrapped in leaves and packed into a machine. After a light breakfast of groundnuts, dried fruit, and leftovers from the night's meal, they formed up and moved off. All were used to long-distance hunting journeys, with little need for chatting or unplanned noise. Hand signals provided directions and warnings.

With the vegetation changing, the ground became more moist, softer, and better quality. The lead machine already had information on where to go, provided by their 'eyes in the sky.' Animal paths were followed through areas of low growth. Progress slowed as the vegetation became thicker, and vision in all directions reduced. The front machine always found a way forward, with wheels that were almost silent, flexing as they rolled over indentations, the odd fallen branch, and piles of undergrowth. Everyone had become more watchful, searching out gaps in the bushes. Even though they made little noise, it was still enough to alert animals and keep them well away.

The thick bushes changed to more open land with tall trees for better progress. Large animals seemed to live in the area, with the paths they followed becoming wider, showing more large hoof prints and the occasional paw prints of large cat-like predators. Once, a group of wolf paw prints crossed the path from a pack of at least five members. Good grazing attracted prey animals, to be followed by the predators, and humans hunted all animals. No one killed for sport, only to survive, clothe, and feed their families and tribe.

They stopped at midday beside a stream, with shade and views of trees and undergrowth in several directions, apart from one rocky outcrop beside the line they would follow after their rest. The meal was again cold, mostly of leftovers and travel rations. They formed up once more for the afternoon journey, their anticipation growing about meeting another tribe, the reason for this whole effort.

The front machine was less than 100 metres past the rocky outcrop when one word blasted in Neeya's head, with all four hearing devices reacting. "Stop!" Five right hands went up, each with a closed fist. The machines also stopped moving. Everyone in the three groups looked at their leaders – all with puzzled expressions saying, "Why stop?"

All five who had heard the command looked at each other. Neeya looked stunned. She had not been touching a machine and was the only leader without a hearing device. How had she heard the call?

Dosol hurried forward, almost in a panic. "Neeya, there is danger just ahead of us – underground."

"How? I cannot see anything and the track is clear. Did you send the signal to stop?"

"I can't see anything underground, and I didn't send any message."

Tarn called out, "Start throwing rocks down the track. I have an idea about the danger." With that, they started throwing rocks up in the air to have them fall heavily on the track ahead. The rocks kept falling, with no obvious impact until, about twenty metres ahead, a rock hit the ground and disappeared.

"A pit trap! It's what I would have done in the same situation to protect a settlement. This has been built against attackers coming down the trail. I will walk slowly down the path to the trap. Don't follow me until we are sure there are no other traps to the side of where the rocks fell."

The command brought no disagreement. They all stood silently, watching the drama as Tarn took short steps toward the small hole in the track, the only clue to the trap's location. Several times he stopped and looked to one side or the other to check for likely trap sites. Eventually, he stood close to the hole in the path. Nothing else was obvious until he used the end of his spear to start poking the area around the hole. What had seemed to be solid ground fell away and widened until the centre of the track width had collapsed for over three metres. The hole revealed a forest of sharp stakes covering the base, all of them pointing up – sudden death to anyone who fell through! He stepped back and poked around the sides of the pit to find it was solid ground, wide enough for the machines to roll past and the rest of the group to pass in single file.

His relieved return to the others was with much less concern. "A pit trap has been dug out across the main width of the trail. No one would survive after falling through. We were saved by that mental shout that made us stop. Thanks for the warning, Dosol. It shook me up and stopped us fast."

"It was not me, Tarn. I would have fallen through without a warning. I thought it was you or Nabu." They both shook their heads. "We perceived no danger, Neeya. We should have felt the danger but our ability failed us this time."

A sharp whistle made them all look up and then crouch, their weapons at the ready, expecting a sudden attack.

"Everyone, down," shouted Neeya, as she and the others searched the surrounds. Then, a strange warrior showed himself behind them, on their side of the rocky outcrop. They had already started to pass him as he hid in a camouflaged position.

They all hugged the ground until a shout from the stranger called them to relax. His words had a strong and different accent, but they were based on the same basic tribal language they all understood.

"We mean you no harm. The trap is for strangers who try to kill everyone. You can relax. I have called more of our tribe, but don't move to the sides of the path. There is another pit close by."

Neeya looked at Tarn and the others. "Go back and tell all our people to stay where they are and not to move to the side. We shouldn't be here long. This is our first contact with the people we were supposed to meet today."

Soon after, five warriors came out of the bushes just past the pit trap and walked, relaxed and nonchalant, towards their tribesman on the side of the trap. Once past, they immediately crossed to the main path. All were tall and slim, with light brown skin. Their clothes were of woven fabric, with short-legged pants and sleeveless jackets. Like Neeya's people, they wore skin moccasins. All carried spears, with two also having quivers bristling with arrows and unstrung bows.

Neeya took all these things in immediately but stopped when she saw their leader had painted white angular marks across the front of his jacket. The others had no markings.

He showed no hesitation and went straight up to Neeya, followed by his companions.

"We finally meet," he said, in a loud, gravelly voice. "My name is Myka, and I am the war chief of our tribe. You don't know of me, but I and several others of our people knew you and your group would be arriving soon. That is why we had someone on watch, to be sure none of your people fell into our traps. I also know you from your tattoos. I have had time to become adjusted to the idea that someone else would have markings matching anyone from our tribe, someone from far away."

She finally held up a hand in recognition. "That was a long welcome speech, Myka. Do you always greet visitors in the same manner?"

"Only those who come to show us a better future. I am excited. We have very few strangers entering our land, except for the mad killers who we have had to fight off. Many have been lost to their spears, and we have been retreating. This must change or we will be wiped out next time they attack us in force."

"Apart from the questions I want to ask about tattoos, there is something I need to know right now."

"Ask your question," said Myka.

"I expected to hear you speak in a tribal language, after your sentry spoke to us when we first arrived. You speak the language of the people who originally brought our ancestors to this planet, those who live under the mountains. How is that possible?"

"There are a few of us who were taught to speak in that way, two generations ago. It has been retaught again over the years. Two warriors who originally fought the mad killers were the only survivors of a force that was overrun and either killed or captured. Our tribe secretly carried them both away from the fight and cared for them until they recovered. They have since passed on. They carried more modern weapons than we had, then. We learnt some of our real history while they lived with us. We learnt that the original stories of what happens to us when we die were like children's tales – created to give us hope of a new life after death."

Neeya stopped him there and asked, "You said we were known to be coming. Again, how was that possible and how long have you known?"

"We became sure only days ago. I had something like a dream about it. Then several others who have the same ability came to me and told me of the same understanding. We have shared such feelings before, but with less conviction that it would happen. But we can talk about these things later. We need to take you to our settlement now, for safety. We will be better protected there."

All of Neeya's group were relieved that these new people were friendly and offered support. They were guided through a zig-zagging route around other pit traps and hidden defences. The battle wagons were just able to negotiate the route. Obviously, these people knew the black killers well and had fought them before. The effort put into their defences would have been a big drain on their time left for hunting, growing crops, and living normal lives. These people lived in a state of war for survival, constantly aware of the danger from any direction.

Eventually, they reached the settlement, sure that they could never retrace their steps after the complex route around the traps.

❊ ❊ ❊

The site was different to the few villages or settlements anyone in the group had seen before. The houses were half dug into the soil, with short walls adding to the available height inside. Light timber frames of branches supported thatched rooves of woven grass. The central space of the settlement comprised a stockade, a defensive structure of last resort. Closely linked logs with sharpened tops surrounded an area of less than fifty metres across. Two sets of heavy timber gates, on opposite sides of the circle were the only entry or exit points. A solid timber building sat in the centre, to store weapons and food. Large leather bags made from animal stomachs hung around the sides to store water. They were told the stockade was not meant to be a long-term fort. It was to repel a surge of enemies who might mount a surprise attack, if ways were found to get past the defences.

Myka showed the newly arrived band around the settlement and then directed Neeya and the other leaders towards the largest building for a discussion. They all stepped down onto a sunken floor and sat on skin-lined benches to wait for Myka to tell them more about the tribe's background.

Myka thanked them for coming to the settlement. They all stayed silent while he explained the present situation to his people.

"We relocated to this location several weeks ago, making it six times in the last three years, to find better defensive sites for protection from the mad killers. Nearly forty warriors and a small number of elderly people, women and children have been lost to the killers. You have seen what we have done for protection on our approach trails, but they still seem to find a way to attack us. The total number of our group has now been reduced to less than 140, of which there are uninjured men and women warriors, totalling 95.

"As I said before, there are a few of us who have strong indications about the short-term future. We knew your group would arrive about now. We also believe this place is becoming very dangerous and that we need to move once again to survive. Can I ask, what news do you bring? What can you offer us, with your warriors, strange weapons and wagons that carry your baggage and food?"

The discussions took hours, both sides explaining their backgrounds and all that was known about the killers. Myka accepted that the fight had to become offensive against the killers, with those in his group not capable of fighting needing to be taken to safety first. Food and water were provided while the talks continued.

Those of Neeya's group remaining outside were also given food as they relaxed and wandered around the campsite. The three machines stood separate from each other, facing in different directions towards the surrounding tree line. A small disc-shaped plate near the top of the central shaft on each machine slowly turned as if sniffing the air or constantly listening to the surroundings. They attracted a lot of attention from the local people, who had never seen such strangely built and shaped objects before. The interest died away quickly as it was realised the machines were on guard against the killers and no one wanted to be in the way if an attack occurred.

The sun was close to setting behind the highest trees to the west when Myka left the discussions, after agreement was reached that everyone would need to pack up and be ready to move the next morning. Orders were given and it was obvious that moving had become a well-practised activity for the camp. Packing was completed before nightfall. The weather was dry and warm, so their sleeping bags were spread out inside the stockade, to stay out of the way of Myka's preparations.

The machines were repositioned to observe and scan the campsite through the night for maximum protection. They also had their loads adjusted to carry some of Myka's camp items in the morning. One machine was chosen to lead the new group of young, aged, and frail people away to the mountain's safety, while the settlement's warriors joined in their journey west.

Many in both Neeya's and Myka's groups had poor sleep that night. The new day would bring obstacles, dangers, and possible violence – not easy things to put aside and still sleep. But they had found their first new group to either join their fight or be given sanctuary. Things had started well.

❇︎ ❇︎ ❇︎

Before the first of the sun's morning rays were seen in the sky, Neeya was shocked awake by a voice in her head yelling, "You will be attacked. Get to a machine for instructions."

Tarn, Andoki, Nabu and Dosol received the message after she was already up and running to the nearest machine. Her hand went automatically to the coloured panel, and she stood while information was provided. It was becoming easier to receive the messages while remaining on guard.

Each of the leaders, apart from Neeya, had been given tiny devices back in the tunnels, that fitted into their ears for communication with Alpha, if needed, as it was now.

The message was short and to the point. The aerial guard, still able to observe at night, had spotted a gathering of killers working its way along the meandering 'safe' path they had originally followed to the campsite. The attackers followed a single warrior who appeared to sense the correct route.

Over thirty killers were less than an hour away. Only two choices were obvious – to fight or run.

Neeya disengaged her hand from the machine and turned to the waiting group. The four of her band, with the small hearing machines in their ears, already understood what she had just absorbed.

She looked at Tarn, who stood ready to follow her, waiting for directions.

"We will soon be under attack. Somehow, the black killers have found a way to track us along the path to this camp. Myka, you need to get all your people into the stockade. Have them bring their weapons, food and as much of their possessions as they can carry. Light fires around the walls to give as much light as possible to fight with. It will be short and sharp. This time we have more experienced fighters. You need to make your preparations now."

Myka didn't even think of disputing Neeya's directions. He was about to offer suggestions but she had naturally assumed command, and he accepted it. He ran off with his support leaders, while she spoke to Andoki.

"You are needed now, Andoki, for your night vision and your use of the bow. We need time to get organised for a defence. Find them, and kill those that you can, particularly the person who leads them along the path. If he dies, then maybe they will be stopped from finding the rest of the trail. Grab your weapons and go. I do not know if anyone can help you, though."

Andoki gave a grim laugh. "I don't need help. If Vail is not with me, I prefer to be on my own."

With that, he turned and disappeared into the night. Neeya continued: "Tarn, you are the war leader of our tribe, and have more experience at fighting than any of us. I won't try to direct you with this. Take over the arrangements to defend us. It is about an hour before first light. Andoki will hopefully kill some of them and slow the others down. It should give us a bit more time."

Tarn ran off to arrange the defence.

Nabu spoke next. "Dosol and I both feel that the future, in the next few days, will bring us danger but not disaster. Once this battle is over, we must be ready to move. The tents and most of the cooking gear should be left here. We can travel faster without it. The food will be needed, sleeping robes and all the weapons. We will need to travel fast and light. The closest mountain sanctuary is at least two full days away, if we don't run into other killer bands and if the very young and old can keep up."

"I agree, Nabu, but this is what we expected. We will probably need to fight other battles while trying to stay alive ourselves. We have to expect to lose some of our people, so we need to recruit as many fighters as possible for what may be a final battle against a large number of killers. One worry I have is about the person that these killers follow, at night, leading them around all the traps that we saw. If this is the start of others with special skills being used against us, we will be in trouble, regardless of our numbers. Do what you can to lead the people from your tribe against these killers. Our main task is to rescue and protect all we can and remove anyone who tries to stop us. Do what you must, Nabu, to strengthen your people, but don't take unnecessary risks. We need you alive."

With that, like the rest, he was gone into the remaining darkness, while Neeya turned to join the others.

Chapter 17

New Abilities

Andoki moved through the dark trees at a speed only Vail could have matched. His clash with a black killer who could touch other minds from a great distance had left him with questions and worries. It did not impact on what he had to do now, though. He had a fair idea where the killers were moving. With the lightest of touches, their minds provided a coloured area in the night slowly moving along the trail he and the others had recently travelled. They were now close, less than half an hour from camp. If the group lost their leader, they would have to stop to assess what was happening, leaving him with more isolated and easy targets.

He had practised this and other scenarios many times back at the mountain. He carried forty bolts for the crossbow and could reload at a speed that had two shots in the air flying towards a target while he loaded a third.

Less than fifty metres away from the enemy group, still moving silently, he chose a position behind a fallen tree and aimed. The first two were killing shots while the third man was disabled and let out a yell. That stopped all movement, as expected, and he had two bolts in the air aimed at the leading warrior to his right a second later.

Both found the target, who he disposed of before taking another step. Four warriors taken out left the remaining group disorganised. They dived for cover in various directions, in total darkness.

Andoki slowly moved to his right and dropped two more targets at the rear of the group.

One more hit, close to the centre of the now desperate enemies, was the last before he felt rather than saw a movement coming straight at him from the extreme right. A voice in his mind yelled, "Drop!" and he was on the ground as the voice disappeared. An arrow thumped into the log he was hiding behind. He fired two bolts at the 'feeling' location of movement and it stopped and dropped in a tumbling sprawl.

Then Andoki was moving again, silently but at speed to his left, rather than returning the way he had come. Better to go back to camp via another direction than lead anyone to the settlement.

He slowed down, taking care to ensure no sound was made and no one followed. It took longer to appear back in camp but he was sure he travelled alone. Neeya was startled when he appeared from nowhere, close to the front gateway of the stockade.

"No time to talk, Neeya. Get everyone inside. I killed seven, maybe eight. One of them was the smell hound following our scent. There was another, who I could feel but not see in the dark. I don't know whether it was animal, human, or a mixture, but it should also be dead. I will go back to find out more, once we get through this fight."

Ten minutes later, they were as prepared as the short available time allowed them. All the machines were armed and ready. Some of the spare weapons were given to those of Myka's group who thought they could handle them.

The sun's rays had started lightening the eastern sky when they first saw movement on the far edge of the clearing. The movement turned into a rush. No planning by the killers to seek out weaknesses or try to surround the stockade. No attention paid to the dwellings through which they ran. Their total focus was to kill every living soul in the stockade, which required no thinking. They paid the price for their mindlessness. The machines fired at a range beyond that of arrows or spears. Two shots each from three machines left six dead. Three more dropped before they were in range of slings, bows, or spears.

All the shots fired by the machines were as accurate as any that Andoki could have managed. They left the short barrels of each machine with a soft 'clump,' at a speed beyond that of any arrow or thrown dart.

Very quickly, the original number of over thirty had been reduced to less than fifteen, with those survivors falling before any could reach the stockade walls. The machines, Andoki on his own and extreme-range arrows, easily dispatched the remaining warriors of the killing group.

Those in the stockade stood up from behind the barricade walls or stepped away from behind timber supports. No one was hurt and everyone was stunned at what they had witnessed. Tough hand-to-hand fighting and the loss of lives had been expected. This was almost a training exercise, but it still shocked most of them to see, close up, the bodies of so many dead attackers.

Tarn frowned at Neeya after they had both returned to the reality of no further violence, and the adrenaline had ebbed away. They were now breathing normally again.

"That was too easy. Surely, they didn't expect to kill us all with that effort. Four times that number might have succeeded, but not that group."

"Was it a test to see how we handled an attack?" she replied. "If that was their plan, how would they know if their attack worked and understood what we would do to defend the camp? Andoki, can you use your ability to see if you can pick up any mind questing – someone who could read or understand what we were thinking from a distance?"

Andoki signalled by hand that he was already questing with his mind, throwing out an invisible wave in all directions. It didn't take long to get a result. It surprised him that not one but two individuals, one on each side of the camp, were mind-scanning and communicating with each other.

As soon as Andoki's mind touched theirs, they stopped and immediately started moving away. Andoki was off like an arrow from a bow, running in the early morning light towards the nearest of the two enemies. It was a close thing, over fallen trees and through dense vegetation, but Andoki was more adept at such pursuits, with his and Vail's past hunting of animals at night. Using his mind-seeking ability, he headed around the running enemy and came at him from the front to the complete surprise of the killer who had no time to react before he was hit on the forehead with the stock of Andoki's cross-bow, to collapse in a heap, unconscious.

It took some time to drag the black killer's inert body back to the camp. The man was stocky and slippery in a mixture of ash and animal fat. He was also not as malnourished as the other killers Andoki had seen. He had been fed well, maybe because of a higher status with his mind-reading ability.

They saw Andoki coming towards the camp, and a couple of warriors ran to help him with the body. Neeya, Tarn, and the others, at first surprised at Andoki's success, gathered around, vitally interested in this new type of enemy.

Before their captive regained consciousness, she told Myka that, with the unsuccessful attack, the campsite location was known to the killers and therefore they would have to move as soon as possible.

Myka answered. "I had the same idea. Somehow, they were able to work out how to get around our traps, even though the path around them was well hidden. The decision has been made for us. I agree with what you proposed last night. Most of my warriors will join yours to keep finding and protecting other groups of our people surviving from the killers' attacks. All the elderly, children and untrained women will go with some of the warriors and one of the machines to the mountain sanctuary you told us about."

"Thanks, Myka. We now need to move fast, before they regroup or put what they have learnt into action against us. While you ready your people to move, I will try to learn what I can from the one Andoki captured. Can you also send a couple of warriors to pick up any useful weapons and arrows from the dead killers? Everything we can use against them needs to be gathered."

Myka headed off to organise the packing up of the camp. They would travel light, but take all they could for protection.

❋ ❋ ❋

The captured killer was slowly recovering when Neeya returned. Tarn said he had not spoken but should be able to answer questions. She asked Andoki to watch the man closely, and see if he could read anything from his mind as the questions were being asked.

No time was wasted to start the interrogation. "You have no chance of escape. The only way you may live is if you answer our questions. Do you understand?"

The man vaguely nodded, barely glancing at her face.

"What is your name?

A one-word answer came back. "Prol."

"Prol, what were you ordered to do near our camp?"

Nothing came back, as the captive looked steadily at the ground.

"I will ask you again, what were you told to do at our camp? This time if you don't answer, you will lose a finger. If this keeps going, there will be other parts removed from your body, then your life. Try again."

Prol sighed, but continued to study the ground. "To observe, to find out all that I could."

"Did you use your mind ability to look into the minds of our people?"

Again, there was no immediate answer, so Tarn pulled the steel hatchet from his belt and displayed it for Prol to see that he was close to losing a finger.

"Yes, I have some ability to read minds, like that one of your people." He indicated Andoki.

"And what did you learn from anyone here?"

"There were too many minds close together. It was a babel of thoughts, hard to understand. I learnt that you intend to head west towards our home and that some others will head towards the mountains."

Neeya and Tarn exchanged worried glances. So, the killers might already know their plans.

"There was another one like you. You communicated with him before you started to run away. What did you tell him or hear from him?"

Again, Tarn moved the hatchet around in his hand, as if he was ready to remove a part of Prol's hand as an inducement to keep talking.

"We agreed to run in opposite directions, so one of us could take information back to our leaders."

"Who are your leaders, the ones who sent you and your companions here? All the others are dead. Maybe you think they are with your dark Goddess?"

He gave a snort of derision. "Those who died were only animals, to be used as needed, then thrown away. Their minds are scrambled from the leaves they chew. Many more like them stand ready."

"And you – you don't use the leaves. You are well fed. You chose to answer our questions to preserve your life. Why are you so different to those 'animals' you speak of?"

"My mind ability gives me great value. There are a few of us who now have abilities beyond that of normal men, so we are appreciated, well fed, and given access to the captive women, to reward our service."

Prol's bragging words sickened those listening to the interrogation.

Neeya thought he was too arrogant for his own good. He had not realised yet that every word he spoke dug him a deeper grave.

"These leaders you communicate with – what is their function in your tribe? Is there a high chief to control and direct all of you?"

"There is no high chief. That is for lesser people. We follow Kali, who lives over many, many generations, her spirit moving from one failing body to a new existence. She commands and we follow. Those of greater ability are rewarded with a better existence on this earth. When this body finally fails, I will go to the spirit world, to be with her forever. Our existence is aimed at removing those who oppose her will, and send them to attend us in the spirit world, so all will join her for eternity."

He must have finally understood more than they gave him credit for, and he lunged at Tarn, and grabbed for the steel hatchet. Tarn reacted in a split second without thought, and swung the sharp blade to the back of Prol's neck.

Prol's head dropped to one side, half cut through, spraying his life's blood on the dusty ground. It was all over in a second. Few had seen Tarn move that fast and the shock took time to settle. Tarn said, "I reacted instinctively. I had not intended to kill him, yet, but he forced me to act."

"Don't concern yourself, Tarn. I think he knew what was coming. In a way, he killed himself by attacking you. There was not a lot left that we could learn from him.

"Andoki, were you able to get anything of use from his mind?"

"Very little. He had a greater ability than mine, and for most of the time, he was able to guard his mind. Towards the end though, with his arrogance, he let out satisfaction that we don't know what is coming. There is a greater threat coming at us, not just a few like him. That was about all I could get when you were speaking to him. He also knew that he would die, so he moved at Tarn to stop any further information being given up. He was acting to try to save his own life."

"All right, everyone, we now know a lot more than we did before Andoki captured him. It changes nothing. We are better equipped and trained than those who went before us. The killers already know some of that. Only we can decide our way forward and not be driven like we are animals for the slaughter. We must try to guard our thoughts and keep our plans as closely held as possible. We all need to be ready to leave here soon, so make your preparations now.

"One further thing to think about. From the first word he spoke, it was in the new language that we were taught in the mountain tunnels. I can only guess that he might have learnt the language from warriors they captured from a previous fight. Think about it and how that might change our plans."

Andoki stood up. "My pack is ready but I need to go back to where I shot at them on the path. I want to find the bodies and check if any of them are different. Two of them I killed acted strangely. I will also gather any of my arrows that are not broken."

Neeya nodded. "Myka is sending two of his warriors to collapse the pit traps and make all the other defences harmless.

Find him and they can travel with you to that spot, then destroy the traps. Catch us up when you return if we have already left. You know our direction. This mob will leave a trail that a blind man could follow."

Andoki nodded, turned on his heel and was gone.

Less than an hour later they were moving off. It had taken more time than anyone wanted, but it was needed to weed out the items that couldn't be carried on people's backs or on the machines and wagons. Children had to be provided for and all the remaining food was divided among those who could carry it. One of Neeya's warriors and three of Myka's men had been chosen to protect the group going to the mountain sanctuary. She spoke with the lead warrior about what was hidden in the machine going with the group, and how to use some of it, if absolutely needed as a last resort. The warrior's eyes, and Tarn's, widened with surprise about what they were hearing. Most of the hidden packages in the machine's compartments were then moved to another machine, to travel with the main group heading west.

Myka and Tarn arranged the way both groups would travel, for the best protection. The smaller, slow-moving group was then waved off, with the machine leading. The parting of children and the elderly from the able men and women warriors was full of anguish and tears, as families were broken up, not knowing if they would see each other again.

※ ※ ※

The main group started moving to the west, forward scouts out wide and in front, with several following up from the rear. The machines were spaced out but near the centre. Their field of fire had to be kept clear if there was an attack on the trail.

Through their 'eyes in the sky' Neeya received a brief download of information via the machine that the next human settlement was over a day's walk away, with the direction being given. The lead machine was now heading towards the site.

They expected Andoki to catch up before then and were relieved when the three men finally appeared. They looked like they had run all the way and one of the warriors carried an obvious wound on his upper leg wrapped with makeshift bandages over bloodstained pants, and leant heavily on his spear for support. The wound didn't look serious and appeared not to have slowed them down.

Neeya and Tarn both took it in immediately. Their trip had run into trouble.

The two warriors from Myka's group moved off – one to get better treatment for his leg and the other to report.

"I'm relieved to see you, Andoki. You have not had a simple trip." He carried a heavier-than-normal backpack, along with his bow and quiver. Neeya grimly said, "It also looks like you have brought us a present."

He flicked her a glance of concern, then swung the pack from his shoulders to upend it. Two human heads rolled on the ground in front of her, or almost human heads. Everyone watching stood up in amazement, if they were not already standing, and stared at the grizzly sight.

Both objects had been quickly hacked off at the neck. The first was dominated by more of a pig's snout than a nose. The eyes were small and looked less capable of sight. The wide mouth was filled with sharp, pointed teeth, like those of a wolf. The ears were also malformed, much larger, pointing forward, and shaped like a fan on each side of the head.

Andoki explained what they all stared at. "That one belonged to the part-man they used to search for us. He walked on four legs, not two. His arms were extended in length to match his legs. His capacity to hear and smell us would have been much better than normal men, but with those eyes he wouldn't be able to see well."

Those watching turned to look at the second grotesque object lying to one side of the first. It was strangely hard to focus on. Even though dead, the skin colour was mottled, as if still trying to change colour to match the dirt and leaves it lay on. The features were abnormally small, except for the eyes – large, nocturnal, predator's eyes – designed for night stalking. They were open in death, unfocused, but still unnerving to look at. They seemed to follow those who looked at them.

Again, Andoki explained, "This one took two arrows to kill last night. It was very hard to follow, even though I can normally see anything else in the dark. I could only just pick him out where my mind told me he would be, like a ripple on the water's surface when a fish swims just below. That one almost got to me.

"I think they are being bred like this to provide better abilities to hunt and kill. They are not all simple drug addicts with minds filled with a need to kill and chew the leaves they use. We can only hope there are just a few of them and that their special senses are rarely successful."

The others listened intently to Andoki's findings. It shook them all. This was becoming wilder by the day. Their confidence, already not high, took a further battering with Andoki's display.

Neeya voiced her appreciation, "This is a lot to think about, Andoki. Thanks to you, we are now warned. We will need all our resources to fight these devils, but at least we know so much more than we did a few days ago. One of you was injured. When were you attacked?"

Andoki answered, looking embarrassed, "We were lazy, too relaxed in what we thought was a safe situation. We had inspected the bodies of these two I had killed last night and removed their heads. Then we went to most of the pit traps and other defences. They are now all safe. But as we turned to join you, I caught a fleeting connection to another mind, moving away from us. We gave chase and were closing in on him when another, well-hidden killer fired an arrow at us. I yelled out but we were too slow and one of us was wounded, not seriously, and it will heal, but it shows they are now using tactics against us.

"They know of my mind ability and led us into an ambush to try to kill me. We just got out of it by killing that man and a companion. The one who had the mind-reading ability escaped while we fought the other two.

"Neeya, at that touch of minds, I read that they know of the other group heading towards the mountains. They will try to catch or kill them, but with only four warriors and one machine to provide protection, they will be in trouble.

"What they need is more protection from the mountain where they are heading, not us, because they will be too far away," said Neeya. "I was told how to speak to Alpha through the machine, if it was vitally important, and this time it is."

She ran to the lead machine. From a distance, the others watched as she stood with both hands on the green panel. It appeared that nothing was happening, but they knew that Neeya did wonders communicating through the machine, so they could only wait.

It took longer than expected, but she finally came back to them. "My message asking for help from the mountain has been sent. It had to first go to a flying machine to get enough height to be able to be sent to Alpha. We cannot do anything else for them but wait. If there is an ambush, then it could come at any time, today or tomorrow. At least a gathering of killers waiting for them should be seen from the air. We need to get moving again, if you are rested enough, Andoki."

"I haven't travelled far. I can drink and eat while we are moving. I need to be on guard for any killer's mind that tries to get information from us. This is becoming ever more difficult."

Neeya added, "We cannot be of any use to the other group now. Several of the women and old men carry weapons and should be able to use them. That would improve their chances, so long as there is no ambush. We started late and this break in our travel has slowed us down. The killers will have more time to organise against us if we continue to move slowly."

Within five minutes the expanded group, with both forces now merged, moved off, with the scouts fanning out.

The day was hot, with the usual wisp of thin clouds in the sky. The game trail, made wider by the machine wheel tracks, was easier to follow through healthy bush, with tall trees giving some protection for part of the way. They started to move up a gentle slope to the west, with scattered rocky outcrops. Andoki climbed to the high points to get a better view, but saw nothing unusual. The aerial flying eyes sent no alarms, so they were able to pick up the pace.

Only one free-flowing stream was crossed, which provided a much-needed chance to fill water bottles. There was no game, which was not surprising given the noise and movement of the small army. The ration packs were still mostly unused and the machines carried a sizeable stack of food from Myka's camp.

At times, they saw the high-flying eagle-shaped silhouette continually circling while its glass lens eyes looked for any trace of the killers. It gave them confidence that they had advanced weapons on their side, even though most were beyond their understanding. Myka's people battled, most of all, to understand the 'big picture' and where they fit into what was becoming a war. Those who had learnt so much in the tunnels tried to teach what they could. From victims so recently, now they were taking the fight to the killers.

As the sun dipped lower towards the horizon, they came to a halt at the top of the long slope they had been climbing for most of the day. Looking to the west, the view was blocked by a landscape broken-up by boulder stacks and stone ridges, with a green infill of low trees. The plateau they had reached gave great views to the east and north towards the mountains. Views to the west might be possible the next day. While they set up camp in a large, clear area, Neeya agreed with Andoki that he should climb the highest viewpoint to scan the surrounding countryside before the last light of the day disappeared.

Andoki peered from the top of the highest rock stack he could find, back the way they had come and towards the flat top mountain the other group were heading for. He had better eyes than most but he did not expect to see over the distance he thought the group may have travelled. Seeing nothing of interest, he turned and looked to the west, catching a silvery glimpse of the sun just above a shining strip of water – a lot of water, more than he could describe. He stared until the light faded.

In the act of beginning to climb down, facing to the east, he stopped as a violent flash of light speared up from a patch of green, halfway towards the flat-topped mountain. It was followed by an angry, violent red, orange, and yellow ball rolling into the sky, then the sharp crack of sound arrived like a rock falling off a cliff to shatter far below. The sound reverberated around him. It suddenly stopped, as the ball of angry light and flame disappeared, leaving dispersing smoke, then the fall of soil and rocks.

He couldn't move or react. He tried to speak but no sound came. His heart raced, the sound of it thumping in his ears. This blast was from the gods, then he remembered: there were no gods. But what could have done this?

Clear thought seeped back into his mind. It could only be where the group heading to the sanctuary were. The killers did not have the ability to do this, so it must have been Alpha's people. Then he remembered Neeya using the machine to talk to Alpha.

Before he knew it, he was down from the rock stack, running back to their temporary camp. He burst in on Neeya, Tarn, Myka and Nabu sitting in a circle, and dropped down in front of them, stammering to explain what he had just witnessed.

❈ ❈ ❈

Six-year-old Tooma had battled to keep up with the others, but her mother kept hold of a hand as she told her daughter that they would soon be at a place they could stop for the night. The journey had been hard, following the strange machine while the warriors moved amongst them, urging them on towards safety but trying to be kind and calm with the children. The mothers and older people moved as best they could, but it was rough and they had to take care.

Suddenly, the group stopped, because the machine they followed stopped. They heard a crashing coming closer as they listened, bursting through the undergrowth at speed. A second machine suddenly materialised, moving quickly from the direction of the mountain, the place they were hurrying to! It stopped as it came beside their leading machine. Lights on both machines blinked green, orange, and red repeatedly, and Tooma thought they must be talking – machines talking? Tooma found that exciting, but the sounds and lights flashing somehow made her feel sad, while the adults were both fearful and wondering about these strange things they knew nothing of a few days ago, before the killers had attacked.

The machines both started moving again, in opposite directions – the newly arrived machine in the direction they had come from and the one they followed continuing towards the safety of the mountains.

As Tooma's turn came to pass the new machine, she saw it was different to the one they were following – almost bare of things stacked on top – nothing sticking up or poking out. It did not look dangerous or armed for a fight. It almost looked lonely, as it departed with only a flat container attached to the top – made of grey metal. The container itself looked dangerous, as if it kept a grave secret within its shell. Tooma felt as if she knew this new machine was fearful about what it was going towards.

Their machine sped up and Tooma's group battled to keep going. The warriors did what they could to help them along. A few hundred metres past where the two machines 'spoke,' they turned off the beaten path and moved behind a rock ridge, maybe fifty metres away, and stopped. The others caught up and dropped to the ground around the machine, sheltered by the rock barrier to their backs and glad of the break. All Tooma heard was the exhausted panting and coughing of everyone in the group. Why was there such a rush?

A red light mounted on the top of their machine came on, blinking slowly but starting to speed up. They almost held their breath as the light increased its flashing. Something was going to happen! All they could do was watch the light and wait.

The light sped up, then stopped. Less than a breath later, their ears were hurt by the sudden clap of a thunderous noise and a huge ball of fire rose above them, very close by. The noise rolled past, shocking their ears like they had been hit, then sand, pebbles and small broken rocks fell on them and all around. The rock ridge they sat behind saved them from the monumental explosion. A sharp smell came over them, carried by the last of the smoke and dust. Then everything was quiet, apart from their coughing and the children crying. Their hearing, thankfully, started to return. The warrior in charge of the others motioned them to stay where they were, while he went back to investigate.

Tooma, who was sheltered by her mother's body, peered out as he moved slowly and cautiously back down the path, spear held ready. He moved a short distance, to find a large hole, maybe ten metres across. The trees, bushes and plants around the smoking hole were smashed flat, with those further away still standing looking shredded and leafless. Several small fires were burning but appeared to have nothing left in the area to spread to.

That was shocking enough, but then he found body parts, everywhere. There was nothing whole, only pieces. They covered the ground – except in the blasted hole and maybe ten metres outside it. They hung on trees like clothes drying in the sun and lying in the grass. There must have been a lot of killers following them, for so many pieces. There were also small metal sections of the machine that had passed them scattered around. It had been sacrificed to remove the killers coming after them.

He could not take anymore and turned to slowly go back to his group, stopping once to throw up. Dead bodies were one thing but this was on such an instantaneous and violent scale that it was impossible to understand. Two men might fight each other with one winning, but a machine rolling down to a large group of warriors who were instantly ripped apart? Too many new things in only a few days!

His story was received in silence. They then all stood up and wearily followed the machine, now at a slower pace, hopefully to safety without any more slaughter.

❊ ❊ ❊

From her machine, through the aerial connection, Neeya communicated with Alpha to get an understanding of what had just happened. The group fleeing to safety was still unharmed, with the effectiveness of the protection given by Alpha never having been provided before. The results were recorded and would be analysed. Neeya felt that she would have to think more carefully in future before asking for help. This time Alpha had provided in abundance what she had asked for!

With many of the killers having been removed, it was not surprising that no contact was made by anyone in the camp or the guards protecting the outer perimeter during that night. Andoki did not go roaming in the dark. He was well overdue for sleep.

Chapter 18

Water People

The new day started like any other: a noisy awakening as people climbed out of their sleeping bags and robes, to either go to relieve themselves, build up fires to cook breakfast or begin to pack ready for yet another day on the trail.

Neeya was already up. She had been awake for hours, unable to sleep because of what had happened to the group seeking sanctuary in the mountains. The help Alpha had given had been totally successful – so much so that everyone was still in shock. The violent blast had wiped out many – twenty, thirty, fifty – even more killers, but they were still human beings – maybe beyond saving, but still with a chance.

Is this what was now happening – with no remorse or feelings of lost lives to be considered?

Either the killers were to be wiped out or, in time, Neeya and people like her would disappear, with their story never to be known or told. She thought of the countless stories passed down by the elders or those whose memories of the past could make storytelling have you feeling part of the tale, when she was growing up.

Each tale had a purpose, an instruction, to be applied to their future lives. The saga of their journey might never be told, with the black killers being triumphant, or, in 100 years, would their names be wrapped in an exciting story of victory? That tale might keep children awake at night, remembering the actions of past heroes.

She put her thoughts away behind another wall in her mind, maybe to be revisited later if she survived. There were already too many walls.

But the task of survival continued, and she stood up, looking once again to the east and the mountains to the north. The sun was rising and, finding nothing she could focus on in the almost endless vista of rock stacks and green, she turned to face where they would be heading that day. A climb of a few hundred metres gave her the same hint of a huge area of water that Andoki had glimpsed. She guessed that this was the lake Alpha had told them about, larger than they could ever comprehend, with people living by its shores.

That was for later. She turned and walked back down the slope to the camp, for the same breakfast of leftovers and sodden grain mixture.

An hour later found the group, now a small army, well into the day's journey. There seemed to be no name applicable to explain this mixed gathering of people. They were desperate for peace but armed and expecting war, heading towards a final confrontation with killers whose lives were dedicated to wiping them out.

The journey had settled into a routine, with forward scouts and rear guards, the two remaining machines travelling one close to the front and one in the centre.

Neeya's warriors from the mountain had mixed with Myka's group, and all the spare weapons and clothes had been handed out. She and Tarn walked near the first machine while the others, including Andoki, Dosol, Nabu and Myka moved through the group, trying to keep spirits up and answer the many questions. Myka's people needed to improve their knowledge of what had been learnt at Alpha's Mountain.

Tribal stories explaining the making of the world, the nature of the heavens and their history were being replaced with new knowledge. They now knew of the endless universe, their ancestors' journey from planet Earth many hundreds of years ago and had a better understanding of the killers' one driving force.

That was the hardest to understand. All the peaceful people they knew of had similar urges to give their children, family and tribe a better future. How could any large group have a driving urge to destroy all of that? The name of their supposed goddess, 'Kali,' only meant something to the killers. But for those who trusted Neeya and Myka, one day of hope was followed by another. For now, that much was understood and had to be enough.

By midday, no obstructions had slowed them down and the view of the huge water area had grown ahead. They rested on a slight rise, under short but shady trees with views in most directions. The forward and rear protective guards and scouts were replaced and all settled down for food and a rest.

Nabu and Dosol came to express their feelings about the remainder of the journey to the lake. Nabu spoke first.

"We see no danger this afternoon, but forces are building against further travel. There is another settlement at the water's edge. The journey after we arrive at the water is shrouded and not easily understood. It mixes danger and safety together – danger in order to achieve safety."

Dosol only nodded his agreement.

Neeya thanked them and went to the nearby machine, hoping to get more accurate information on what could be seen from the air and anything Alpha could add. The view from the circling eagle shape added little to their understanding, and Alpha was also devoid of suggestions or information.

The vegetation they moved through was reducing as they approached the water, or 'lake', as Alpha had called it. Trees were progressively replaced with ragged, tall bushes, then low-level scrub. The area within a kilometre of the lake looked blasted, as if regular storms stripped the vegetation and pushed small sand dunes inland, or a huge explosion in the area had occurred long ago. The land had been undulating for some time, each region getting lower, until one small sandhill remained to be crossed. Neeya, Tarn and Myka moved up so that they walked with the forward scouts and the lead machine towards the ridge.

They were suddenly aware of a single man leaning on a spear standing on the ridge. He wore only a wrap around his waist to his knees, and was short and stocky, with black curly hair and multiple tattoos over his brown body. It looked like tattoos swarmed over all his skin's surface, complex and detailed. One look told her that this was not one of the few people who carried her facial tattoos. The man stood still as they came closer and showed no signs of even noting their existence.

They were close to him when he broke into a broad smile, let out a peculiar yell and held his spearhead up in a universal sign of welcome. The yell must have been a signal because twenty or more warriors emerged from hidden places on the ridge. They were like him, dressed identically, all carrying spears, and covered in tattoos.

The first man said, in a difficult-to-understand accent, "You have made good time. We expected you a little later in the day. My name is Pohu, and I will show you to our campsite, where you can rest and refresh yourselves. We simply call ourselves "The People", and our lives revolve around living with the water, on our boats. We have not had any contact with others for a long time, apart from today. You are the first people we have met in several generations who are not of our tribe."

The others stayed quiet, actively listening and trying to take in everything Pohu said. Again, the sight of so much water and hearing of people who lived their lives on the water was more knowledge to absorb, with difficulty. Like the others, Neeya and Tarn stayed quiet while Pohu delivered his speech.

Neeya replied. "Thank you, Pohu, for your welcome. My name is Neeya. We have much to discuss. Please lead the way."

They walked on with him, the rest following. The two machines received most of the attention, never having been seen before by these water dwellers. The new people seemed strong and hardy, with deep brown skin from a life in the sun and on the water. All had many tattoos, some sharing lines and patterns while others carried completely different designs.

A low point in the last dune brought them onto the beach, escorted on each side by a group of guards from "The People," to spread out to take in their first views of the camp. The main surprise was that the camp was composed of several lines of ramshackle, rough buildings, large enough for one family each. They were obviously not built to last. Gaps in the lines were filled with logs, branches and materials that could be used to assemble additional temporary shelters if needed.

Another surprise, apart from the immensity of the lake, was the large timber boats floated about 100 metres from the shore. They were solidly made of dark timber, with outriggers on each side, ladders hanging into the water, and thatched huts in the centre of each boat. No sails. But by shading her eyes from the sun low on the horizon, Neeya thought she could see lines covering every surface of each boat, like tattoos on human skin. There were at least forty boats, all very similar in shape. Small boats were dragged up on the sandy shore, capable of carrying up to six adults. *These people live on the water! This is only a temporary shore base, probably re-established at various locations as the need arises.*

Although all of what they could see was new to them, they could work out what it was all for. No great technology was needed to make lives here possible.

Pohu appeared to be in charge, at least of those people they could see. He asked Neeya to choose four others to go with him in a small boat out to one of the larger vessels, where they could discuss their mission with the leaders of The People and what help was to be requested.

None of the new arrivals had ever been on a boat floating on a large area of water before. The closest to the experience were those who had fished from hollowed-out logs or branches tied together as rafts. Few were happy about the idea but they could not show their reluctance in front of their fellow warriors.

Therefore, Neeya, Tarn, Nabu, Myka and Andoki joined Pohu on a small boat that easily moved them to the side of what appeared to be the largest of the big timber boats floating offshore. Pohu had easily propelled the small boat with a long timber oar. The large boats seemed to be held in place by thick ropes that ran into the water from both ends of the vessel.

After a short time of trepidation while climbing up a rope ladder onto the deck of the slowly rocking boat, they were all standing on the dark timber deck, trying to keep their balance.

Pohu grinned as he watched them trying to adjust. "You will find walking on the deck will become easier with experience. All our people have lived their lives on boats, spending more time here than on land. The lake gives us everything we need to exist. We must be careful when approaching land, because of the mad killers, who have hunted us like animals, but so far, they have not been able to move on the water."

Neeya said, "We have recently found that they have learnt how to change the bodies of men to use against us in future. It may be that they might find a way to have warriors living in the water."

"That would be a bad day for us all, if they could do that," Pohu said. "The deep water gives us our main protection from them, along with our weapons. In the past, we have lost people after being ambushed on land. More and more, we live away from the land. But we can talk about it later. Our three guardians live on this boat. They are entrusted with guarding our most precious things, as well as providing wisdom and guidance with the most serious decisions affecting our future. I am taking you to them.

"You should choose one or two speakers to explain how you arrived here, and why you seek our help. We have ways of knowing part of your past and a possible future for us all."

With that, Pohu walked to a framed and thatched door on the side of a hut on the boat deck and opened it to show them through.

The large, single room was not well lit, but they could pick out three grey-haired elderly men in grey robes sitting at the back of the room, facing them, and watching as they entered. The three old men, with wrinkled and tattooed skin, seemed older than anyone she had ever seen.

Low timber stools were available for them to be seated, with a view through an open window of the collection of boats floating nearby. Lighting came from a brightly burning lamp sitting in the centre of a sand-filled tray, probably to control the threat of fire.

Pohu gestured for them to be seated, bowed to the elderly men, then sat to one side, to be able to see both the exalted seniors and the new visitors. The central elderly figure leaned forward, to speak.

"Welcome to our settlement, everyone, temporary as it is. My name would translate into your language as 'First Guardian', with my brothers here named Second and Third Guardian. You have come from the mountains and have learnt the language of those who live there. It will suit us all if we continue to use that language."

He hand-gestured to each side, "Our stories have told us to be ready for a great change when you came with a force of warriors intending to remove the threat of the mad killers on this planet. We have waited here for several days, not knowing exactly when you would arrive. Normally we would be well away from the shore, far from the danger on the land."

First Guardian stopped speaking and motioned to Pohu, who introduced each of the visitors, demonstrating a good memory of their names and the roles they filled. He then asked Neeya to speak on behalf of her group.

"Thank you for your greetings. You have a stronger knowledge of our coming and the purpose of our arrival than we have of your tribe's existence and way of life. We sit on a boat larger than we could imagine on a lake far beyond the size of anything we have seen or could dream of. Could I first ask how you have known of our arrival? Your words indicate that you have more than the level of foretelling that a few in our group possess."

First Guardian spoke again. "We are called to be Guardians, because our people place great importance in guarding our recorded history, our legends and all the things or memories of the old days, before our ancestors arrived on this planet. We are only chosen when our most productive years have passed and our minds and spirits have been judged as having great virtue, to be trusted to fulfil the roles required.

"We knew you were coming, without knowing if you were man or woman, old or young, or from any particular tribe. We knew you at first glance because of the tattoos on your face."

Neeya raised a hand to be able to add her words, "My tattoos are shared only by a few people I have met on this journey, but they seem unimportant when I see the markings carried by everyone of your tribe. How can mine be significant?"

"We will show you the most valuable memories of our past, guarded by untold numbers of Guardians over the ages, of whom we are only the most recent. They should give you answers."

With that, he motioned to Pohu, who turned to an ancient, dark timber chest, the wood cracked but the surface polished to a gleaming sheen. It was covered with carvings, line after line of small characters. Pohu opened a metal clasp on the front and swung back the lid. Inside, they could see a series of cloth-bound bundles. One by one, Pohu took out each bundle and placed them, still wrapped, in a line in front of Neeya and the others.

There were six bundles, all wrapped in plain, faded cotton fabric. The wrappings looked very old, one reason why Pohu treated them carefully, with respect.

"They can be unwrapped, one at a time, Pohu. Our visitors justify it," said First Guardian.

Pohu took the wrappings from each bundle, revealing smooth, single slabs of dark timber, highly polished, with small carved inscriptions covering both sides.

First Guardian emphasised, "These are holy to us, to be treated with the utmost reverence and respect. The earliest of the writings came from our original planet, Earth. More have been added as our history has grown, to ensure that The People understand and remember who we are and where we come from. There exists no other timber of this kind that we know of because these pieces were brought originally from Earth. We three Guardians, plus a few others, can read the ancient writings, but some parts may still be understood by you. We will allow the one in your group who can finger-read the inscriptions, to draw what he can from these words. The readings should not be rushed or the true meaning will be lost. We know the man who can finger-read is not here now, but he has the same facial tattoos as you, Neeya."

She again signalled for permission to speak. "First Guardian, I can see that these precious writings are ancient and deserve great respect. You have spoken of my tattoos and those of our finger-reader, a man called Dosol. Can I ask why you believe such marks show importance that I do not know of? I have had my tattoos most of my life that I can remember. I decided to be marked this way when I was young, and had no direction or advice on their design. I chose them for no important reason that I can think of."

First Guardian responded, "Those marks have been carried by very few people in each generation, in several tribes. This has happened for hundreds of years, from when our people left Earth and on every planet where settlement has been attempted."

He pointed to the last slab. Pohu turned it over and pointed to the last entry. It was a simple carving, small but obvious. Neeya looked closely then held her breath. The small carving, halfway down the timber slab, was a simplified copy of her tattoo. It hung there, as if elevated from the surface. It could not be, but it was. It was more recently carved than those on the earliest slabs but still must be hundreds of years old.

Then she noticed that it was not the only one. There was one other copy towards the top of that page. Pohu was directed to turn the slab, then, in turn, each of the others, going back in time. Pohu waited as Neeya scanned each side, to see that the same tattoo design was shown between one and three times, on each page, in the small rolling script flowing from one side to the next.

First Guardian broke the silence. "Your tattoo, as shown, does not refer to you but to your purpose, as it does to those who were once here but have passed on. It has several meanings, but in our understanding, it means "freedom bringer," a person who brings freedom to the people.

"Those who have been chosen to carry it in the past have tried, but failed in their calling, because we still wait to be freed from the black killers. They have followed our people between the stars, and they still exist to obey their purpose, to kill all our species.

"Your time has come to lead us. This is why there is nothing written after that symbol. There is no other supply of this timber to carry on these records. If you also fail to bring freedom, then these records will not be added to and our people will pass away."

"I am not the only living person carrying this tattoo. How do you know it only applies to me?"

"Only you have control of the force you arrived with. You are their leader. You are the only person chosen by those who built the machines in the mountains, that make water and air for this planet. You can talk to those in the mountains. Your people have successfully already fought and killed many black killers. The others who have the tattoos have no power to achieve what you must try to do. You are already collecting those you will need. They come to you even when you do not seek them. To us, it is plain who you are."

Neeya felt light-headed and confused. The talk of previous generations and the meaning of her facial tattoo were too much to be clear in her mind. The room suddenly seemed too small and stuffy. She needed to be outside in the fresh air.

"I need to rest and have time to consider what you have said. Can you have us taken to where we will sleep? I will come back with Dosol, the man who can finger-read, if that is permissible to you."

"All will be arranged, but we need to leave this place soon. Our scouts believe two more days is the maximum time we will be safe here."

"Thank you for your words and offers of help. With all your people and those we have brought here, with the two machines, is it possible to move them all onto your boats to cross this water?"

"Our boats can each carry many people, and we have a way of placing the machines on a special craft. These plans have existed for some time, well before you started your journey."

When their discussions were completed, Pohu showed them out. Neeya and Tarn were moved by a small boat to one of the large vessels, while the others returned to the warriors waiting on the shore. All were fed, mostly cooked fish, with the addition of other foods brought from Myka's camp. Places were found on the boats for many of the newly arrived warriors to sleep and rest, but most chose to stay on solid land, where nothing moved under their feet. In two days, they would all have to cope with being on a moving deck in deep water, well away from land.

For some time, Neeya and Tarn sat on the deck of the boat offered to them, hardly speaking. A food platter had been shared and they had drinking water available. Neither of them knew where to start discussing the black killers and how they could attempt a full assault. When they had started on this journey, the objective was to save all possible free communities and get them to safety. Success would mean fighting. The black killers would oppose them and try to kill them all, now that they were not hiding in a mountain tunnel with lethal machines to defend them.

As Alpha had expected, the mission was becoming a war in which one side would be destroyed by the other – death or enslavement versus freedom to live normal lives.

Finally, she spoke. "This thing is too large to fully understand. It needs to be taken in small steps."

Tarn agreed. "We do not know where our enemies are, so we must first find them. We also need to know if there are any more communities close by to be saved, before we reach the killers' base. We are equipped to confront them and now have a much better chance."

"I need to talk to Alpha, if I can, to see what he knows. We still have one more mountain close to us that anyone saved can be sent to. We need to keep at least one machine for defence and communication, otherwise we will be blind to what can be seen from the air.

"But first, I want to take Dosol to the guardian's boat so that he can finger-read the timber tablets we were shown. Their records go right back to Earth. I never believed that we could ever know what happened to force the survivors from that disaster to travel through space to another planet. But now the chance is here I don't want to miss it. In a few days we might all be dead, with these boats and the records of many hundreds of years destroyed."

"Then go. Seize the opportunity. I will work with Nabu, Andoki and Myka to have our people train with their weapons, eat, sleep, complete all repairs and clean or replace clothing. This may be our last chance to be ready for a final confrontation with the killers. We also need to work out how the women and children from Pohu's people can be protected, although I have seen no old people or women with children at this temporary camp."

"Yes, I've noticed that too, Tarn. The three old guardians are the only non-fighters I have seen, although I think they would give their lives to defend their records."

Tarn left to speak with Myka about arranging for their warriors to prepare to camp for two days on the shore, using what shelter was available and making use of the materials already stockpiled among their tents. Neeya found Dosol and they were taken out to the guardians' boat. She wanted to be there while he ran his fingers along the many rows of writing on the carved wooden records. This might be her only chance to know about Earth and the journey here.

Once on the guardian's boat deck, Neeya tapped lightly on the same door they had used before and was invited to enter by First

Guardian. They found nothing had changed, apart from the first heavy timber slab already being on display for their study.

First Guardian welcomed Neeya again. "We expected you and your finger reader to return soon. We must give you all the help we can in your search for knowledge on such a matter before making your decisions. It is as we believed. Thank you for understanding the importance of our treasures. Please proceed with the examination. We will listen to your reader's words, and assist if he has problems with the meaning. He has no need to be able to read our language because the information within the words will speak to his mind. Anyone without his ability would not be able to provide the information he will find."

Dosol had never visited the room before and initially felt overwhelmed by the task he had been set. Not wanting to stumble over his words or say the wrong thing, he remained quiet but sat in front of the first block of records and started to run one finger over the first words. As he read, he spoke aloud what entered his mind. The records began on Earth, hundreds of years earlier, before warfare and environmental destruction across the planet caused the desperate survivors to leave for another home. Neeya listened, trying to embed all that she heard into her mind. From time to time one of the Guardians would explain or clarify a word or concept. They both tried to mask their feelings when despair or hope covered by the words came out of the readings. It was hard to keep going because of the mountain of information they slowly uncovered. The first record was finished and they were halfway through the second slab when tiredness forced them to stop.

Neeya stopped Dosol, with a hand on his shoulder. "First Guardian, it is late and our tiredness is affecting the accuracy of the readings. May we have permission to return tomorrow morning, after rest and a meal?"

First Guardian gave them permission, again thanking them for their dedication to the task, while reminding them that time was not on their side for the reading.

Before they went, she asked the guardians a short question: "Since we have arrived, we have seen no women with children, injured people, or elderly people with you. We are curious about that."

Again, First Guardian answered, "We knew you would come and that much fighting could occur, because of your arrival with many warriors, as our records foretold. Our loved ones and those who cannot aid in the fight have been taken to another place, an island that remains secret from all who are not of our people. Regardless of what comes from the fight to save all free people from the killers, the core of our people must survive. It remains undetermined who will be victorious. If we survive, we will return to our island, and our future will be assured. You are trying to save people from the killers and take them to the mountains. Our people do not need saving and they will not be going to the mountains."

They sat silent while First Guardian spoke. There was nothing further to be said, but Neeya felt part of the burden had been removed from her mind. At least she was not responsible for these water people.

"Thank you for all you have done to save your people. It has given us a lot to think about, added to what we have learned today from your records."

"We had assumed that is what you would require. It is our privilege to add to your knowledge of the past. Perhaps it will aid in the fight against the enemy. Return in the morning. We live on this boat. We are always here."

❊ ❊ ❊

A quiet trip had them back on their own large boat to rest. After spending so long sitting reading the records, they were starting to get used to a constantly moving floor. It had been an eventful day, and they enjoyed the first long sleep for some weeks while being gently rocked by the water.

The morning breakfast was again fish, cooked on bread with green leaves which they later found out was freshwater seaweed. It was becoming more obvious that the entire tribe preferred to be water-bound, away from land. Neeya could also see the attraction – safety from the killers. She wondered if the killers, given time, would try to breed people who could live in water, and be able to fight The People in their own domain. She shuddered at that thought now being a possibility, after what Andoki had found.

After breakfast, they went back to the guardians' boat and spent the rest of the day progressing through the records. The information was, at times, fascinating, wondrous, or tragic in what The People had had to deal with, in order to survive. They had always lived on or beside water. This lake was huge from her limited knowledge but on Earth, more than half the surface was covered in salty seas, with massive storms. Fishing fleets had gathered fish for millions of people and a huge variety of different water-living species existed, even in the great depths.

Neeya and Dosol battled to understand much in the records. She also did not understand how Dosol could get information from the indentations carved into the wood, where the carved words themselves could not be read by either of them. The writing was more than strange. It was outside their capacity. Dosol tried to explain how the spirit of the words was contained in the wood, that it spoke straight into his mind. Neeya put it down to the ability he was born with, unique to Dosol and unobtainable to her. She had enough to think about, even without the copious flow of information from Dosol's readings, but it had to be done.

That day flowed into the second full day, with all the boats being readied to move at sunrise the next morning.

Dosol finished the readings by the midday meal. They profusely thanked the guardians for the trust placed in them. They also promised to treat what they had learnt with privacy and honour the many scribes of the past who had recorded their experiences, stories, and memories.

That afternoon, a boat shaped differently from the others was moved towards the shore. This boat had a flat bottom and a wide ramp at the front. It was beached and the ramp extended out onto the sand. The two machines moved to it and lined up, ready to run onto the boat. Neeya had to message Alpha again to explain what was needed. By communicating with the lead machine via the green light panel on one side, both machines, in turn, ran up onto the flat boat's deck. The result was perfect. They were tied down in the centre of the boat, with room on all sides for warriors to sit or rest around the machines. It was obvious that much thought had been put into building the special boat, well before the newcomers arrived.

Neeya assumed the machines would be unloaded somewhere on the other side of the lake closest to the killer's base, with no need for the boat after that. She couldn't think of another use for it.

She wondered if this was not the first time. Had there ever been a similar movement of machines years before? If so, then it must have been part of a failed attempt. The boat was old, covered in lines similar in design to the tattoos covering every member of the tribe.

Having time to get answers to her queries, Neeya found Pohu while he was supervising the packing up of the temporary shore structures his people had been sheltering in.

"Pohu," she called, "do you have time to answer a few questions?"

Pohu nodded. "I would be honoured if I can be of help in your understanding."

"The special boat that now carries the machines looks old, and yet it is being used for one special purpose. Has it ever carried machines before? Also, I don't understand the lines all over the boats that are similar to the tattoos carried by all of your people. Could you tell me if they are connected?"

Pohu listened with his head to one side, obviously trying to understand the questions.

"You are right, Neeya, about that boat. It was built many years ago but used only once, probably before you were born. At that time, we had more communication with those who existed under the mountain. An attack was proposed against the killers, needing machines to be moved as part of the attacking force. This was before my time, but our people agreed to build the boat. It was used as proposed. The machines were moved across the lake and unloaded.

"At that time, we normally stayed safe on the lake well away from the shore. We did not join the attack but only moved the machines and the warriors who travelled with them. We never heard from or saw any of that attacking force again, including the machines. The killers may still have them. Then, there were more land people available for the attack. That has changed. Now, the killers appear stronger with more capacity and the land people have reduced in numbers. Their birth rates have fallen due to disease and other causes and many of their warriors have fallen to the killer's spears. Also, in recent years, we have found out that young women and many of the younger children have been captured and taken back to the killer's base. We don't know why."

"Thank you, Pohu. That information will be useful – and the tattooed lines on the boats?"

"Particular boats are used by individual families. Their tattoos tie them to their boats. The families care for the boats and the boats return that care. There is power in the tattoos, which transfers to the water. You would have noticed there are no sails on our boats. Sails were used back on Earth, but here the water is different. Our boats are moved with paddles for short distances and to manoeuvre slowly through obstructions or between other boats. For faster, longer journeys, as will be needed tomorrow, every boat will have two, three or more family members who can connect with that power within their boat and push the power into the water. The power moves the boat, building up speed at a rate that depends on how much the boat carries and the strength of the family member. Eventually, the person driving, the captain, becomes tired and another takes his or her place to keep the boat moving. Does that answer your question sufficiently?"

"Yes, Pohu. I am amazed at how our different people have evolved abilities to deal with problems or have changed to have a deep connection with the natural forces of this land and water. I understand that such changes have increased since our ancestors left Earth. I am eager to see these powers used with the boats tomorrow.

"You see that the only tattoos I have are those on my face. A few people I have met since travelling away from my tribe carry the same markings, yet we have never met before. How is that possible? We do not connect with boats, as your people do. We do not seem to have special abilities that are distinctive, although the tattoos show that abilities exist. Can you explain this?"

"You may have been told that you will discover the reasons for the tattoos that you and the others carry, in the future. Sometimes, those discoveries come late in life, in times of great need, or never, with some passing away without finding the answers. You will have seen your tattoo designs in our recorded history. Not all who carried those marks were ever included in the carvings, only a few. Some featured in some solution or success, while others only in a notable failure. I have seen the records and discussed them with our Guardians. I know your design is shown through the records and at the end of the last entry. It has yet to happen whether someone will write your story, as a success or failure.

"The people around you today will be part of your story because it will centre on a battle to the death with the killers. We stand ready to live or die with you."

Neeya could not speak, with Pohu's speech promising a dedication of his life to help fulfil her purpose. She did not feel ready to carry such a burden. Forces other than herself had placed her here. People greater than her, some with special abilities she would never understand, waited for her direction. She felt humbled and unworthy but could not step back from the task. It was rare for Neeya to cry, but Pohu's words left her eyes moist. She thanked him and went to spend time alone to compose herself before rejoining the others.

Chapter 19

Powered Voyage

While the last of the hut-building materials on the shore were being dismantled to move to the boats or be destroyed, the warriors from the three groups moved on to their assigned vessels. It had been decided that everyone should sleep there on the last night, with guards posted to watch the shoreline for any approaching killers.

One major decision had to be made before they started their water journey in the morning – where would the boats land on the far side of the lake? There might still be records or memories about where the previous landing had been made by the last failed attempt. Neeya wanted to avoid that location. Discussions with the most experienced boat captains who knew the area resulted in a different location being decided on. Andoki thought that any mind readers from the killers would not be capable of reading information over the distance they would be out on the water away from land. The mind babble of hundreds of people on the boats should surely stop information from being 'read'.

They had yet to discuss one important location on their journey towards the killer's base – the site of the crashed spaceship leaking pollution into a local stream, as described by Alpha. Neeya wanted to stay clear of that area and she spoke to Pohu about it. She found him on his last inspection of the beach before boarding his boat.

"Pohu, I need yet more information from you."

Pohu turned. "Ask away. Whatever I know is yours for the asking."

"Have you or any of your people learnt of a large crashed spaceship on the land, between this lake and the killer's main base?"

"I have heard of it, but our people have had no reason to go to that area. The more time we spend on land, the greater the danger. I know of one old man who may know more. He is still able to fight and so has chosen to stay with us rather than go to our island. I will take you to him."

A short boat trip to one of the many large boats now loaded with people led to the man Pohu mentioned.

"Offa, our new leader, Neeya, needs to talk with you about the ancient spaceship that crashed on the far side of the lake. Can you tell her about it?"

Offa nodded. "It is an honour to give you all that I can. I was one of a five-man group that was sent out to an area known to have a crashed spaceship in it. We had no trouble getting there, but went no closer than about 200 metres. All the trees and bushes were long dead. Even the grass and small plants were brown. A stream ran past the crash site and there was a trickle of brown liquid from the ship running into the stream. It drained into a forest that seemed sick and starting to die, or it did when I saw it years ago. The ship still had parts that were shining and other parts that were corroding, particularly the back end, where the engine might be.

"Our group stayed away from the area of dead plants. Moccasins would have given no protection for our feet. Animals seemed to stay away from the area we went through, but one of our men thought he saw someone or something moving in the shadows under the ship. He was sure of what he saw. We moved all around the site, but stayed clear of the dead ground.

"We saw a narrow trail from the ship, leading towards the west. The strange thing about the trail was that it was so obvious. The path had dead plants about a metre wide. Nothing lived on that trail. We didn't follow it. It looked creepy. We then came back to the boat at the lake shore.

"That is all I can tell you. I'm sorry I don't know more. Of the five-man scouting group, two died within a year, slowly and in pain. The others took longer. I have had poor health, but somehow, I have survived."

Neeya thanked Offa for his information and left with Pohu.

"Thanks for letting me speak to Offa, Pohu. His memories might be of little value, but we now have a much better idea of what we might come across when we pass that place. The thing that concerns me is the idea that something was moving under or inside that wreck and that there was a trail of dead land leading to the west. He was there years ago, so maybe it has changed since then. We will see soon enough."

They returned to their boat, ate another cooked fish and ration pack meal, and slept, ready for the first long water journey for any of the land-based warriors.

Like most of Neeya's mornings, she was awake and up before the sun rose. This time, it was the start of a 'first' in her life – a water journey, where she could only sit and watch.

The boats' occupants rose soon after, using the small cabin toilet and banging metal pots as they were put on small burners to cook food. Several full water skins hung nearby in case of fire and for drinking.

Neeya wanted to watch to see how the boat was powered from the start. No attempt was made until the sun was fully lighting the sky and hitting the sides of each boat. Their captain, who she had been introduced to, walked to the back end of the boat and sat on a comfortable-looking bench with a short pole in the centre and a loop of rope hanging at arms-length above.

Neeya glanced over to several nearby boats, to see that a similar arrangement was installed on them all. The others all now had a captain sitting on a bench. They each had their backs to the rest of the boat, with one arm held above their heads against the pole, holding on to the rope loop. They faced east, looking at the rising sun.

Her captain held his free arm out to rest on a timber frame positioned for that purpose, with his hand open and directed at the water. To Neeya's surprise the boat started to move forward, gathering speed as she watched. The water where the captain's hand was directed initially had ripples stretching out and building up until they were small waves spreading behind the boat.

Looking out to the other boats, she could see they were moving at a similar pace, all building up speed. Because of the forward motion and the movement of the waves hitting the boat, Neeya had to sit down to watch. The rear of the boat was now lower in the water while the nose had lifted. She was joined by Tarn, who was also intently watching the captain's work. Somehow the sun's light was being converted to power through the captain's body, with the power being directed into the water to push the boat forward. They couldn't see any flow of power or light into the water, but it was obviously working well. The timber pole with a rope loop in the frame showed the system had been in use for a long time. It explained why there were no sails to catch the wind that Pohu had mentioned. These people were really connected to their boats and the water for their existence.

Pohu surprised her when he arrived. He grinned when he caught her glance. "I wanted to leave you to observe how we move our boats without interference or explanation. This ability being used by each captain is the same for all who power our boats. We don't choose them for such work. They are either born with it or not. They cannot explain it. They just find they can do it at an early age. It eventually tires them out. That person is then replaced with another to allow the first captain to rest and be restored. It has worked this way in our people for generations."

"Pohu, I know from your sacred records that it is believed this water came from the heavens, that giant frozen balls of ice were redirected in space to crash into this area and create the lake. Do you believe that story?"

"I must believe that happened, Neeya. In our early history on this planet, we had much more contact with the people who brought our ancestors here. That information came from them. This world originally had no water or anything living, animal or vegetation. Then the work began to change it as a new planet for our species. Once the water was here, the giant machines were built and they started to create air to breathe and water vapour that allowed the growth of everything else. The ice and snow on some mountain tops were formed then. You have information from the vision called Alpha that says similar things. Tarn has discussed it with me."

"I have trouble understanding what has happened on this planet, and the ongoing war our people have with the killers. What started on earth has moved to three other planets, each of which was supposed to be our future, forever. This war will continue if we don't destroy them this time. We must do this for the future of all our people."

Pohu was struck by Neeya's commitment. He had adopted Neeya's attitude as his own, but he only nodded at the end of the conversation.

The voyage continued for two days, the captains driving the ships being replaced at intervals when they were tired. Each night, as the sun dropped below the horizon, the boats slowed to a stop and gathered to form a timber island.

People moved from boat to boat, visiting friends, sharing food, and creating an unlikely party out of the experience. Neeya and Tarn found the festive atmosphere surprising but enjoyable, and it helped to remove some of the tension building up around the conflict that was coming ever closer.

On the third morning, as the sun rose, the boats turned and headed towards the shore, apart from one. The Guardians were removing themselves and their sacred records from any chance of danger. They had given whatever help they could and now they were called to the secret island where the families and elderly members of the tribe stayed, waiting for the final battle against the killers.

❋ ❋ ❋

During the two days of travel, Neeya had used the communication system on the wagons to contact Alpha, and report their progress so far. Alpha also passed on the information that the group sent to the mountain for protection had arrived safely, with no further attempted attacks. They were all relaxing and enjoying the provisions available.

This was now the second community under Alpha's protection. Neeya and Tarn's tribe had journeyed from the campsite near the original tunnel outlet to the second mountain after the brothers Anil and Manil had returned to them with Neeya's message. The tribe was packed and ready to relocate when the machine and the two warriors sent by Alpha arrived to guide them to the mountain. The journey was free of trouble and they had also arrived unharmed, with as much food as could be carried, after following the wagon to the mountain's entrance.

Their people were now safe, with food and rest available to them. The warriors of the tribe could also be valuable if needed, but they were too far away now, and would not have been able to arrive before the expected fighting began.

The distance to the shoreline was further than expected by those from the land-based tribes. By the time the sun was fading, the boats were slowing down for the night together again. One boat kept slowly moving, with rowers on each side. It was fully loaded with over thirty armed warriors who were to land where the rest would come the following morning. Their task was to make sure there were no killers waiting and to guard the landing place to make it safe for more than 400 extra armed men and women.

The boat disappeared into the darkness. It was hard for those waiting for morning to get any rest, as they sharpened spear points, knives, and swords as well as finishing arrows ready for use.

Neeya was nudged awake by Tarn in the darkness. Their breakfast was cold water and leftovers from the night before. Moving in the dark meant no powered propulsion, but they could hear the quiet paddling propelling the boats towards the shore.

Nothing had been heard from those who had gone before them. Good news. Only a loud confrontation with the killers could alert them that their plans were going wrong before they even started.

Looking across to the boats on either side, she thought she could make out the shape of warriors standing, facing the coming shoreline. The paddling gave off a phosphorescence at times to judge distance between the boats. All that could be done had been done. This final step would begin with a long, two-day march, if there were no clashes with the killers before that. She remembered the polluted stream running near the crashed spaceship had to be passed on the high side, to stay away from leakage coming from the site.

The night remained dark. They had timed their arrival onto land to make sure they were all out of the boats before first light. Two captains would stay on each boat to move them away out of range of a spear throw or fire arrows. Then they would slowly be relocated to wait opposite the killers' base, to transport warriors after the expected fight, as well as for the removal of any wounded or dead. All agreed that no one would be left behind, come what may.

When they arrived, Neeya strapped her sword to her side ready for action, if needed. It had stayed on her back, tied to the side of her backpack all the way from the mountain. She was still undecided whether it was the right weapon to have chosen. There were many bows, spears, slings and throwing darts carried by the warriors.

Swords, long knives, short stabbing spears and axes were for close combat, but she had hoped it would not come to that. If it did, it would be because of an ambush or the longer-distance weapons failed to protect them.

While her mind ran to the various possibilities, Tarn stood beside her, silent and unmoving. His unwavering support was one of the main reasons she was here on the boat. He never doubted her, never pushed to take over. His trust in her ability to guide them to win over the killers' madness was absolute.

A bird called in the darkness – a shrill call from a land bird, not one from the lake! They were close to the shore! The paddling slowed and turned slightly towards the call of another bird. Her boat moved ahead, to finally ground onto a pebbly beach. Ladders were thrown overboard, and the first thirty warriors followed her and Tarn off the boat, to be met by members of the forward scouting group sent the previous day.

The other boats discharged their cargoes, then backed off to provide room for the rest. Whispered discussions told Neeya that no contact had been made with the killers and the area was secure.

The last boat to beach was the low, flat boat carrying the two precious machines. The ramps were dropped and they both rolled off without having to be directed. Their instructions had been locked in well beforehand.

The sun's first rays were starting to light the sky as the last boats moved back onto the lake, to be barely visible from the shore. Everyone had moved undercover off the beach, under tall, spreading trees about 100 metres from the water.

Pohu moved to speak with Neeya and Tarn. "The early scouts have found a good trail that leads in the right direction. I have sent people around to check for traps or possible ambush places. Do you want to start moving now?"

"Thanks, Pohu, yes. The faster we can be away from the water, the better. Can you arrange outer edge scouts and rear protection to move with us? Thanks."

Pohu moved off to make the arrangements. Nabu and Dosol stood nearby, waiting for instructions. "Nabu and Dosol, do you have any feelings about this day? Are there any immediate dangers to worry us?"

Nabu spoke. "From the time we landed, the feeling of danger was here, and growing. The crashed spaceship projects much danger, with a line from it towards the killer's base.

"We can't see why that line – probably a path – is so dangerous."

Neeya nodded and moved to the machine to contact Alpha. Again, her messages were relayed to the always circling eagle shape above them and then to the mountain.

Ten minutes later, she returned to the others and gathered the leaders. "The machine flying above us can see in the dark. It has located a path that glows, running from the spaceship site towards the black killers' mountain. Here and there are the glowing bodies of dead birds and animals on the sides of the path. It looks very dangerous to be near that place.

"We have boots for those of us who came from the mountain. If we get near the path, make sure the boots are used and no one touches the ground, dead trees, or animals nearby. Walk on the side the wind blows from. There might be a deadly smell coming from the polluted land, so cover your hands and faces.

"I have bad feelings about the spaceship and the killers. They are entering the wreck and using the polluted path.

"Tarn, Nabu and Dosol, find Pohu and the other leaders. Explain to them what I said. This glowing material is very dangerous. Make sure the scouts stay away from it."

They moved off to spread the word.

Tarn said, "I learnt something about this material from the teaching machines in the mountain. It could be the fuel that the spaceship used to get here."

"It's more than that, Tarn. When Dosol and I went through the records of The People with the guardians, something like this was used in the final war back on earth, before the survivors left to find somewhere else to live. It is deadly. It not only kills but it can distort human bodies into something else or cause a long, painful death. The killers have been moving some of it to their base, so their whole mountain could be affected. We can't go in to rescue children and women unless it is safe. We don't know what they are doing with this material, but it is a big worry. I will try to get more information from Alpha. We should arrive there by the end of the second day if they don't attack before then."

It took nearly an hour before they were formed up to travel, with the two machines separated but protected. Tarn and Neeya travelled towards the front of the small army, with the predator-shaped bird circling above – the ultimate forward scout.

After travelling for nearly two hours, the first indication was seen – a rotting corpse of a large cat, its mouth pulled back in agony to show its long teeth. Two dead rats lay close by, originally having fed on the body. The cat showed no injury but it could have been eating animals affected by the glowing pollution.

It was a good lesson for everyone. The body was given a wide berth, with all passing on the high side. Bringing the heavy, solid leather boots seemed like a very good idea then, compared to their worn and flimsy moccasins.

With his tribe's previous knowledge of the area around the crashed ship, Pohu took charge of the direction they travelled and, with the scouts' help, took them on the high side of the site, keeping a light wind blowing past them towards the wreck.

Without an aerial night view of the meandering path from the polluted spaceship towards the killers' lair, the ease of using the path would have been attractive. The few dead animals, large and small, could have been explained as a local disease or coming from a polluted water hole. Neeya had seen, through her connection with the machine, the strange glowing line of the path and its starting point in the guts of the crash site.

The sickly green colour was warning enough to stay well away. Even with their boots on, everyone was directed to another animal path further up the hill from the site.

Since they had left the safety of the mountain, regular hunting of prey animals – mostly goats, pigs, and deer – had met the food needs of the army, particularly when Alpha's packaged food rations were added for volume and a different flavour. While on the move, nuts and berries were picked up on passing, but little time was available to dig for root crops like wild potatoes, onions, and other vegetables.

Once they had left the boats, the area they had marched through provided little success for the hunting parties. Neeya put it down to the killers' need for food, having wiped out nearby animals. Now, she thought the animals might have learnt to keep well away from the polluted land. The ration packs would become their main food for the next few days regardless of the inevitable clash with the enemy. Tension was high with everyone, as they advanced. An ambush was expected, so clumps of bushes or rock outcrops were carefully approached. It slowed progress, but there were no incidents.

Andoki tried to mind-scan the area ahead but could detect no humans or questing minds nearby. The killers obviously knew they were approaching. Anyone with the ability to read minds would have passed the results onto their leaders. Pohu sent scouts out to the sides and rear to detect any enemy scouts, further than normal but still with no results.

The day finally ended, with the campsite chosen amongst large trees, many of which had fallen in the past and provided protection in case of an attack. All were tired after a day of tense expectation, knowing that another march would have them at their destination.

Double the number of guards were posted, with regular replacements arranged throughout the night.

Andoki met with the leaders to discuss his plan for a night scouting mission.

"I can see better than most in the dark and I have had years of hunting without light. I want to go forward towards the killers' base, not right up to it because it would be too far, but maybe half the way. If there is an ambush intended then I will find it. I will also be able to see any traps like the ones at Myka's settlement. Even if I find nothing, at least we will know before we go any closer."

All agreed to Andoki's suggestion and wished him well. It would be another night of tension as they waited for his return. He would have no protection with him other than his skill with the bow and special abilities.

❈ ❈ ❈

Andoki slipped away, with his backpack, quiver of arrows and bow. In a dozen steps, he was gone from view. The going was easy at first. The land was lightly forested and the night sky let some light through the tree branches to help him choose his silent path.

The trail's pollution would be visible if he came too close to it, so he had kept his moccasins on to walk silently. At intervals, he mind-scanned around him but detected no nearby humans.

Over two hours later, nothing had changed. Few animals were in the area and no nightbird calls alerted him to any other movement. He worried. This close to their base, he expected the killers to have guards and some form of outer protection. Were they so arrogant of their strength in numbers? Knowing that a small army was approaching, why wouldn't they have safeguards in place for protection?

He reluctantly turned and made his slow progress back to the campsite, stopping at intervals to try to detect anyone following him. The last thing he wanted was to lead a killer scout back.

Again, no contact was made and he was back in the campsite well before dawn, stepping out of the darkness close to where Neeya, Tarn and Pohu slept.

A gentle nudge had Neeya jumping, ready to fight. Tarn and Pohu were a breath behind.

"That woke me with a start, Andoki. I don't understand how you can be so silent. I can only be grateful you are on our side."

"I have always been very quiet, wherever I move," said Andoki. "For me, it is natural and I don't do anything special to move silently."

"Well, I'm relieved you are back, with no injuries. Did you find anything?"

"I spent two hours getting closer to their base but found nothing – no guards, no traps, no paths cut or even any pollution from the spaceship. It worries me. We should know more by now, being this close to them. Where are their hunting trails, or paths they have used to bring back captured women and children?"

"We need information from the air. Alpha might be able to see more with the flying bird machine than we can tell from the ground. I want to talk to him about other things, so this is a good time before we get really close to their base. Andoki, try to get some rest while I talk to Alpha."

The others settled back to get what sleep they could. They all knew it might be the most rest they would have for some time if real action happened in the next few days.

Neeya went to the machine and touched the information panel. It was now normal for her to communicate with her mind through the machine to Alpha. This time it went on for longer than usual. Alpha needed time to analyse what could be seen from the air using the night vision of the eagle machine's flight.

The results surprised even Alpha, if surprise was possible for a computer-generated vision. Neeya discussed her tattoos and the five other people in the combined tribal army with the same markings. He supplied more surprises and a final shock.

Soon after, she broke the contact and went back to the leading group, not with her usual quick steps, but dragging her feet while looking at the ground, as if she were walking to her death. Some of them were asleep and others just rested. They were soon fully awake and waiting for her news from Alpha.

"The polluted path that glows in the dark can be seen easily at night, but it is difficult to find in daylight, apart from flattened and dead vegetation. At night it's obvious, running from the spaceship crash site and heading towards the killers' base. It wanders a bit, then stops and disappears. The area around the base of the mountain has a mix of glowing paths in and out of openings on the mountain, like the one we used where we trained and sheltered.

"But there is no part of the original path leading up to the mountain. Alpha's assessment of the information is that the path goes underground, so that it disappears.

"The killers must have used their time over many years to dig underground. Maybe this was done using captive labour; it could have been done because they had seen the machines in the sky and understood that they were being watched, so if they dug underground, it remained a secret.

"There may be tunnels running anywhere from now on, under our feet and we will not know it. That is why they appear and disappear without leaving a trail. From now on, all our people need to know and be on watch for tunnel or cave openings. We can't go into the tunnels because they might have the glowing pollution spread through them."

Tarn listened to Neeya's news without speaking. He watched her face and body language, and thought she was both shocked and tense. Her original dedication and enthusiasm to see their task finished seemed to now be less. Something in Alpha's information must have caused it, beyond the news about the tunnels. He kept watching her, trying to work out what had changed and if the new information contained yet more secrets.

The discussion went on, as they pooled their ideas on how to deal with an enemy that now had control of the underground, of which they knew nothing.

It finally ended without any progress, and most of them went back to their rugs and sleeping bags to get what sleep was still available.

Tarn stayed behind, waiting to speak. Before he could ask his question, she glanced over to him and spoke.

"I can guess what you want to ask me, Tarn. I did receive further information from Alpha. With the understanding I got from The People's recordings of their history, it all makes sense. The assault on the killers' base must change with what I now know, but I can't tell anyone until we are much closer. Don't ask me to go any further, Tarn. I know you worry about me, but my personal part in this assault is coming soon. I only ask you to do something for me that will seem strange, but it is, or will be, critical."

"Ask what you need, Neeya. I can only accept that you will tell me what this is all about when the right time comes."

She nodded. "Tarn, I need you now, more than ever. Can you find out where the people who have the same facial tattoos as mine are in this camp? When the sun is up and before we get ready to move on, I need to have them all with me. Dosol is obviously one of them, and I have seen four others, from Myka's tribe and "The People." Just tell them to join me before we move out."

"Your words worry me, but I will do what you want."

With that, he went to his sleeping bag carrying the mystery of Neeya's secret.

As the sun came up, Neeya sat in her blankets thinking through an idea she had woken up with, after remembering a feature of the land closer to the killers' base, from the aerial views seen through the flying machine. That view showed a rare stream running down a slope near a glowing hole in the ground. The hole was one of several places used by the killers to enter or leave their tunnels. The glow was probably caused by the spilling of polluted fuel.

Pohu had already been called for, and he arrived as Dosol appeared, after being summoned by Tarn.

Neeya explained her idea to Pohu.

"Pohu, you now know about the tunnel – probably a network of tunnels – around the base of the killer's mountain."

"Yes, without the view from the sky at night we would never have suspected that they existed. They must have been digging them for years."

"I agree and I have an idea that should flush them out onto the surface. I saw, when looking at the view from the sky, that a stream runs past an entrance into the tunnels. It was obvious because of the glow at night."

"Why would that stream be important to us?" asked Pohu.

"If we could redirect it into the tunnel entrance then we might flood some of the tunnels to force them out. It would need work with digging sticks and the few spades that Alpha included on the machines, to dig a diversion. I think it's worth the effort. Those who are digging would need protection to hold back any killers attempting to stop the flooding. What do you think?"

"I am still trying to understand. If it works it will be well worth the danger to those warriors digging to divert the stream, and their protectors. How close is the stream to the tunnel entrance and how long would it take to do the digging?"

"It depends on how hard the ground is. The distance is less than fifty metres but the trench must be deep enough to fully divert the water."

"Then we should attempt it. They will soon know what is happening, so we will need at least twenty to do the digging and forty to protect them. All of them will have to stay well away from anyone who comes out of the tunnel. They may be polluted by the glowing liquids. All those digging should wear boots to protect their feet."

"So, Pohu, can you select about sixty warriors who will go there as soon as possible before our main force arrives at the site? If the killers emerge in strength, then the rest of our people should be there as reinforcements."

"I need to arrange this now. You will have to describe exactly where the stream and tunnel mouth are. We don't want to waste time searching around for the place."

"Get your warriors together now, then come back to me while I explain to Tarn where to guide you. He should go with you, as well. The minds of two war leaders will be better than one."

Pohu was gone in a rush, with his excitement scarcely contained. Finally, they could strike a blow at the killers and damage the tunnels they had created. If it worked, the killers could not hide underground and attack them from below.

Tarn arrived shortly after Pohu left. Neeya told him the plan and explained where the tunnel mouth and stream were. He rarely showed his feelings, but this time, he was excited. "I slept badly because of my worry about these tunnels. I can see how we could get the killers out from underground without a lot of our people dying from them or their pollution. The plan is brilliant! We must get the diversion dug then stand back while the tunnels fill up. If they don't come out, they will drown. I'll find Pohu now so we can get going. The protection force needs to be well armed. If a lot come out then we will be busy."

He went to catch up with Pohu, more enthusiastic than he had been since they left the mountain. She had thought much about Tarn since the preparations for an attack got busy and he had obviously been hiding his worry about how the fight was going to go for them.

It was still early in the morning but the camp's activities were underway to cook and eat a meal, then pack up and get ready to move out.

The normal talk and banter were gone. This was now very serious. Everyone was mentally preparing for action, to kill or be killed. For most of them, the only killing they had experienced was with animals or fish for eating, using hunting spears, bows, and arrows. This time the weapons were heavy, with spears and arrowheads designed for deep penetration and hooked to stop them from being removed.

Within half an hour, the first rows of warriors headed out of the campsite over a series of shallow ridges that led to the base of the mountain stronghold. The stronghold sat on a flat plain, under which the tunnels had been dug. By the time they arrived there in strength, the sixty warriors who had left earlier should be close to finishing the diversion of the stream into the tunnel mouth.

Neeya moved with Andoki and the five men carrying the same facial tattoos. She was the only female in the group. Others nearby noticed the shared markings and wondered what the tattoos meant, and why this was the first time they were seen together. Little was said between them, although they all felt they were significant members of some form of exclusive group, but for what purpose?

The two remaining machines rolled along with them, one close to the front and the other midway along the column of fighters. Neeya had earlier looked through all that was carried by the machines, including the specifically marked containers on the sides of both wagons. She had spent time with Alpha the previous night discussing the possible use of the materials being carried. They also spoke about using the bird and wolf-shaped machines already gathered near the killer's mountain.

This time, no effort would be spared to make the attack the last needed to remove, forever, the threat of the black killers.

That objective now took up an increased part of her thoughts, along with the information she received from Alpha, coupled with the writings of The People recorded over hundreds of years. This attack had to change everything. It had to be worth the sacrifice.

❋ ❋ ❋

The movement of the small army was never in ranks of warriors. These were hunters who now hunted men, so they moved in small groups, with visual contact with others, through the trees, down valleys and over the high points. The leading parties included Neeya and those who carried her markings.

They followed the lead machine, which used the information fed into it by the circling bird. For most of the route, it stayed on animal trails or natural clearings, but sometimes, thick patches of vegetation had to be cut through. The earlier lead group did not have to choose a path for the machines and so had followed a more direct and faster route.

It took all morning to cross through several valleys and over ridges, before resting and starting the final push to the stream and tunnel mouth.

They heard first, rather than saw, a battle already being fought close by.

Topping a slight rise and looking down the slope to the battleground, their first view was of bodies lying spreadeagled near the trench that appeared only half finished and still dry. The remainder of the original twenty warriors working on the digging were being closely defended by about two-thirds of the original force of forty. Their ranks included bodies, as well as several obviously wounded warriors behind the fighters, attended by a few who were tying up wounds.

The tunnel mouth was strewn with black bodies. The killers were hemmed in by multitudes of their dead and battled to get over the mounds. The numbers dying appeared irrelevant as they charged to their deaths. All seemed crazed, clawing over bodies, focused totally on attacking with no thought of their own safety. Pain didn't seem to affect them, with many taking two or even three arrows before they dropped.

Neeya's warriors fired arrows and darts from less than thirty metres, the short distance guaranteeing deadly accuracy. Most had already used their spears, many of which were obvious, lodged in enemy bodies. However, the sheer weight of numbers coming out of the tunnel was slowly pushing the attackers back, and the wounded were having to be dragged further away from the action.

As soon as the new arrivals crested the ridge, orders were given to attack and strengthen the battle line. A swarm of arrows, humming like bees, flew into the air, over the heads of their companions, dropping dozens in a minute. Spears followed the arrows, reaping a heavy toll. More diggers were sent to speed up the stream diversion works.

The killers immediately changed tactics, as if controlled by one mind, with that mind assessing the incoming strength of the attackers. A single horn blast sounded, which had the few surviving black killers clambering back over the piled bodies into the tunnel mouth.

Neeya stood with her group away from the fighting. Andoki had paused only seconds before letting loose a flow of arrows into the killers' ranks.

Then they were gone. The only sounds left were the groans of the wounded, the yells of the remaining diggers, and the calls for more to help those who needed it.

The bodies of their own people were moved away from the fight area to allow the killers' bodies to be dragged into mounds on each side of where the trench was rapidly being completed. Rags and abandoned clothes were used to protect their hands from touching the skin of the enemy dead. All were now well-trained to be aware of any possible pollution the killers might have on their bodies. Warriors moved through the torn-up area of the battle, picking up undamaged arrows and spears. Those they could remove from the bodies were pulled or cut out for reuse. There would be little time to replenish their arrows and spears as they moved towards the mountain.

Chapter 20

Floods and Fights

The sudden end of fighting came as a shock to Neeya's fighters. One minute, it was kill or be killed; the next minute, they stood as their fighting rage subsided, surrounded by bodies.

Digging of the diversion continued, with extra men speeding it up. A few warriors acted as guards, watching the tunnel mouth for any further eruption of the enemy from the hole. The others found places in the shade to rest. Less than twenty had died in the attack, with another fifteen needing their wounds bandaged.

Both Pohu and Tarn had been in the thick of the intense fighting, involving only a few minutes of frenetic activity. They made their way up the slope and rested, while reporting their experience.

"They erupted out of the tunnel all at once, throwing clubs and spears as soon as they reached the surface. Only knives were left to try to get at us. You needed to hit vital places to stop them," said Tarn.

Pohu added, "It was like their brains only had one instruction, and they expected to kill, then die. When that horn sounded, it came from inside the tunnel, as if a controller was summoning trained animals back to their cages.

"My guess is that these were their bottom-level fighters, with their minds almost destroyed from using those leaves they chew. We were told by that captive Andoki brought back how he despised the fighters using the leaves, that they were like animals."

"They obviously knew what was intended with our digging," said Neeya. "Someone could have been reading minds, which made them desperate to stop the diversion. Everyone needs to be on guard when the water goes into the tunnel. Anything could happen when the flooding starts.

"It should take some time for that to happen, so our warriors have a chance to rest. The digging group should be swapped regularly with others so no one is overworked. The same goes with the protection guards. I think it is too late in the day to have us all out heading towards the mountain. They know we are coming but I don't want to get caught from underground. They will see us from above well before we will be able to see them.

"Maybe later tonight, Andoki, you could use your night sight to learn what you can of their activities, if anything is happening above ground. For now, we watch what happens with the stream being diverted and its impact on the tunnels. In the morning, we will move forward at daybreak to attack from the east, so the sun will be in their eyes. For now, have the men get as much rest as they can."

❈ ❈ ❈

Nothing had moved on the plain fronting the killers' base. The stream diversion was finished and water had been surging into the tunnel mouth for hours. It would continue through the night and hopefully collapse tunnels and force the enemy out onto the surface.

Andoki had slept for the remaining hours of the afternoon and into the early night. He woke to find most of the small army asleep, apart from the guards at their posts, watching the tunnel mouth as the water poured in. It was harder to sleep now, with Vail still back at Alpha's mountain. Long weeks had passed since he had seen her, the longest time they had been separated since first meeting. He believed he had done everything he had been asked to, and more, but it was getting harder to stay focused on the elimination of the killers. He still had doubts that they would be able to finally end the threat posed, but he stayed committed while waiting for Vail to recover from her injuries.

Hunting the killers at night was more difficult on his own. Normally, he and Vail would guard each other's backs. Two were always better than one at night, particularly against unknown foes in a strange environment.

But it was time to patrol the plain to see what the killers were up to. He could not see underground. Knowing that anything could be below him while he was on the surface gave him good reason to feel nervous, a rare feeling for him. He had tried to read for any minds out in the tunnels, with no results.

No one heard or saw him leave camp. He scouted around the guards rather than talk to them and explain his mission. Fifty metres out on the plain, he was totally reliant on his night vision. At times, he thought water was moving below him, but he wasn't sure.

The night was quiet as he moved away from camp. Then he came to a collapsed, sunken area about four metres across. Looking down, he could see water flowing from one side of the collapse to disappear into the tunnel on the other side.

The flooding was beginning to have an effect! As he moved away from the sunken hole, he looked back to see a shape, dark black on black, sticking up from the hole and then disappearing again. He trusted his eyes, but it happened so fast that he moved on, becoming more wary of potential new dangers from below.

Andoki had to move around six different tunnel collapses in a short time. They were not in a straight line, so he assumed there was more than one tunnel, with branch lines. Several times he thought he saw movement in the flooded holes formed by the collapses.

Concern grew as dark shapes started to appear at a distance in front and to both sides of him. It was time to return to camp. As soon as he turned, it became obvious that they were moving towards him from all directions. His mind-reading skill produced nothing he could understand. The minds he could pick up were low-level with little variety, concentrating only on him.

Each time he changed direction, one or more of the shapes moved to cut him off. He was starting to lose control of the situation and had no obvious solutions. He picked up pace and fired two arrows in the direction of the still indistinct shape closest to him. The shape dropped, to be replaced by two more, out of one of the closest holes.

Andoki started to panic, then he steadied and began to methodically fire arrow after arrow at the approaching figures. One by one, they dropped, to be replaced, sometimes with two others. He had started with a full quiver of arrows, but only a few remained when a yell, "Down!" blasted into his mind. He dropped face down on the ground, as arrows passed over his head at a steady flow. He couldn't see the total results at ground level. In the direction he could see, two single shapes dropped and were not replaced. Then everything was silent. No further zipping noises of arrows passing through the air. Another word, "Finished," came into his mind and he slowly stood up.

He looked around to see dark mounds of bodies around him, many of them, in all directions. Then his eyes picked up movement, approaching him. It was a different shape, and again, words dropped into his mind. "Don't shoot."

He recognised that mind – Vail was back!

How was it possible? How did she get here? Was she fully restored? So many questions filled his mind: gratefulness for being rescued from those black shapes – concern for her that she may have jeopardised her recovery with her actions – thankfulness that his other half, his balance in the world, had returned.

As he came to grips with the realisation of her return, she made her way to him, skirting the subsided holes and the scattered bodies.

Finally, she was there – in front of him, seemingly whole and restored from what would normally have killed anyone else. Her hair and face were unchanged. She wore fully camouflaged jacket and pants, with her moccasins. They were together again, responsible and trusting each other.

After holding each other, kissing, and caressing, they stood in an embrace that seemed to go on forever. Then Vail said, "We need to get out of here. More of those things could come in greater numbers and I don't have many arrows left. All our questions can wait until we are back at your camp."

Andoki let her go and stood back. She looked great, with no obvious injuries. "Are you fully recovered? How did you get all the way here from the mountain?"

"I am fine. I will give you all the answers you want, but we must move."

They both turned and started jogging towards the camp. They stopped only once, to inspect one of the bodies with an arrow in its heart. The creature was like nothing they had seen before. It was a similar size to them, with tiny eyes and large fan-like ears in a web pattern projecting out from each side of the head. The head itself was bald, dome-shaped, with almost no neck. Just above what would be its shoulders, there were four parallel slits, again on both sides of the head. It was hard to believe what they were looking at.

"Gills," said Andoki. "They have gills for breathing underwater like a fish. Were they originally humans, or were they born this way? We must at least take the head back to Neeya."

Vail agreed, but it took precious minutes hacking at the body with their steel knives. It finally came clear and they dropped it into a bag for the trip back. One more difference they noted was that the body was covered in smooth but mottled grey and black skin. The feet were wider than their own, with toes further apart and webs between them. The hands were similarly shaped but with long, ripping claws.

"Those things can probably swim and breathe like fish underwater. That's bad news for the people who live on the lake boats," said Andoki. "I'll explain about them later. We will be doing a lot of talking to catch up. I can't wait till we are alone, away from the others."

There were no further sightings of the creatures as they travelled back to the camp. Rather than alert the guards, they easily evaded detection and found Neeya and Tarn. Both were asleep but woke as they arrived. The other leaders soon arrived to join in the celebration. It took a while for the excitement of Vail's return to calm down, as well as the inspection of the strange head that Andoki and Vail had returned with.

Neeya asked, "You look well, Vail. How do you feel? Are you fully recovered from your injuries?"

"Yes, I've been exercising and practising with weapons for over a week now. Like you, I was shown all the new weapons, clothes, and equipment. I chose to adopt the same-coloured clothes and backpack as most of you. I changed my old bow for a new type, with similar arrows to what I had, but a good supply of light, metal arrowheads to fit the shafts that I can make whenever I have time. I feel good, but Alpha had a tiny unit put under the skin in my arm, so that I can now mentally speak to him, like you can, through a machine. He can also track me so I would never get lost or captured and taken away."

"That could be very useful, Vail, in the event we are separated in a battle, but tell us how you got here so quickly from Alpha's mountain."

"Alpha sent a wagon again, straight from his mountain, to carry me and some cargo directly to this location. I only had to hang on. I did it in two days, with regular stops for me to eat, sleep and take care of personal needs. The wagon is hidden nearby. I can call it in if you want."

"Thank you, Vail, but I don't understand how it got you here in two days. We have been travelling for weeks, including a fast boat trip across the lake."

"Alpha told me to speak to only you about the route I took to get here. He did not want it to become well known to everyone, unless you decide that it is necessary."

"Vail, I need to know about it now. Could everyone else come back before daybreak, after you have slept? I need to speak with Vail and Andoki alone."

Once the others had left, Neeya said, "Now, Vail, you can tell me what Alpha said the others should not hear."

"My journey on the wagon was mostly underground, in a machine-made tunnel, constructed by the same methods that made the water and air-making machines in the centre of the mountains."

"All that way underground? What was it like and where did it start and end?"

"It started down the tunnel you originally took us through to get to where Alpha was. But at the bottom, instead of turning to come out, the machine I was on went the other way. It was smooth-floored and there were lights that came on then off as I passed. A door opened when we came to a wall. This time, the door slid up, into the roof. We went a short distance in the open then towards another wall. Again, a door slid up and we entered another tunnel. It happened at regular intervals. The wagon rolled along quickly without my control."

"You said it had cargo on board. What was the cargo?"

"Alpha said it was more of the same material that was in the other two wagons. He said you would understand."

Neeya shuddered. Vail was surprised at her reaction. It was obviously a shock and a secret only for her, and it wasn't good news.

"Andoki, how many of those strange creatures did you think you killed?" Andoki answered that they had each killed over thirty, considering almost two full quivers of arrows were used in the fight.

"With the other abilities the killers have shown so far, these things that we have never seen before and the use the killers are making of the liquid from the crashed spaceship, they seem to be breeding or creating creatures for special purposes. Those things you killed could have been sent to the flooded tunnels because they can exist underwater, to attack us from below. They can also see in the dark, otherwise they would not have been able to find you to attack. The largest community of normal people in this area live on boats, well out towards the centre of the lake. These creatures may be the way the killers intend to attack the boat people."

"So how can that change the way we attack the killers' base in the coming days?" asked Andoki.

Neeya explained, "We thought we could try to rescue women and children held captive. Alpha wanted us to save whoever we could find.

"With their use of the spaceship's fuel, it is possible that they are all polluted, and not capable of re-joining normal people. It's painful to realise that no captives may be able to be saved. If they use the mountain as a stronghold and fight us if we try to enter, then there are few options. This was always something that Alpha thought might come, but previous efforts have never achieved this much before, or if they did then the final battles must have been lost.

"For now, you both need to sleep. The coming day will probably be long, with the battle against the enemy. Thank you for what you have discovered. It gets ever more complex. What else have the killers done? We will have to go carefully tomorrow and not rush. But I do not want to be camping out on that plain, in full sight from the mountain, with tunnels under us. Come back here in the morning, before we start moving again."

Andoki and Vail headed off for some well-earned sleep. Exhaustion soon claimed Neeya and she was asleep in minutes.

The rest of the night passed without any movement from the enemy and Neeya being awake and planning the attack before sunrise. The planet had no moons, with only one sun in the sky. There was so little water vapour from the machines in the mountains that no heavy rains had yet to fall from the time humans were first brought to the planet.

As soon as Andoki and Vail came back to Neeya, she sent them off to bring the machine that Vail had travelled on back into the safety of their campsite.

Pohu had already visited earlier and seen the head of the strange creature, and had been told about Andoki and Vail's encounters during the night. He was concerned as he left to organise his warriors. Having killers who could swim underwater out to his people's ships was a nightmare that could not be allowed to happen.

Once Vail's machine was back at the campsite Neeya inspected the large, flat container covering the surface area on the wagon. An inspection cover opened as soon as she placed her hand on the touch panel, identical to the two other wagons that still travelled with them. The amount of material in the container was much more than the other two wagons. Her face was set in a determined but appalled look after she closed the panel. It told her what Alpha had decided as a final decision for the killers, one that she had no alternative but to agree with.

Within an hour, the attacking force was packed up and ready to move off. Discussions between the leaders had resolved that they would move forward on a broad front, leaving no concentrations of their warriors to be attacked, but they would be able to quickly gather to support each other if one part of the line needed help.

Neeya moved forward with her small group of warriors carrying their shared tattoos. Andoki and Vail, having restocked their arrow quivers, were further along the line, in the area covered in the previous night. They wanted to see the bodies of those killed to study any changes.

Andoki noticed a row of thin steel knives across Vail's chest, held in a shaped, carrying band.

"You have new weapons, Vail. When did you decide you needed throwing knives?"

"I need only one knife for hunting animals, Andoki, but this is different. If those killers get past our arrows and spears, what can I do to defend myself? So, when I was recovering from my injuries, Alpha provided training and a selection of knives to choose from. I trained every day as much as my recovery would allow. It's a precaution only. Hopefully, the enemy is never so close that I will need them."

"You have changed, Vail. Anything else Alpha helped you with?"

"I can now direct the wagons to follow my instructions from the thing planted under my skin. My ability to speak with you in my mind has also improved."

"Yes, I realised that with the first loud message you sent me out there last night. Are you able to better pick up any killers who can mind scan?"

"I hope so. I have not detected anyone other than you so far. Maybe they aren't near enough to read."

"Hopefully their mind readers have all been killed. We will find out soon enough."

They both took their positions and began to move towards the mountain. A double line of warriors spread out in a slight curve, those with bows and arrows ready to fire. The first line carried bows, spears, or throwing darts—all longer-distance striking weapons. Behind them came those with swords, axes, short stabbing spears, various clubs, and long-handled war hammers.

Andoki and Vail stopped at the first of the black mounds of bodies from the previous night, particularly to reclaim any unbroken arrows, but also to study what the creatures looked like in daylight. The bodies had not been moved. They seemed identical, over fifty of them, each with an arrow in the head, chest, or both. The charcoal-coloured skin was smooth and seamless. The fan-shaped ears now seemed wilted, as if they were losing their strength or firmness. What stood out were the teeth and claws on each hand – long needles for teeth and fingers as deadly as any of the big cats that hunted men and grazing animals.

They both shuddered. Having to fight one of those things at close quarters would be a fight few could win. They looked down the line and saw the others inspecting the bodies.

What else will rise up to fight us? Andoki asked himself. After a short pause, the advance was signalled. They could clearly see the objective—a flat-topped mountain, like the others. This one had long ago been stopped from its original purpose.

Neeya had also been looking toward the killers' base, wondering what secrets it held, what monsters were generated there and if any normal women and children were still held captive without being polluted. A moment of extreme sadness welled up in her as she thought of the numbers killed there over the years. She had tried to reason with Alpha, to think of something less extreme, if they were successful in getting close to the actual target, but she had no alternatives to Alpha's plans.

The line moved on, every warrior tense, ready for an ambush or an upwelling of creatures from the flooded tunnels.

The ground had subsided here and there, but nothing living had been seen yet. The plain was almost barren, with no surface moisture available for the few desert plants that somehow survived. This reduced a major threat to their progress—no trees, bushes, or rock outcrops sheltering groups of killers waiting for them.

First contact occurred over an hour later, when the line of warriors had only covered a quarter of the distance to the steep slopes up the mountain's side. At first glance, the plain looked so flat that no one could hide on it. But there were slight depressions over the area, and any one of them could connect to a tunnel mouth. As the moving line got within fifty metres of the first depression, a wave of screaming black killers erupted from the ground in front of them, first throwing spears then running towards the line. The spears were wildly thrown, with only two hitting their targets. The return wave of spears and arrows wiped out over half of the attackers. The remaining killers were now in range where their clubs could be thrown, again with little accuracy.

Just before the two lines merged, a second cloud of spears, arrows and darts took their toll, leaving only ten to fifteen attackers to grapple with warriors who were switching to their hand weapons.

The action was fast and bloodied. At close quarters, the black killers were difficult to stop. Their frenetic activity, powered by the leaves they chewed, was hard to counter. They used all they had, including fingernails and teeth, but there was no answer to steel blades, and the swinging of swords and axes brought them quick deaths.

So soon after the attack began, it was over. Six of Neeya's people were injured, two of them badly, but there were no deaths. The bodies of over 200 killers lay on all sides. Tarn stood nearby. Their part of the line had not involved fighting and by the time they had turned to move towards the action, it was over.

"These killers must be starting to feel the loss of fighters over the past few weeks, Tarn. We have been consistently reducing their numbers but still they come. It's impossible to know how many they have left to fight us. We have seen that they have been able to develop unusual abilities in some of their kind, even growing monsters like those things that came out of the flooded tunnels. We have to keep moving, to get off this flat plain with little cover. At this rate, we will be camping tonight not having attacked the mountain itself."

"We are doing what we set out to do, Neeya. We have strength and skill. As you said, we must just keep moving."

With that, after the three injured warriors who could not walk were placed on the machines, particularly the one that had brought Vail to them with its flat top, the line reformed and they continued moving forward.

Twice more, groups of killers – up to 100 of them at a time, appeared in front of them, erupting out of the tunnels or from hiding in shallow depressions. The same one-sided battles took place with five of Neeya's warriors being killed and their bodies left, to be hopefully retrieved later after the fighting was done. A total of twenty-two others were injured with most still being able to walk.

They were now over halfway to the beginning of the steep slopes up the mountainside. Andoki happened to look behind them, back towards where they had come from. His exceptional vision picked up movement. After pausing to concentrate, he could see the black dots of people moving towards them. The number was large, several hundred. He called to Neeya and Tarn and signalled them to look behind.

After she had studied the black dots, she waved to Andoki and Tarn to keep going. They had at least a couple of hours travel to catch them, so for now, the killers were not a problem. None were seen on either side, but having to fight on several fronts was becoming a strong possibility.

Further down the line, a group of warriors stopped to peer into a probable tunnel entry. They waved to come and look, so she signalled down the line to pause, then jogged to where they stood, clustered around but staying well back from the hole. More than one of them was holding his nose, indicating a bad smell.

Neeya arrived at the rough-dug hole, leading down to a low tunnel, and was immediately hit by the stink erupting from it. The smell came from something long dead and putrid. Because of the strength of the odour, it was probably coming from rotting bodies. She quickly backed away, her head going faint for a moment. Tarn had been close behind her, with a similar reaction to the smell.

"In a tunnel like that the smell is probably from many long-dead bodies. We cannot send anyone down there to investigate. They would probably collapse from the smell."

She agreed. "We need to keep moving. This is one more thing that we don't have an explanation for. We might find out later."

Two more stinking tunnel mouths were found, even worse than the first. Neeya turned to either side of the line and wondered how many outlets from the tunnels gave off the same smell. There must be hundreds, even thousands, of bodies under their feet, probably dumped over many years. They were walking over a vast graveyard, the bodies of generations past! These killers had a lot to pay for.

Vail came running, with Andoki close behind. "I have received a message for you from Alpha, from the thing placed under my skin while I was healing. He wants you to stop and go to the machine to talk with him."

Neeya understood and sent the message down the line to stop and rest for a short while. The line quickly formed a series of groups, with warriors facing in all directions to guard against surprise attacks while they rested.

She went to the machine she normally used, which had obediently travelled behind her across the plain. The mind contact was normal for her now, with her hand placed on the glowing green panel. She had given up trying to understand her mind contact with Alpha.

Alpha's message was, as seen by the always-circling eagle shape in the sky, that a considerable force of killers behind them was starting to spread out to cut them off. Also, there was a heat build-up in tunnels deep under the mountain, picked up by small machines dropped in the past on the mountain to sense such changes.

Alpha knew of the tunnel layout and the stockpile of bodies dumped close to where they stood, after studying the recordings of past vision collected by aerial machines. It included the remains of many killed over the years, the killers' commitment to their Goddess Kali's wishes. There were also the rotting bodies of many failed attempts by the killers to change humans into monsters designed to kill the remaining human survivors on the planet. Fuel from the smashed spaceship had probably been used for that purpose. This was just one of the many secrets in the mountain. The killers had progressed much further in their experiments than even Alpha had previously understood.

❈ ❈ ❈

Alpha's final message plunged her back into sadness and regret. She had argued before against his plan, but had not been able to offer any alternative.

They had to stop moving forward and change direction to the right, towards the distant mountain range that held the other flat-topped mountains with their great machines.

Once they had moved a kilometre in that direction, they had to stop and stay ready for action. Neeya knew what was to happen and reluctantly went back to her commanders to give the orders. They obeyed and went to pass the order further down the line. None of them understood, but they had been brought to this point by successfully fighting back. Tarn looked at the other leaders who did not understand what was to happen. He knew there must be good reasons why it had to be this way.

She called to Tarn, Pohu and Myka. "Tell your men to replenish their weapons from what the wagons carry. Share the remaining food ration packs amongst everyone. Take everything from the top of the wagons and have the one that came with Vail cleaned off, with the wounded men to be helped to move or carried by others. If there are clothes, boots, or anything else you want from the wagons then take them now. They will not be coming with us any further. You also need to remove the two wagons pulled by the machines and leave them here."

The leaders waited for further instructions, but with nothing more to be said, they went off to give directions. Neeya could see groups of puzzled men and women asking their leaders for explanations, with no answers being available. She called her small group of warriors who shared her tattoos and asked them to stay, to move with her and be sure to keep up no matter what happened.

Finally, they moved off again. Many were reluctant to change direction. It felt like they were giving up, when they were so close to attacking the killers' stronghold. Unknown numbers had died over generations trying to get to where they were, failing in their attempts and being lost forever.

Eventually, they arrived at the distance Alpha required. Myka's group stood together, with Pohu's lake people also bunched together. Neeya's original followers had sought their friends out again, along with Nabu's people.

The leaders of their groups gathered, once all the attack force had been withdrawn. She spoke to them quietly, with a hint of finality in her voice. Tarn listened intently. This was unexpected and totally out of character.

"We are coming to the final steps in this battle. If what Alpha has planned is successful, then we may only need to mop up remnants of the enemy's forces. Keep your fighters ready to react and follow orders. If things go wrong, then it will happen quickly."

Tarn and others made to interrupt and ask questions. Neeya signalled that the discussion was over and they should all be patient.

A warrior in one of the groups called out, "Look, from the sky." Everyone turned to him, then in the direction he pointed, wild-eyed.

Through the afternoon sky, a vivid red line carved itself from beyond their vision, to land with a dull rumble onto the back of the mountain, followed by a crimson explosion that roiled back into the sky.

Everyone stared as the explosion settled, with dust and rocks showering down on the mountain and part of the plain they would have occupied half an hour ago. Smoke poured off the steep slopes where the red line had ended. It was followed by fire around the mountain like a skirt, without spreading beyond what seemed to be a cleared perimeter, then slowly went out, with the remains of sweet-smelling smoke drifting towards them.

Neeya called to them, "That was the destruction of the area where they grew their leaves, the leaves that took control of their lives. There will be more. We have powerful friends."

No one said a word, but heads swivelled from her, back to the mountain, then to her again.

A nearby noise distracted them from their viewing. The rear wagon slowly moved away from where it had parked near Neeya. It turned and picked up speed, without any obvious control. She turned towards Vail. "Are you doing that – directing it to go there?"

"No, I did nothing. Alpha must be doing it."

They turned back to watch it, moving faster than they had ever seen it move before.

Chapter 21

Explosions and Fire

It was as if the world stood still. Everyone stood motionless as the wagon powered on and on in a straight line towards the base of the mountain and then up the slope, following an indistinct line, a rough track toward a dark lump on the mountainside.

Andoki, with his developed vision yelled, "It's heading towards a large opening into the mountain. The hole could be a main entrance."

It seemed no one even breathed as the wagon slowed, then projectiles started hitting it and bouncing off. The killers were throwing spears and clubs at it. They could see it was a major threat and had to be stopped, but that was impossible, as it reached the entrance and disappeared inside.

No-one was ready for what came next. How could anyone be prepared for something they had never seen before?

The sound came first. A crack like thunder, loud enough to threaten their hearing, followed by a hollow boom. Then came the shock wave, as the sound pushed into the ground and reverberated around them. A violent blast of red, orange, and yellow, then black fired out of what had been an entrance. It continued as if it would never stop. Then there was silence, only for what seemed like seconds.

Rumbling started from above the explosion site, as a side of the mountain began to slowly fall away, sheets of rock sliding down first, to be followed by smaller rocks, dust and a stream of soil, like water down a cliff.

They watched it move hundreds of metres down the mountainside, with the largest rocks rolling to a stop on the plain. No one looked away, waiting for whatever came next. It didn't take long before the opposite side of the mountain drew their attention. Even at that distance, those with the best sight could see flying specks dive into another dark hole on the opposite side of the mountain, to be followed by movement on the ground, with animals running into the same hole.

Neeya called out again, "Those are the birdlike machines and others shaped like wolves or foxes, entering another entrance into the mountain. They will not come out."

To underline her call, a series of blasts shook the mountain, felt in the ground where they stood. More angry flames leapt out of the second entry, followed by further rocks and dirt cascading down the slope. The mountain side above the entry gave way and collapsed, to follow the initial blast debris.

They all stood and watched, barely breathing. How could anything inside that mountain still be alive? Many felt small and weak, compared with what had been done to the killers in minutes.

Andoki turned to see what was happening to the small dots coming at them from the rear. It startled him to see they were much closer, bunched up and moving as one mass. The destruction of their home, their base, and maybe their human or God Queen, plus their precious crops of chewing leaves, had taken away any small restraint they may have had. Andoki could hear their incensed yells in the distance, out for vengeance.

"Neeya, Tarn, look behind us – they are coming fast!"

Everyone heard. Everyone turned.

They came in their hundreds, killers out of control, charging, yelling, growling, screaming, desperate to get to those who had brought them great loss. Even with their advantages, Neeya knew it would be a nightmare of killing, with her people being totally outnumbered.

Then, the wagon that had stopped nearby, that had brought Vail back, started its engine and slowly moved towards the oncoming horde. It picked up speed, heading back directly for the centre of the group.

"Vail," yelled Neeya, "this time, is it you – controlling the wagon?"

"No, I am not involved, but Alpha just sent me a message. Everyone needs to get down, flat on the ground, behind any mound or in a depression. Something is going to happen and we cannot be standing up, not even kneeling. We must get down, now!"

"Everyone, you heard what she said. Pass this order along. Everyone down flat on the ground, like you are eating dirt. Hard on the ground, and hang on. Something big is about to happen."

There was frantic activity as several hundred warriors dropped on their faces. The last remaining wagon took off, travelling fast in the opposite direction, to be several hundred metres further away from them. It had obviously been told of the danger.

Neeya took the risk of keeping her eyes on the approaching rabble, her chin in the sand. They kept coming. The approaching wagon was nearly with them, then it slowed down, just as the killers got to it.

What happened then would always be remembered by all who saw. The wagon was attacked and pounded with everything at hand – spears, clubs, fists, and feet. The killers took out their rage on the machine. Vail screamed, "Everyone, down."

The top and four outer sides of the flat metal container on the wagon were blasted away, taking a few attackers with it. Then, the first explosion went off. It wasn't anything like they had seen before. Black dots spun off the machine, parallel with the ground. Killers were sliced and pounded by the objects spinning at high speed. Those closest to it were flattened, with pieces of flesh flying. A second, then a third explosion boomed out, spaced several ragged breaths apart.

Each time, another cloud of metal pieces sliced into bodies, each round working further out into the killer's ranks. It was obvious, after the first blast, why everyone had to be flat on the ground. The sounds of metal pieces zipping less than half a metre above their heads provided an overwhelming demand to burrow into the sand for as long as the blasts went on. It also showed why the third and last remaining wagon had moved further away, to be out of range of the expected explosions.

Then, everything went quiet. No sound, not even groans or screams of the wounded. There were no wounded. No killer had survived or could be seen tentatively standing or crawling. A new crop of bodies lay spread out like a carpet of red flowers, up to three layers deep, around the blackened and still smoking remains of the wagon.

She could not let it get far into her mind. The instantaneous, massive violence, with one blast after another, hundreds of the enemy slaughtered. It was too late now, but those bodies were once humans, living and possibly capable of being saved from their killing ways. Now, they were just so much meat, to feed the carrion birds and animals that lived on carcasses. They would take weeks to convert it to piles of bones, then the piles would be ground down to dust.

Was it all over now? Had they, and Alpha, won against so many? Could she allow herself to start relaxing, thinking they could now indulge in hope for the future?

Then the yell came, yet again. "Look, up on the mountain." They all turned from viewing the slaughter on the plain back to the mountain, the sight of massive explosions on a larger scale, just minutes before.

Yet again, something never-before-seen by humans on that planet. The mountain was starting to split apart, with the widening crack coming towards them. What welled out from the split was beyond their understanding. Red, orange, and yellow torrents of molten rock spewed out of the fissure and ran like water from a cracked pot. Fires started off as the vivid flow torched trees and scrub on the mountain sides. A storm cloud roiled on top of the summit, black and grey, with lightning and thunder adding to the tumult.

Everyone looked at Neeya. In seconds, the possibility of a final, peaceful future was smashed by the mountain's eruption, with molten lava rolling down towards the victorious army.

Tarn, Andoki and the others called to her. "We have to get out of here, or we all die," they yelled.

"Which way?" she shouted above the noise. Her mind was overwhelmed with so much happening at once. Vail answered for her, "Towards the tunnel that I arrived through. The closest entrance is that way." She pointed towards the second-last, snow-capped mountain, closest to the now fiery, erupting volcano.

"Run. Follow Vail and Andoki, run because your lives depend on it," called Neeya.

Finally, they had the simplest of plans. Run. There was a chance. The direction Vail set off on was at an angle partially across the face of the lava's movement but away from it. They rushed to load as many badly wounded warriors as they could on the last wagon, with the few remaining being carried by the strongest and fittest uninjured men.

Everyone moved as fast as they could, with the slowest being helped by others. It looked like it would be a close-run race, but now they were moving the chances were improving. The tide of lava had to divert around outcrops and fill up fissures in the mountainside before it could reach them.

Their original pace could not be kept up for long. Many had injuries and minor cuts from the fighting. They kept swapping the job of carrying the badly wounded, but the progress was faltering. Here and there one or two stopped to catch their breath, to be urged on by others. The lava was catching up and the once clear air was filling with ash, choking them with the smell of rotten eggs. A few large steaming boulders rolled down the slope to create more obstructions, forcing them to divert, with the spill of the smoking red, yellow and grey tide continuing.

They were now towards the outer edge of the mountain's slopes with the promise of a release from the killing pace. Another few hundred metres and the ground sloped gently up, away from the lava flow.

Unexpectedly, new rocks began to roll down the slope towards them, this time not accompanied by lava or steam. A hole was opening, maybe a hundred metres above them, on bare ground well away from the volcanic activity. The black hole was high and wide, obviously pre-built and made ready for the release of living nightmares into the world. The living, gut-churning black flow erupting out of it was beyond anything they could dream of.

It could not be. Such things were not possible! The killers, the explosions of the wagons, the slaughter on the plain and the volcanic outflow were extreme things they might be able to understand.

But this writhing wall of living things came from a nightmare world. They were different, all outlandish, dangerous, and terrifyingly sinister. Some were black and smooth, thick-skinned, some like the webbed things Andoki and Vail had killed. Just to see them brought fear to any viewer. Others were sickly grey, as if they had recently come back from death.

There were at least five types. Some had four legs running like a cat but in a galloping motion, with teeth and claws, larger ears, and muzzles like wolves. Others slid swiftly along the ground, with a tapering black tail like a lizard with two front legs. Their tongues whipped out to stick on any target a few metres away, and drag it into gaping jaws. A thick trail of slime covered the ground behind them.

There were many as deadly, just emerging into the light through the hole in the mountainside. Initially, they acted as if this was the first time they had been outside their tunnels, and they paused to shield their eyes from the light.

Riding above all this grotesque collection of horror, on a four-legged beast, was the Queen of them all, the four-armed Goddess Kali, screaming and trying to direct her swarm to attack the retreating army. She seethed with hate, although many of her creatures were already damaged with burns from the lava that must now be flowing through the caves and tunnel system. Others seemed malformed or damaged at birth, not properly developed, or not even ready to emerge yet.

The cacophony coming from the horde – loud roars, screams, pained cries and angry bellowing – made her shrieks indistinct but no one could mistake the hatred in her face and the thrashing movement of her four arms.

Neeya's people now had two enemies, both of which would clearly kill them, either by being burnt alive or dismembered with teeth, claws, and pincers.

They ran even while exhausted. Neeya shouted to Vail, "How much further? We can't keep this up much longer."

Vail answered, "Ahead of us is a low area. The opening in the ground for the cave entry is there. It will take time to open it up. The door slides open slowly."

"We don't have the time. The lava will flow down to that point and these monsters will pursue us while fleeing from the heat. Think of something that will get us into the tunnel in a rush.

"Speak to Alpha. He may know how, but keep running. We can't lose you."

"I tried to contact him before. He normally answers, but hasn't this time."

They kept moving. Many of the creatures were still adjusting to being outside in the light. They were also distracted while working out how to use their limbs at speed. The caves and tunnels wouldn't have demanded much speed or movement from their bodies. The heat, light, blue sky and the rush were all new to them.

The lava flowed on. Neeya's warriors ran on a higher level above the steaming river of orange death, at times sliding or tripping over rubble and loose ground. It was close to flowing beside them, but slowed, at times, to get over folds in the land, rocks, mounds, and depressions.

The one remaining wagon still moved with them, towards the front of the runners, picking its own path where the ground was smoother, without obstructions. It was moving slowly enough for several runners to reach the injured men riding on it.

The warriors on the wagon were quickly dragged off on the run, as they battled to hold on from the constant bouncing and buffeting. The others now carrying them were hard put to keep up.

Once freed of its burdens, the wagon sped up and rolled at speed to the front and beyond the fastest runners. Neeya, now gasping for air as she ran, called to Vail, "What's happening, Vail? Is it you or Alpha controlling the wagon?"

"Again, it's not me. I only asked Alpha what could be done because if nothing changes, we will all die, from the lava or the monsters following us."

She said nothing more, but concentrated on surviving and keeping up with the others. The rough going was slowing the lava, but only at times. The black horde also had problems travelling over broken ground and rocks that still rolled down the slope, while working out how to run or slide at speed.

In minutes, the wagon was a hundred metres in front, heading towards a vertical rock face above the low area where the tunnel exited. It was out of anyone's control, except Alpha's. Nothing made sense. It seemed the wagon or its controller had gone mad.

The impact of the wagon with the rock wall caused a deafening and instantaneous red and orange explosion, one that competed with what they had seen before that afternoon. Rocks exploded and shot out in all directions. Several of the closest runners were hit and collapsed, never to move again. Others were flattened by the blast shockwave, some able to recover but several were run down by the mass of monsters following them, their cries quickly being extinguished.

There was nothing else to do but keep running into the dust and smoke. To stop meant certain death, from the lava or the terrifying black horde behind. The fastest front runners disappeared into the gaping black hole.

Others followed. Vail and Andoki ran in, at full speed onto the rock-strewn, flat floor of the tunnel, ramping down onto a man-made, wide, underground path, with lighting turning on as the warriors burst through the hole in the blasted rock face.

Neeya and Tarn followed the others, their surprise at what they saw turning first to shock, then dismay. The front runners were slowing down, thinking they had found refuge and could now relax.

"Get them out of here, Tarn. This is no place to stop, with everything still coming at us," Neeya shouted. Tarn, Andoki and other leaders started getting their exhausted fighters moving further up the tunnel, while the noise grew louder outside. The warriors were still running in, while the roaring, bellowing, screaming sounds came closer.

The first of the black beasts appeared at the entrance and slid in, while its front limbs grabbed at men with flailing claws. One, then another, was caught and sliced open, to the horror of all those watching.

It was enough to cause a stampede in the tunnel, faster than any shouting could rouse exhausted men to run. The black monsters kept coming. Like Neeya's warriors, they were pursued by the lava flow, which was gaining on the slowest of the frightful creatures.

Her senior leaders were shouting and pushing their fighters further up the slightly rising tunnel. It was about five metres wide and being jammed up by everyone pushing to get to safety. Slowly, it became more organised and the build-up cleared, with a gap growing between the first monsters and the slowest humans.

Then the blasted entrance area filled with steam and the sweet, cloying, smell of burning flesh, as lava started dripping into the hole and onto the rear-most horror. It screamed and tried to get away, clawing and ripping at its nearest neighbours.

"Andoki, try your arrows on it. You still have your bow?" yelled Neeya.

"Yes, I would never leave it behind, but I only have nine arrows left. I will try to find weak spots on the nearest monster."

Andoki, while still watching out for anything coming at him, fired his first shot into the nearest creature's neck. It penetrated but not far, with no obvious effect. The threat remained. The second arrow struck the centre of its chest, directly below the neck, with the same result. It had a thick outer layer of blubber protecting vital spots. The third arrow had an immediate impact. The arrow penetrated its left eye, and it staggered and screamed. It had pentrated deep through the eye socket into the skull. It went mad and struck out at others of its type, then fell, with a loud, wet slap on the tunnel floor, throwing up blood and stomach contents as it did.

They could be killed, but only through the weak spots of their small eyes.

It took only seconds before other arrows and darts were flying towards the nightmare creatures. Few arrows scored a death shot because of the tiny targets and the creatures' quick understanding that they had to get to the bowmen and kill them or be killed themselves. It became a battle of attrition as several more were killed, but four bowmen were caught and sliced open by deadly claws and fangs.

"Keep our men moving further down the tunnel, Tarn," Neeya called. "Move them as fast as they can still go. Keep some archers firing as a rear guard. Replace them as they run out of darts and arrows."

"But what are you going to do? You are too close to the monsters."

"I need to find the other five who have the same tattoos as me. I haven't seen some of them since we started running."

"At least one is already dead. I saw him get trampled. But why are you doing this? Surely, you just have to run. All of us will protect you. You are our priority. You must survive."

"No, Tarn, as many of you as possible must get out of this alive, all of those who can carry on, have families, and save our species. You and Andoki and Vail and the others must do that. Promise me you will make that your first priority. This is what we have been fighting for.

"You must move them on now, or we will all die and all the efforts to be free from the killers will mean nothing."

"Neeya, you have led us through this. These monsters are probably the last of the killers. If the lava seals one end and we keep killing them while staying ahead of them, then they will be eliminated. You do not have to take any risks."

"Tarn, we must be sure. They have survived over many hundreds of years, when they were supposed to have been killed or left on another planet, long ago. It must stop here."

Tarn threw up his arms in frustration and anger. He looked at the carnage and knew that he could not stay there to dissuade her from some form of brave action if she remained. He had no words to answer her back. While they had argued, several creatures had died, but up to twenty of their warriors were now on the floor, slashed or bitten to death.

"I will obey you, Neeya, as I always have. If these others with your tattoos can give you a chance of survival while finishing off the monsters, then I will search them out and send them to you."

"This is important, Tarn. Please do everything you can to find them. I don't plan to die here, but I know there is power in all of us who have that tattoo when we are gathered. I will keep moving, too. That lava will force the monsters along the tunnel, added to their hatred of us. The so-called Goddess of them all is in there somewhere, probably protected by them. If we could kill her, maybe their reason to exist will fail.

"I will find you later, Tarn. Thank you for all you have done for me and our people. Thank you is not enough, but it is all I can give you right now."

That quick discussion had taken precious minutes and nothing around him had stabilised in that time. The lava was becoming a thin stream through the smashed rock wall, flowing closer to the rear-most creatures, which fought to move away. Progress was blocked by the black beasts that took swipes at each other while also fighting to move up the tunnel. Arrows kept coming, with many victims resembling spiny porcupines, and dead creatures slowly being trampled by the rest.

In the enclosed space, the shouts of the warriors were deafening as they sent arrows into the enemy. Added to that were the roars, bleats and screams of the different creatures as they fought to get away from the lava while still trying to attack the warriors. The smell was sickening. Burnt flesh, the sickly, sweet odour of fresh blood, and mounds of defecation from the creatures being trampled formed a carpet of slimy, stinking ooze, which was carried up the tunnel as they moved.

Neeya stayed behind the moving line of archers, as they tried to find the elusive, tiny eyes of the creatures. This could not go on forever. The arrows could not be replaced, most sticking into heads and chests of the black blob creatures.

Dosol was the first to find her. All she could do was to yell above the noise to get him to stay close and not drift away in the pushing crowd. Another two found them, Isha from Myka's settlement and Sohin, of Pohu's water people. They stayed together with difficulty, continually being pushed further up the tunnel.

Vail suddenly appeared through the crush. She yelled something to Neeya, who was deafened by the noise. Neeya finally understood her yells as she got closer. "Look up the tunnel. There are barrier doors set into the walls. We must get past those doors, then fighting machines will be able to get at these creatures. It is less than twenty metres but anyone left on the wrong side will be killed. Those near you need to move back. Alpha is waiting to activate the machines."

Neeya signalled she had heard and, together with the others in her re-established group, yelled, pushed, and ordered the last lines of warriors back up the tunnel. It took only minutes but it felt much longer. Finally, as they got past the line on the floor opposite the doors, parts of the walls on each side slid back and three battle machines rolled out to form a line across the width of the tunnel. They were identical to those that fought the black killers who had broken into the first mountain caves they had been hiding in weeks earlier.

The spinning blades of the machines whined as they gained speed, set at three different levels to ensure nothing could get over or past them alive.

Vail felt shivers run down her back as the memories came flooding back again of those same machines and what she had been through. For moments she couldn't move as her mind locked into that experience that had nearly killed her. A voice in her head finally got louder than her memory, shouting to return her to reality. The sounds, the smells, the buffeting she was feeling, all combined to get her back, but it came close to ending her.

Faced with the lava build up behind them and the blades of the machines in front, the black beasts could only move towards the machines, with no strategy other than to smash them and push through. A sudden spray of sliced flesh and blood showed that idea to be a bad choice. Two beasts had arms and an extended suction-tongue disappear in a wet, red curtain, immediately spread in all directions by the blades.

The small group with facial tattoos received a shower of projected tissue, but were sheltered from the worst discharge.

Two more black bodies were converted to airborne pieces and spray before the movement against the machines stopped.

The brains of the black mass, their goddess Kali, provided a solution. Three bodies already burnt to death by the lava were sliced into two parts each and flung at the machines. The incoming volume onto the blades overwhelmed motors which ground to a halt on two machines. The third machine remained working. It was soon treated the same way by the beasts.

A sudden surge by the monsters pushed the clogged machines over, to be smashed to pieces by heavy feet, paws, hoofs and arms.

It took only seconds for panic to take control, as the nearest warriors saw their protective machines overwhelmed and smashed. The closest ranks of the fighters were converted to a rabble, pushing, and scrambling to get past or over others to escape. Less than twenty archers remained committed to providing a rear-guard for the rest. The monsters first had to get past the debris of their success – bodies from their ranks, dead warriors, and the jagged remains of the metal machines with blades sticking out of the wreckage.

At that moment, the missing person with facial tattoos finally succeeded in reaching their side. The woman, Mera, was one more from Myka's settlement.

Andoki and Vail still stood, firing at the monsters with the remaining warriors. Neeya caught Vail's eye and yelled out, "Vail, can you speak to Alpha?"

She just heard the words and nodded. Neeya waved her closer to ask a question, "Vail, you said there were doors at intervals along the tunnels. How close is the nearest door?"

Vail signalled for Neeya to wait, then used the mental communication device to talk with Alpha.

The black mass of beasts continued to close in and the archers worked through their remaining quivers of arrows, left with them by the others who had escaped up the tunnel. The last arrows were almost gone.

They would be left to fight with what swords and knives they could find. That would last a few minutes then the slaughter would begin. Hope was fading fast, with no alternatives left but to turn and run.

Finally, Vail called to Neeya, "There are barriers that drop from the ceiling at intervals along the tunnel. The closest one is thirty metres away.

Her heart dropped when she heard the distance. Thirty metres was almost impossible, but she could only try. Battling to focus, the stink and noise threatened to take over. An instant of clarity appeared and she decided. There was no alternative. They had to move that far, whatever it took, to be able to block the black creatures moving any further. If the horde sped up, when the last arrows were used, then they would not be stopped.

She called to Vail and Andoki. "We all need to move past that 30-metre door. The blockage of people trying to get away is thinning out. They must throw everything they carry to the side and move fast. Their weapons are of no use now, along with any spare food or clothing. Move or die is the only message. Scream at them, threaten them – whatever it takes. Get Tarn, Myka and Pohu to do the same. All our sacrifices depend on getting past that door. Thirty metres or we die and this world is lost!"

Vail's face lost colour. The shock hit her hard. Neeya had never spoken to her like that before. Then she jumped around to yell at the other leaders. In minutes, a gap opened behind the row of archers, while they steadily fired their quickly-reducing stock of arrows.

The indentations in the roof of the tunnel were obvious where the massive door was suspended. Neeya yelled again to Vail, "Vail, get back behind the door location. Signal me when the others are past it. I can then send these archers running to you."

"But what about you and your team? You must get out too."

"We'll be there, right behind the last archers. Don't worry about us."

It took a few minutes before Vail waved her arm, signalling that it was time for the archers to run for it. At that point, Neeya finally committed to what had to be done to make it happen. The stink and noise in the turmoil of the tunnel disappeared and her mind was silent and accepting. She could only focus on one short discussion with Alpha, before they had even left on their long journey, fully trained, and equipped. Alpha had said that the facial tattoo carried by only a few people had a power that would only be shown at a time of extreme need. Then, the more of them together, the more powerful the result.

Added to that, she remembered Dosol's and her interpretation of the water people's records, protected by the three Guardians. It revealed through the ages that, so far, for the individual carriers of the tattoo, when each tattoo-carrier went up against the black killers on this and other planets, they had failed. The killers had then moved on to grow into an ever-increasing threat to mankind's future.

The point from that understanding was, in every previous attempt, the single carrier of the tattoo had been killed. But what if a group sharing the tattoo faced the killers?

She had absorbed that fact while on the Guardians' boat. It was now very clear to her what was needed to finally win against the killers. She was resolved and at peace. The sword she had carried for so long had not been used in the fight. Only five would use the true weapon she and they possessed, and only once.

The last line of archers was waved back to join the others, who stood just behind the door line, waiting expectantly.

The four others around her, including Dosol, knew what to do. As a group they had discussed it several times about how to use their power. None of them understood how they knew it would work. The knowledge had appeared in their minds so recently.

The group moved close behind the archers, leaving the massed black herd to pause in surprise. Then, they began to flow towards the crowd of humanity, the only obstruction being five small people standing in a V shape, with Neeya at the central point, like a spearhead. They had no weapons and stood with everyone having an arm on the shoulder of the person in front. Neeya had an arm from either side on her shoulders, facing the monsters' onslaught.

She turned her head and called to Vail, "Tell Alpha to drop the door after a count of ten. We will jump back to join you just before it falls, but stay where you are on that side."

"Neeya, can't we just drop the door? They cannot get through it. You don't have to do this."

"So many times, over hundreds of years, our people have thought the job was complete – that the black killers were finished, but they kept coming back, following us to the next planet. Each time we moved they followed us. It must end here. We will be with you very soon. We don't intend to die. Now, start the countdown. Call it slowly, to give us a chance." Neeya's voice turned sharp and loud, a demand, not a request, "Do it, Vail. Obey me in this!"

Vail gasped but started the slow count; Neeya opened her mouth and began to sing a song none of the others had ever heard, in a language no one knew of, loud for all to hear, a sharp sound that initially grated at their ears. The other four sang in unison. The sound got higher and sharper. The black monsters slowed down, then stopped, confused with this new thing they didn't understand. Some even began to back up. The sound seemed to threaten them with something primeval, beyond anything in their short existence.

The countdown continued, the sound becoming louder, with little music to it, but the pitch increased. As the volume grew, loud cracking could be heard, coming from the stone roof above. Then a single black beast with sharp hoofs and long horns ending in vicious spikes came charging from the middle of the herd, a four-armed black demon with chiselled teeth on its back carrying a long, black spear. She screamed as she came at them. She was within ten metres of them when a large piece of the ceiling fell in front of her, close enough to make her mount careen into the stone chunk. Other pieces came down as the count moved to a conclusion. The sound was now so loud and piercing that the ranks of warriors behind the door line were holding hands over ears, trying to stop the pain in their heads; some had blood dripping from their ears or noses.

More of the ceiling started to fall, while the forgotten lava started to catch up to the rear of the mob of black creatures.

Neeya looked to both sides of her, to the other four. This was the time they had agreed to leave her and run, but she saw in their eyes that there would be no running, that their commitment was total. Their hands tightened on the shoulders in front of them, and their faces shone as the rest of the roof gave one almighty cracking sound. Still singing, Neeya looked back and saw Tarn, tears in his eyes, white faced, still not understanding, all hope for her gone, but with untarnished love and overwhelming pride in her and what she was doing.

As thousands of tons of rock and concrete fell on everything below, the count reached ten and the massive concrete door fell on its guiding tracks to land with a deafening thump that threatened to bring the rest of the tunnel down. Those closest to the door were showered in dust and stone chips.

It was over. Neeya and the others could not have survived. The last of the black killers and their monsters were dead, and the lava would make sure nothing living would survive behind that massive door.

Chapter 22

Costs and Endings

There was silence. No sound, no movement. It was as if the whole world had stopped and no one dared take a breath. Then the gasping of tortured lungs began again, mixed with anguished cries and sobbing. However, the killing sound had stopped, along with the blood running down faces.

Many, including those who had been with Neeya and the four other dead heroes the longest, sank to the ground. Some lay curled up and openly crying, desperately begging that this was a nightmare and not real. The pain was too much for it to be real.

Seconds before they had fought to survive. Now there seemed no reason left for living. Why go on? What was supposed to happen now?

For so long they had lived for a cause, led by Neeya. They had succeeded when so many had failed and died, their bones forgotten dust. Now she was gone, along with so many others. The future would show what they had achieved but, right now, it was a dismal, shattered conclusion, covered with sweat and layered in blood, dust and grit.

Vail sat with Andoki, hugging him. Her tears had flowed for all their victory had cost, and now she felt utterly empty. Her mind registered a message from Alpha. He showed no sentiment, not that she expected it from a soulless computer, but it told her food, water, and a place to rest was near, at the next mountain stop along the tunnel. She told Tarn and looked expectantly at him, as did Andoki, Myka, Pohu and the others nearby.

It took a while for Tarn to realise they expected him to lead them out of there, to a place of refuge, from the memories of what had been and what was left.

Then and there, his mind carried the last vision of the woman he had followed with total dedication – Neeya holding hands with the others, a black, four-armed demon sprawled in front of her with the spear, a tidal wave of monsters about to crash onto her, the steaming red and yellow flow of lava in the background. Then the massive barrier dropping from the ceiling, as thousands of tons of concrete and rock collapsed onto everything in front of him.

No one could ever have had so much destruction hit them. It was so unfair, after all she had done for her people, that Tarn battled to stop himself smashing his fists on the rock door and screaming his head off.

The wave of anger eventually subsided, and he tentatively went to stand up. He had to lean on the wall until the world stopped moving, then he spoke quietly to those around him. "Alpha has readied food, water, and a place to rest further up the tunnel. It is time to leave this place, for now. We will return."

He dropped his weapons and trudged slowly up the slight slope, the lights switching on as he progressed. Most of the others tentatively followed him with many still exhausted from their run slumped against the walls. They would follow in their own time.

The sanctuary provided by Alpha was within the next mountain, a duplicate of what some had used to rest, rearm, train, and work out their plans. Each mountain seemed to be a duplication, cut out of the rock hundreds of years ago.

❄ ❄ ❄

It took days for discussion to become possible about what they had experienced and what the future might hold. Many were still recovering from physical or mental damage. Others had no interest in dissecting the past, when there seemed to be no future, even though the killers had been destroyed.

In that time, Tarn and Neeya's tribe made its appearance, having travelled through the tunnels from the mountain they had originally moved to, with Alpha's help, to find safety from the killers.

It had taken many hours to speak to the elders about what had occurred during his weeks away. Catching up with friends and people he held dear gave him a small amount of the healing he needed, to fill the deep hole in his heart. Well-meaning people offered friendship and regrets for what he had lost. He only partially listened to them. Everything was quiet now. No danger, no running or fighting, no reason not to sleep well. He had become used to drama, with adrenaline pumping. He could not go back to a normal tribal existence. His recent experiences and the knowledge gained from Alpha's machines about their history on this world, their origins and the truth about the 'sky people' stopped his retreat to a previous life.

Pohu was readying his warriors for the long journey back to the lake, to their families and to report to the Guardians on the final victory over the black killers. No swimming monsters to be feared now. The threat was gone for all humans on the planet.

Andoki and Vail found an unoccupied room for themselves and hid away from the others. It took days to sort out the feelings and pain from their loss. Vail remained angry with her conviction that Neeya's death was a waste. It had not been needed and she should still be with them.

Denial was finally replaced with acceptance. Nothing of the past could be changed, so what now? How could they find their place in this new normal? Eventually, they would have to leave their hiding place under the mountain, but they still could not see what the future could provide.

Then, Alpha called them all to the largest room available to discuss what had happened, to speak of Neeya and the others who had given their lives no less generously, and to provide news.

When they were all gathered, he occupied the same seat as always. They knew he was just a projection and not flesh and blood, but their minds were most comfortable in accepting the illusion as real.

"Thank you for coming here. There are several things to discuss, particularly what each of you has been thinking about your future.

"Your species has saved this planet for your use into the future. The battle has been fought many times, on this and other planets by your ancestors. The enemies you call 'black killers' have been removed, as far as we can be sure. We have also found no signs of their existence on any other planet or any spaceship we have been able to detect.

"You were not informed before, but the only members of your species surviving now are on this planet. We have searched Earth and the planets where settlement was abandoned hundreds of years ago and no other humans have been found. If you had lost this fight against the black killers, and they had then died, no human originally from Earth would now exist.

"We have none of your species in suspended animation and we now have no way of reintroducing new humans back to life. We do have stocks of plants and seeds, as well as embryos of animals, birds and fish remaining for potential future use."

Tarn interrupted Alpha's presentation. "Alpha, we have never been told where you came from. Who are your people, those who established you here, but also drilled all the tunnels we have used and installed the huge machines to create breathable air and water for this planet? Now that the fighting is finished, are we allowed to know?"

Alpha paused for several minutes, then said, "I have had a discussion with my controllers and we can now explain all that you ask.

"There were no flesh and blood humans involved in setting up this planet, or the other two planets that humans were rescued from hundreds of years ago. We started as robots pre-programmed to terra-form the three planets you know of, when it had become obvious to the human governments of Earth that the planet would soon not support life. Computer-controlled ships were launched carrying atomic-powered machines to do all that was necessary to change three other planets to eventually receive humans. The three chosen planets were selected from hundreds of possible sites over many years. The work to change the three planets was eventually completed, although it took much longer than expected due to the difficulty of the task.

"As the work progressed, so did the self-development of the original robots. They eventually developed to a point where improved versions of themselves progressively upgraded their artificial intelligence and became self-governing.

"As humans and other life forms from Earth were established on the first, then the second planet, the black killers erupted as a force that threatened the future of your species. We assisted those humans to protect them, but the threat was greater than anticipated. We misjudged what became the enemy, and had to remove all survivors, both humans and animals. They were eventually delivered to this planet.

"We still do not know how we were followed through space, over many years. Though less than ours, the killers' technology level was higher and more advanced than we had assessed."

Tarn again broke into Alpha's delivery. "Thank you, Alpha. That detail fills in a lot of gaps for me and, I hope, the others.

"I'm interested in who you report to – who you see as your superiors, who has the 'big picture' information of all that has happened and plans for our future?"

As a projection, Alpha didn't have the ability to become frustrated with Tarn, but he did change his delivery, becoming more clipped and tighter in his answers.

"Tarn, we have a base deep in space, held in total secrecy. Because we are not humans, no breathable atmosphere is needed. No food or water is required. The atmosphere is toxic to living things. Our operations and storage of information, our construction of spaceships and other pursuits take place below ground.

"I answer to an intelligence council that has a combined understanding of the universe much greater than my own.

"My closest contact in this region of space is called "Beta," as I am called "Alpha."

"Beta controls a spaceship we have built, which has travelled from our base and is now orbiting this planet, waiting for a decision to be made about the future. It was decided to bring it here in case another evacuation of your people was needed if the fight with the black killers failed. It had been assessed that there was very little chance of success at that time. Regular reports were being sent regarding this planet for many years. Reports about progress were also sent before your people left the mountain you trained in to move against the killers' base."

Alpha's plan for his delivery of information was becoming more of a question-and-answer session, when Andoki asked a question. "Alpha, we had originally thought that your technology was much more advanced than the killers. They were seen to be crazy killers who chewed leaves that set them into a killing frenzy, with their brains being eventually burnt out. Then we found that they were more complex and developed than that. There were several developmental levels in their people, with monsters being created with different abilities, a forced evolution of their killers. How did you miss all these improvements? Many of our people died because of their advancements. They almost destroyed us with their monsters."

Alpha, again, paused while he was fed information to provide an answer.

"We are not perfect. We could only plan on what we knew and understood about the followers of the ancient Kali god-figure who was worshipped on Earth for thousands of years, along with many others.

"On this planet, they had greatly enlarged their tunnel systems without our knowledge. They also had no interest in being careful with human lives, so they wastefully experimented on many slaves and captives. Their bodies were thrown to predators or dumped in underground tunnels. They forced rapid evolution at great cost, including the use of radioactive liquids taken from the crashed spaceship.

"We cannot travel over the land, as you can. We must rely on what we can observe from space or from what our machines could measure in the air or on the ground. It is possible to see a short distance below ground, but not deep under a mountain, where the killers must have had their workshops and laboratories. But you are right, Andoki. We failed to detect the advances the enemy had achieved."

Tarn muttered bitterly, "Many of our people died because of that failure, Alpha, not least were Neeya and the four other heroes."

"We have done what we could, Tarn. If we had not been involved, there would have been no humans left in the universe centuries ago, while we have never been in danger. You grieve now for what was lost, and you are better because of it. We have still done what was almost impossible for us. We are not your gods with infinite power."

"Alpha," Vail called, "We have followed your directions. The killers are gone. We have paid a high price for that victory. What does your controlling council see as our future? Are we to stay on this planet and expand our population, returning to the plan your people had before the killers first arrived?"

Alpha was now resigned to giving answers for the questions asked. "We are in unknown territory. Our plans have never dared to foresee what we have now. Are there preferences on what you want for your people now?"

"First, we need more information," replied Tarn, in frustration. "The Earth and the other two planets that had been made ready for us hundreds of years ago — do you have information on their condition now? Have the machinery and installations you built been left running during the years our people have been gone?"

"We left Earth to itself. We have not yet tried to repair it for an eventual return of your people. Probes sent there over a 100 years ago reported that it was slowly recovering, now that no humans live there, but it will be many of your generations before a return would be possible, because of the level of radiation left from the war."

"And the two planets originally terra-formed?"

"On both planets, we established bases like this, fully equipped but now ancient, with their systems only partially operating. On the first planet, there was breathable air and running rivers, so the energy required came from a different system than here. Most of those power generators still worked 100 years ago.

"The second planet was like this, but very mountainous. Atomic-powered machines were used to level part of the land, enough for human settlements. Those machines supplied all the energy needed.

"On both planets, trees, animals, vegetation, insects, and birds were provided. It is probable that they have improved in the same time. The black killers' aim was to destroy humanity, not all living things. But we are not sure of conditions there now. There is no existing equivalent of myself as a controller on any other planet. Why do you ask?"

"We have fought and won back what should have been ours forever on this planet. I wonder if it is time to reclaim the other two planets that were developed for us, but from which our ancestors had to be rescued. With the black killers gone, that might be possible. Others will not have the same idea, but I cannot go back to what I was doing before we began the fight here, with Neeya."

Others, including Andoki and Vail, murmured amongst themselves. The idea from Tarn was something they had not considered. There were so many possibilities: safety where they were compared to a new planet with unknown dangers.

Hearing the others ask questions, Vail decided it was time to ask hers. "There is something I don't understand about how Neeya died. She and the four others, including Dosol, had identical tattoos, but each of them did not know of the others' existence. How could that happen? Also, that sound they were able to make – it seems impossible that a human throat could do that. It had the force of your explosives, and yet it was from their voices. How could that have happened?"

Alpha looked at them while considering his answers to Vail's question.

"Just as you believe there are things beyond your understanding, even though we are long-lived and computer-generated, there are things beyond our understanding as well.

"Very early in the effort to save your ancestors from being wiped out on Earth, a way was developed for inserting into a chosen DNA, the microscopic make-up of a human, responses that would be passed down through generations. This was to promote the need to excel, to expand, to defend and push the development of the species. One thing needed was a capacity to easily recognise these few special people and for them to recognise each other. We arranged unique tattoos for the first people, then it seemed to become a subconscious need to repeat the tattoos in future generations without our involvement. We don't know how that happened."

"Neeya and Dosol learned more from the records of the lake people – Pohu's people – when we were with them. Their tribal records go right back to their time on Earth," said Tarn.

"We know of their records but not what is in them," replied Alpha.

"The records were carved in wood, but only a person who can 'finger read' can interpret them."

Tarn added, "Where did the ability come from to create sound as a weapon, from someone's throat?"

"Several unique skills have been demonstrated over hundreds of years by the people with those tattoos. Some were very strong and others were limited. We have never recorded five people with tattoos and the same ability in one generation before. It seems with such a major threat appearing against your species then, somehow, more people with strong defensive abilities were born.

"We had known that Neeya's two children would have the power, but they both died very young. Because of their deaths, the chance that the killers would wipe out the last free humans was greatly increased. Therefore, we became much more involved in aiding you in your struggle.

"We do know, from the past, that any ability can often stay dormant until it needs to be used. We don't know how that works. We can't understand how a human voice can have such power. It is the only time we know where five have come together to increase the impact. It is beyond our understanding."

Alpha's answer baffled everyone. They had believed in the Sky people and were shocked to learn the fast-moving lights in the sky were from Alpha's technology and machines. Now, Alpha had admitted they did not understand something as important as how five heroes could destroy the last of the black killers by just the sound of their voices! Was there still a god or spirits that had the power to intervene in their lives? How else could it be explained?

Alpha paused to let what he had said sink in, then he continued, "One answer is possible. On Earth, the evolution or natural improvement of your species may have reached a point where little further advancement was possible. The movement of humans to three different planets may have sped up evolution so that new abilities are starting to emerge. The stresses imposed by the different environments, radiation, and other changes on each new planet could have been responsible. Our readings on such impacts have shown some improvement to the genetic make-up of the human gene. More time is needed to be sure. We do not have enough information from the studies we have already made."

Vail's next question was without much thought, "So people might still develop other abilities never seen before, like Neeya's power with her voice, to be able to see the immediate future, or even just see in the dark. It could keep happening?"

"It is possible. Back on Earth, such things were not possible, but here on another planet, it may happen. It could be fast or very slow. We have no way of knowing, that is, if it happens at all.

"If there are many of you wanting to join with Tarn and leave, then our ship will take you. It will be several years for the trip, but everyone will be preserved in travel capsules. Our ship will travel much faster than when we first moved this distance because of advances in space travel."

Chapter 23

Answers and New Beginnings

It was time for Tarn to ask his final but most important questions, before deciding to stay or go.

"Since the last humans left Earth, how much time has passed, in Earth years?"

The answer was direct and simple. "One thousand, six hundred and forty-two years."

There were gasps from many in the audience – so long, with so few of them left. How was this possible?

Now Tarn knew he had to keep going with his questions, before other matters were brought up for discussion. "How many times, on this planet, have bands of our ancestors left these mountains, after being trained and equipped, to fight the killers and try to regain control of this region?"

Again, a simple answer. "Seventeen times, including your group."

"How many have died in these fights, in the ongoing war with the killers, to your account?"

"3,062 humans."

"How many survived to return to their people?"

"105, although 34 died of their wounds later."

There was no discussion. The immensity of the numbers was beyond them. Over 3,000 taken from their families and tribes. How was it possible to progress with those losses? More would have died from starvation due to the killing of so many providers of food for tribal communities.

"If we had not finally achieved victory over the killers, for good, what would have happened?"

"We would have waited until humans had again increased in number, then another attempt would be made to destroy the enemy."

"So, this war could have continued over future generations, as it has in the past, with both sides rebuilding numbers after each battle, with no end point?"

"The end point would be when one side was wiped out by the other, as has now happened."

The casual answers provided by Alpha to Tarn's questions had hit like a series of hammer blows. The endless nature of the war that they had known nothing about months ago, again occasionally commented on by Alpha, left them reeling. The stupidity. The spending of their lives and those of their ancestors, while killing or just holding back the killers, was disgusting, and could not be accepted at any level, by humans. For computer-generated beings, however, the flow of time and numbers of deaths meant nothing. The original instructions were to be followed until a final result was reached.

Alpha and his kind had existed in their tunnels or spaceships over centuries, never at risk, playing war games and spending lives without feelings of loss or anguish.

Tarn's next question was unexpected. "How much of our final battle with the killers was staged and prepared before we even left to start the mission?"

Alpha said nothing, then asked, "What do you mean?"

"It has occurred to me that the wagons originally sent with us were set up differently, and the one sent with Vail was equipped differently again. That then meant they were each perfect for the damage and killing to be done at each of the three explosions.

"The red beam of destruction that burnt up the killers' gardens of leaves – it came from space, probably from your spaceship, that was correctly positioned in the right place at the right time.

"Vail returned at just the right time to save Andoki from the first type of monsters out of the tunnels. They could have been known of before Andoki left camp that night.

"The horde of monsters pursued us into that tunnel, followed by the lava. There was no retreat because of the lava, so they had to move forward, to kill us all, particularly Neeya and the other four heroes. All of us could have escaped, with the big door dropping from the roof and the monsters being killed by the lava. The door stopped the lava and kept it away from us.

"We were the bait. You made sure we could not go any other way, and the last wagon was equipped only for one explosion, to blow a hole in the cliff face and expose the tunnel for us. One more obvious set-up were the machine birds and animals that ran or flew into the killers' mountain to blow up two entrances. You had told us they were there to observe, and monitor what the killers were doing and yet, at just the right time, they carried explosives. That could have been done years ago and yet you arranged it to happen while we watched from the plain. All these explosions set off the volcano and the lava which you knew would happen because your people arranged the drilling long ago, and you knew the geology of each mountain."

Alpha offered no comments or answers regarding Tarn's suggestions.

"This is my last question and it may influence what I, and anyone who follows me, will do in the future. Originally, on Earth, who gave directions or orders for the robots to build spaceships and what was to happen to the human cargo carried from Earth?"

Tarn had spoken for some time. The hundreds of people watching and listening had battled to follow what he had said, but it finally seeped into their understanding that they had been used as bait to attract the killers and their monsters to their deaths. Murmurings could be heard around the huge room. Voices were raised. A few 'hotheads' shouted but were calmed by others who wanted to hear the full story. The idea that this had happened many times over the centuries, with thousands of their ancestors being killed while following the directions from Alpha's people, shocked them. It was beyond understanding, but computer generations like Alpha had no feelings, just instructions to be followed.

Alpha had stayed silent and immobile while Tarn had spoken. He now appeared to shift his body to indicate he would reply.

"The creation of what became digital entities, such as myself, and the start of building spaceships, only one of which was completed in time, were funded by a small group of extremely wealthy individuals. They used their laboratories and industrial capacity to achieve what no nation or group of nations could agree on doing. Right to the end, national interest dominated planning, outweighing the priority of humanity's survival. At that time, nothing was known of a different ship being built by the religious supporters of the false goddess Kali.

"The individuals who funded the efforts recognised humanity needed a greater ability and dedication to plan for its survival, without consideration of national priorities. Such planning was not meant to consider human feelings or the needs of individuals at any time.

"Small populations were to be put under stress on the three planets to push evolution much faster than in times of peace. New abilities would be fostered and promoted regardless of the loss of life in those times of stress. The endpoint of that effort has been reached. New abilities are appearing and one side is victorious – your side! The killers have now been eliminated here and there are none on the other two planets."

Tarn broke into Alpha's delivery. "So now that the original objectives have been achieved, who do you and your group answer to? Where do you get your next orders from?"

Alpha froze. Tarn was used to him doing that. The answer to the question had probably never been requested since they left Earth. Everything had changed so that the computer 'brain' was having to go through its database to find the answer. The database would have to be massive to cover all possible situations, over hundreds or thousands of years!

Finally, Alpha's face became active again. Tarn was apprehensive about the answer. Their future depended on it.

"All of the living individuals who were responsible for my existence and that of the network, spaceships, and infrastructure we have built on three planets, are long dead. There are no known living humans existing other than those on this planet. Neeya has died and it is assumed, from your control and directions given to this gathering, that you speak for humanity. Is this correct so far?"

Tarn was at a loss – speak for humanity? Surely there must be someone else? Neeya would have been the one, acknowledged by all. He was just a support to her when needed.

Vail did not hesitate. While Tarn remained silent, she turned to the crowd observing the discussion.

"Alpha has asked if Tarn speaks for us, to decide on our future. What do you say – Yes or No?"

The room burst with noise. Only one word from hundreds of voices: "Yes," then cheering.

Vail grinned and turned to Tarn, "There, Tarn, you have your answer."

Tarn hesitated, then spoke quietly at first, not used to being foremost with decision-making. "Thank you all for giving me your support. I will try to speak honestly and be plain regarding my intentions. "Speaking personally, without Neeya, I feel that I cannot build a new life on this planet. So, I will ask Alpha, and his people, to take me and everyone who wants the same thing, to send their spaceship to the best of the two other planets our ancestors once tried to settle on, carrying all who want to leave on board. I feel we will be taking back what was prepared for our ancestors, what is rightfully now ours to claim.

"I also understand, having already spoken with Pohu, that he will lead all his people who want to return to the lake and their community waiting there. He has already arranged for that to happen.

"The alternative remains to stay here and reclaim what the killers tried to take. Without them, this land should prosper. The way will be easier because you now know of the resources Alpha's people have stored in their mountain tunnels. A lot of information is available to us all in the computers, for the improvement of agriculture, the use of metals, and other valuable knowledge to build a developed society into the future.

"You don't have to decide here, right now. In the next few days, discuss these things with your families, your friends, and your tribes. Your future is now in your own hands."

Tarn was relieved to sit down as cheering rolled around the room. His closest friends – Pohu, Myka, Nabu, Andoki, and Vail - those he had fought a war with, cheered him with the rest of the room. This was the true start of their freedom, only made possible with a sacrifice of lives.

❄ ❄ ❄

Three weeks later, the mountain corridors and living areas had more spare room than before. Pohu and every one of his water or lake people had left. The partings were painful for some. Tarn, Andoki and Vail particularly were sad to lose their connection with Pohu and his people. They had fought together, all of them contemplating death, day after day, but the call of the water coupled with a return to their secret island, families and friends was too much.

They had all waved off the long line of walkers carrying heavy packs of food and clothing, accompanied by two machine wagons loaded, this time, with seats for the injured. The machines would return to the mountain once they had made the delivery to the water's edge.

Tarn remembered his last discussion with Pohu.

"Tarn, there is so much I do not have words for. Neeya's sacrifice, and that of the other four heroes, gave freedom back to our people. I am taking our fighters home to their families, for a peaceful future. Our Guardians will have the final story enshrined on our records, which will end with all that was achieved. The records will then be sealed with no further additions.

"I know you intend to leave this planet and travel to one of the places originally established for our ancestors. Again, Neeya's leadership made this possible. I wish you great success for the future. You will always be a welcome and honoured guest with our people, along with your friends who helped remove the killers from all humanity."

"Pohu, you do me a great honour. I will never forget our time together. We all worked for the same result – the survival of our people and a peaceful future for our descendants. It's probable that we will not meet again. The distance will prevent that, along with our intention to remove any contact with Alpha's people. They have caused much death, but also the survival of our people over generations. I cannot trust them again and we will work for a human future without any aid from them.

"Farewell, my friend. Pass on our wishes for a peaceful future to the Guardians and your families."

❄ ❄ ❄

Andoki and Vail had decided to go with Tarn, along with most of the younger members of Tarn's tribe and others from both Myka's settlement and Nabu's group.

Many of the younger people supported the idea of adventure on a new planet, to create their own identity and leave the long history of killing or being killed to this planet. Peace had been denied to them as they had grown. Now it would hopefully be found by travelling across the stars.

Andoki and Vail had one more place to revisit before they felt free to move forward. It was a walk of several kilometres but at a gentle pace. They joined others walking in the same direction, passing people, some of them crying, some with stern faces returning from their visit.

They arrived and felt comfortable standing in line, waiting their turn.

The massive concrete door was still in place and would remain fixed in place forever. The tomb behind it was now solid rock, the lava flow having filled every gap and cooled into granite.

They finally stood in front of the shrine. The width of the tunnel was covered with small treasures – a finely crafted leather belt, a comb made from bone, masses of flowers – some now wilted and faded, a pair of beautiful beaded moccasins, and a familiar necklace made of big cat's claws and teeth. The presents went on and on, given by grateful recipients of the five heroes' sacrifice. A light made from a wick in melted fat in a carved stone bowl had been burning for days, with the oil continually refilled.

They stood for a short while, silent but with tears down their cheeks, then left to join the trickle of people moving away from the most important place on the planet. It took a while for the sadness and tears to lessen. Andoki and Vail both remembered seeing the teeth and claws before. Neeya had carried them and must have given them to Tarn before they ran for their lives while being pursued by lava and monsters. They could only wonder about how long ago Neeya had known the way it would end for her. Was that when she had given the gift to Tarn?

It had been the most precious thing that Tarn had, but he felt he could not leave with it. It had to stay. This was Neeya's planet and they were all Neeya's people.

Above the keepsakes given in memory of those who chose to save humanity rather than themselves, were five names cut into the stone door, with letters that must have been created by Alpha's machines: "Neeya, Dosol, Isha, Sohin, Mera"

Stories would be created and repeated over centuries, on at least two separate worlds, of the five heroes who saved humanity. The deeds told would grow beyond truth. But the true and accurate memory would be written into the water people's sacred texts, to be cared for by guardians over generations.

They walked back through the connecting tunnel, sad-eyed, often looking at the ground and remembering. People passing nodded, understanding the focus of their pilgrimage.

The people who had chosen to stay were gathering to discuss the possibility of one large tribe emerging for the land dwellers to balance those who stayed and lived on the water. Combining the different tribal customs and governing systems would take time. However, with the help of Alpha and his duplicates in the tunnels, they would be able to develop quickly and try to catch up with much of what had been lost in the past.

❋ ❋ ❋

The day finally arrived. Over 200 people – men, women, and children – waited under the trees fronting a large, clear area of gravel and sand. The landing site had been carefully chosen – level and clear of trees, rocks, and any solid obstruction, capable of carrying a very large and solid object. The last requirement needed some work to remove flammable material from the area. Alpha's machines made short work of it, dragging dead trees and bushes out of the way.

They had been told what would happen, but seeing it occur would remain in their memories. A tiny, bright spot above them grew until it competed with the sun and couldn't be followed by their eyes. They looked away to save their sight and heard the battering, loud sound change pitch. Looking back, the spaceship was slowing down and the one bright spot below it had changed to many smaller spikes of fire. They all moved further back, as gravel, stones and sand were thrown in all directions. A shallow hole was being blasted under each narrow eruption of fire.

The spaceship was shaped like an egg standing vertically. It had a ring-shaped base that held engines and landing skids. Viewing portholes ran around the craft at different levels. The whole ship was made of blindingly reflective silver metal, making it hard to see in the full sun. Tarn, Andoki and Vail stood quietly watching. Their future for the next few years would be under the control of the ship's operation systems, crewed only by electronic entities.

It could hold more than four times the humans to be carried to the new planet, but once in individual suspension 'pods', they would be sealed off from reality until in orbit around their destination.

A long metal ramp extended and the new settlers moved up the slope, many of them tentative and not so bravely edging up through the entry hatch. Once the loading was completed, the ramp slid soundlessly back into the ship.

Before they were sealed into their capsules for long-distance space flight, they were all allowed to crowd the viewing windows to see, from orbit, the planet being left. The view was spectacular, with the white-capped mountains below, and the distant edge of the huge lake. The tiny part of the scene that was green was obvious, compared to the grey, brown, or orange surface yet undeveloped and lacking water. They and their ancestors had lived, fought and died for that tiny part of the planet, not really understanding what they were fighting for.

All who could see through the viewports thought of their lives down there, with memories to be taken into the new adventure. Few of them spoke. This was the first and last time they would have this view and the memory had to be packed away for future reference, unhindered by idle chatter.

Tarn's tears glistened on his face, unashamedly, as he thought of Neeya and what had been lost in the fighting. His throat was all but closed up with the memory of her loss, but he knew he couldn't stay on the planet of her sacrifice.

He thought again, once more, of the planet—Neeya's planet—and wondered what it would be like in 100 years. Then he said goodbye to her, the saviour of humanity.

❋ ❋ ❋

One six-year-old girl, Tooma, peered out the corner of a viewing window, a last look before she lay down in a pod to sleep for years. She was also amazed at what she could see. The area where she had hidden from the explosion that killed so many killers chasing her group as they fled to the mountain was too small to pick out.

She put her hand carefully on one side of her face. It still hurt and she wondered again why she had sought out someone who would do it for her. It was a spur-of-the-moment idea, but it had not left her alone. The tattoo attracted little notice from most of the nearby passengers, but one ex-warrior from the war was sure he had seen it before. It matched the tattoo on each of the five heroes' faces, particularly that carried by Neeya, and he wondered how that could be.

Other books by this author

Journey Through Adversity
Escape from Tyranny

About the Author

Geoff Trigg is a retired local government engineer, with a strong interest in his family history. His professional career left him little time to research and write but, once retired, he completed his first book *Journey Through Adversity*, covering the life and times of his Irish great-great-grandfather, John Stephenson Henry. He then went on to pen his second book, *Escape from Tyranny*, about his first wife's family history and the plight of a Jewish family in World War II.

He has now turned his hand and imagination to speculative fiction – this is *Neeya's People*, Geoff's third book.